THE ADULT

JOE STRETCH

THE ADULT

JONATHAN CAPE

LONDON

Published by Jonathan Cape 2012

2 4 6 8 10 9 7 5 3 1

First published in Great Britain in 2012 by
Jonathan Cape
Random House, 20 Vauxhall Bridge Road,
London SW1V 2SA

www.vintage-books.co.uk

Addresses for companies within The Random House Group Limited
can be found at: www.randomhouse.co.uk/offices.htm

The Random House Group Limited Reg. No. 954009

A CIP catalogue record for this book is available from the British Library

ISBN 9780224096478

The Random House Group Limited supports the Forest Stewardship
Council (FSC®), the leading international forest-certification organisation.
Our books carrying the FSC label are printed on FSC®-certified paper.
FSC is the only forest-certification scheme endorsed by the leading
environmental organisations, including Greenpeace. Our paper procurement
policy can be found at www.randomhouse.co.uk/environment

Typeset in Bembo by Palimpsest Book Production Limited,
Falkirk, Stirlingshire

Printed and bound in Great Britain by
Clays Ltd, St Ives PLC

For Tony Weymouth
1938–2010

Education, education, education.

Tony Blair

PRIVATE LIFE

1

In my sister's diary she describes, often with an unbearable sense of loss, the mid-nineties. Elaine describes how she and Nathan Lustard attended raves at the Midland in Morecambe and how once, at dawn, she gave him a blow job on the beach among the cockles, the crabs and people. I love this image.

I was born in 1982. I grew up knowing my childhood and my adulthood would take place in different centuries. I can hardly remember anything about my first five years except a peach leather couch and a fake gas fire. This morning, at the smoothie stand, Peta spat a pip at me to try and cheer me up. I have responded by giving her the silent treatment and by coming outside to eat. The sun is shining. The mustard bricks of the Arndale tower catch the light and it looks like a vertical Spanish beach, the windows laid out like towels. When Peta and I bicker, the smoothie stand becomes small and so I spend my lunch hours doing laps of the Arndale Centre. Today I visited Poundland in the glass wing, where I purchased this notepad and sprayed my wrists with Lynx Africa. I enjoy the glass wing because of its natural light. As I returned to the stand, I looked through the ceiling and witnessed an aeroplane crossing the sky. The truth is, I'm not sure whether the smell of my wrists recalls my own puberty or Elaine's.

We serve a lot of goths at the smoothie stand. They ask for energy drinks. Peta, my manager, won't do them and I think that's right. She does boosters, which aren't the same. I think I'd have been a goth if I hadn't been so committed to table-tennis. I'd have stuck to the principles though. One called Peta a slut and filmed her reaction on his phone. He ordered a 'Top of the Morning!' and it really broke her spirits.

Our pitch sits between a grocer's and a sushi bar. For three years I have diced apples, mushed bananas, squashed grapes, grated ginger, peeled kiwis, juiced oranges and pressed 'go' on the blender. The secret to my new smoothie is its optimistic name; just to order a 'Top of the Morning!' gives the customers a lift.

I've been giving a lot of consideration lately to the issue of what does and what does not constitute 'a life'. Between my bedsit, my job and my visits to Walkabout, the Australian pub where I watch the Premiership, I seem to have nailed some planks of driftwood together, if you see what I mean. Though of course I'm not happy. I walk up Hanover Street each morning at six, sometimes singing Whitney Houston quietly. In 1993, her cover of 'I Will Always Love You' is replaced at the top of the UK singles chart by 2 Unlimited's 'No Limit'. I remember listening to this with my sister. 'This is it, Jim,' she said. Elaine's breasts were developing. She bounced on her bed wearing silk, midnight-blue pyjamas. 'There's no limits!'

My bedsit has one striking feature; a column by the door that I describe as deco. The whole place stinks. My bed's broken; I sleep on its slope. The inside of my fridge is like a room in a modern art gallery – bare, bright white and then the odd disturbing object. My one window is Edwardian and won't close. A community of little moths is standing on the bathroom ceiling. I look up when I pee and say hello. No matter how many times I clean the oven, it emits noxious smoke when I switch it on. I am eating too much Advent calendar and I think it's the lowest-quality chocolate. I have a sweat problem. I should go on daytime television. My brain's inside my head like an avocado's stone. Having said that, 'Top of the Morning!' is currently outselling any smoothie Peta comes up with by two or three sales to one. And it's her stand!

In his 1957 essay, 'The White Negro', Norman Mailer describes how white people became cool. He says coolness becomes possible when people live under threat. For black people, the threat is white people. For white people, he says, it is the atom bomb. I'm on my lunch hour again. For lunch, I took alternate bites from a chunk of Cheddar and a beef tomato. Mailer says white people begin to act cool when they realise they are living in cities that can be annihilated without warning or become radio-active instantly. When individuals can be reduced to nothing except some hair and some teeth on a pavement, everyone has something to gain from becoming cool. At least, I think that's the long and short of it.

Peta just joined me for a cigarette. She's threatened to plunge a banana into my anus the next time I bend over. She swore in Polish, blowing smoke towards the electronic doors of Primark.

'What are you doing, Jim?'

'Writing.'

'Why?'

'I'm not sure.'

It's one month since I crashed Kate Reynolds's hire car. A month since she withdrew money from the cashpoint and handed me enough for a bag of satsumas and my train ticket. I don't want to write about Kate Reynolds. I love her, it's true, but I don't want to write about her. I would inevitably turn her into a kind of sombre and opinionated sex doll. The reader, if there is one, might have heard of my family. If that's not the case, then all the better. I shall write about my family and also my thoughts on the moon landing and how I became a fruit-crusher. I'll write about the career of the child actor Macaulay Culkin and about a pube that grew from my friend Harry King in the winter of 1992, and about a time capsule we buried beneath the infants' playground that summer.

Peta moans about emigrating to Manchester and not London. She says the north of England is grimmer than Katowice. It reminds me of how in October 1989, shortly after the Berlin Wall fell, a weasel was found dead on the playing field, and, while most of the school went to surround it, I asked Harry King whether he and I were Westerners or Easterners. 'We're neither, Jim,' he said. In the distance, children paraded the perimeter of the field, carrying the dead animal on the tip of a fallen tree-branch. 'We're Northerners.'

We moved in the February of 1989, from Stroud, in a silver Ford Escort. Elaine and I played magnetic draughts on the back seat and each hid a sweet wrapper in Mum's perm. In the weeks before the move, she referred to it as 'our main attempt at happiness'. Our cat, Pop, crapped in her travel cage and Mum swivelled in her seat and smiled. The journey passed quickly and we arrived before the removal van. We stood in the village square, outside our new house, a three-storey Georgian terrace, grey brick with white window frames and sills. The village was Ridley, in Cumbria, in the north-west of England and it was one of those crisp winter days. Mum said she couldn't believe we were there and Dad smoked to prove we were. Children lounged on the steps of a war memorial, which was a stone column for both wars. A post van was parked outside the post office with its rear doors ajar. Outside our new house stood an ornate lamp post, erected in 1863 to commemorate the wedding of Queen Victoria's son, later Edward VII, a king whom my mother, in the years that followed, if she looked out into the square at night to see the lamp post lit-up against the dark, would sometimes describe as a 'sexaholic'. I stood beside the lamp post and kept my eye on a group of elderly villagers who were gathered outside the butcher's. They were framed by the shop's large window, where fake vine leaves and pheasants hung, some plucked, some waiting to be. A bell above the bakery door rang and a woman stepped out into the cold clutching a loaf of bread and eating a jam tart. A man with white hair and a black moustache walked a sandwich board out onto the pavement in front of the pub. He leant against it and sighed visibly into the chill, looking across at us.

'Bliss,' Mum said.

The removal van spent a long time reversing into place. 'You've got *masses* of room,' Mum said, waving it back, wearing leggings, ankle-boots and her grey leather jacket, holding her hefty fringe from her eyes. 'Bit more . . . Bit more . . .'

The elderly villagers turned away when the van collided with the low wall around our doorstep. Mum frowned at the rubble and then started laughing. 'What a start,' she said. Removal men shovelled up the scattered bricks and paraded our possessions between the van and the house. 'We can *live* here.' She stroked the gold bell of a gramophone as it was carried past. Later, she bought a pheasant from the butcher. She pulled it from a carrier bag and laid it on the kitchen table. We were all there – Elaine, Dad, Pop and I – surrounded by boxes of pans, cookbooks and crockery. 'It's the England I'd forgotten,' Mum said. She layered her hands on Dad's shoulder and added, 'I've hated the eighties, Julian. Haven't I?' She picked up the pheasant and looked into its dry, hollow eye sockets. 'I let our secret slip in the butcher's, I'm afraid,' she said, pushing her fingertip into the bird's open beak. 'But people knew already, it was all very obvious. They've heard of us.'

Dad took his cigarettes from the table and left the kitchen. Mum shook the dead pheasant at him as he departed. It crossed my mind that lives must contain many attempts at happiness and that calling one attempt your 'main attempt' was a mistake. We ate quiche that first night and talked about eating the pheasant. Elaine said it was immoral and was like slaughtering whales only way worse as we had options. 'I don't agree, Elaine. I don't mind that they shoot them. It isn't about class here.' Mum pierced a green bean with her fork. 'Round here it's about survival. And speaking of which, guys . . . isn't this delicious?'

Within a week there was an article about us in the village newsletter. The headline read: FAMILY BRINGS FAME TO RIDLEY. Within two weeks, Elaine had been kicked out of Brownies for making Tawny Owl cry. After twice trying the King's Arms in the square, Dad drank at the Royal Hotel on the outskirts of Ridley. At Sunday school, I made a paper aeroplane and launched it during the Lord's Prayer. It narrowly missed the bowed head of the Reverend and slid beneath the piano.

2

For breakfast today, I ate several squares of an Advent calendar. Peta's granted me the day off and I shall use the time to write very simply about my maternal grandfather. My maternal grandfather was called Charlie Albright. He played double bass, managed a shoe shop and read the sleeves of jazz records very intensely as though they were Russian novels. He was too young to serve in the war and this led to a feud in the 1950s with Godfrey Albright, his elder brother, who bayoneted what Mum describes as 'numerous Italians' at the Battle of Monte Cassino in 1944. Godfrey settled in Harrogate after the war and sold insurance. He married but never had children, whereas Charlie Albright had four, four daughters, all born between 1950 and 1958, a period in the West where white people are engaged in a project of 'becoming cool' which, according to Norman Mailer, begins earlier in the twentieth century. 'We're *late* baby boomers.' That was how Mum saw it. She performed a cartwheel in her forties and planted her hand on a bumblebee. In 1960, Godfrey Albright's wife broke a coronation mug during a conversation about television. Godfrey went upstairs, took his Beretta, climbed into the bathtub, pulled his greatcoat over his body and shot himself. His wife gathered the pieces of the cup and walked out into the street.

My maternal grandfather, Charlie Albright, did not shoot himself. He wanted his daughters to become professional entertainers. He thought that entertainment would be the great healer of the post-war West. Charlie wanted his daughters to make people laugh or cry or think and then get paid with a cheque and for them to pay the tax on that cheque so that when he was asked what it was his four daughters did, he could say, 'They are all entertainers.' In the early sixties, in a terraced house in

Stroud, Charlie Albright would slink his dessert spoon into his bowl and announce the end of teatime. 'It's the song-and-dance hour. The rug's a stage, girls. The living room's the Albert Hall.'

Over the course of the sixties, standing on the rug in a neat ensemble, the four Albright sisters grew tall and beautiful. There was Elizabeth, the youngest, who came to prominence in a production of *Educating Rita* staged at the National in 1984. Reviews heralded a breakthrough performance by a glamorous young actress with perfect comic timing. Having subsequently made several memorable appearances on television, including a short run in an ongoing crime drama, Elizabeth, by the early nineties, was looking to make the transition to the West End and even Broadway. She described herself as 'a reluctant man-eater, put on this earth for musical theatre.' She had a blonde shriek of a perm, shrunken eyes and no children.

Irene Albright, the eldest, was timid, neurotic and the greatest soprano of her generation. Aged thirty-four, she appeared on the BBC's *Desert Island Discs* and spoke lovingly of her father and bashfully of her achievements, including her appearances opposite Placido Domingo, which had given rise to seminal opera recordings. She remarked that she 'just liked singing'. For her one luxury, which each guest must choose to take to the fictional desert island, Irene Albright chose 'my daughter, Jess'. Roy Plomley, the host, told her humans were forbidden. 'In that case I'll take silence,' Irene said. She once told me *Hook* was her favourite film.

Then there were the middle daughters. Jayne Albright attributed her success in Hollywood to being fractionally less insane than the other producers. She was the calmest sister, the third daughter. She was sheltered by her elders, Mum and Irene, and somehow elevated by Elizabeth, the loudest and youngest. Jayne's success in Los Angeles appeared so natural and serene, it was hard to believe it wasn't a kind of fate. She used sleeping pills. In 1996, she became the first of the four sisters to abandon the perm. Unlike Irene and Elizabeth, Jayne worked behind the scenes in the entertainment industry, the merits of which seemed to speak for themselves. Aged ten, I listened at the kitchen door as she explained that 'The hardest thing about being English in LA is the dating. I don't know how to *fuck* an American.' I went upstairs, chose a bra from her suitcase and fastened it to my pillow. Having filled both cotton cups with pairs of my socks, I kissed them and kissed up and down each black strap, saying love words to where I imagined Jayne's head.

There was a family joke. When we gathered in restaurants to celebrate opening nights or awards, one of the sisters would tap a champagne flute with a teaspoon and ask, 'Why are we called the Albrights?' At which point, the rest of the sisters, their boyfriends, husbands, even the children would reply in unison, 'Because we're *all stars!*' The joke is among my earliest memories. By 1990, it was really getting overworked. I remember Elizabeth Albright standing in a Paris restaurant, not far from the Garnier Opera House, wearing a black sequined dress and choker. 'Sorry, everyone,' she said, tapping her espresso cup. 'Sorry, but could someone help me, please? I can't quite remember why it is we're called the Albrights. Seriously, any ideas?'

Millicent Albright, my mum, met my dad on 22 July 1969 in North Wales. She was eighteen, slim and bookish, I think, and visiting Bangor ahead of studying there. 'I was standing on the corner of Stryd Fawr and Friars Road.' Mum told the story at my sister's wedding in 1999 while balanced on a chair in an east London pub. 'And there he was, this *guy*, that's what your father was, Elaine, a clean-shaven *guy* who asked if I liked astrophysics. It was the morning after the moon landing, you see. I had a train to catch, I told him, which was true. He thought I was rude, which I don't think I was, though Bangor wasn't my first choice. We exchanged names and he said he hoped we'd run into each other come September, which we didn't, not really. Cut to five years later, I'm standing on the banks of the Serpentine in Hyde Park, on my lunch hour from teacher training, when suddenly there he is, standing right beside me, staring across the water with a beautiful beard. And what a lovely idea – that five years earlier we'd discussed space travel on the corner of Stryd Fawr and Friars Road. We wandered round the lake together towards Marble Arch.'

'I never *wanted* to be famous.' That's what Mum says. I once threw up into her hands apropos of nothing. When she poured it onto the car park, where tree roots had risen and torn the concrete, we discovered a pound coin. She shook it clean and let me keep it.

On a hot summer's day in 1991, I helped Harry King clean his dad's car. Harry King was a pea-headed blond whose mum was on the rota for mowing the graveyard. His nose ran relentlessly when we first met; he drew snot into his mouth with his tongue. His dad was a solicitor. His godfather was a local MP, a Tory who wrote novels set among the theatres and brothels of High Georgian London and who had a reputation for waistcoats. 'What is it with your family, Jim?' Harry King was smart and memorably frisbeed the crust of a cowpat right over the school. His dad's car was a VW Beetle, a cream convertible. 'I mean, what do you personally think is so special about you all?' I scrubbed a hubcap with an old toothbrush with damaged bristles. Harry dropped a sponge into a washing-up bowl and crouched in the shade beside me. 'Because the thing is, I've thought about it quite a lot. And the thing is, Jim, your mum sings a lot, sure, and she grabs me and makes me dance around your kitchen. But the thing is, she's not famous. Your aunts are, sure. But your mum just teaches.'

Later that month, Elizabeth Albright was guest of honour at the Ridley Summer Fair. Harry's dad drove her slowly down Main Street with the roof down, as people clapped from the pavement. This was during Elizabeth's crime drama days. Elaine and I sat under the old lamp post, waiting for our aunt to pass by. Later, there was a fancy-dress contest, and I thought if I did keepy-ups dressed as Gary Lineker, I might win, so I put on shorts and a white T-shirt and rehearsed a smile in my wardrobe's mirror.

I lied about football in 1991. In September, Harry and I began playing for Kendal Under 11s. We were the only boys from our school on the team and we quickly realised that on Monday mornings we were able to exaggerate our roles. 'They're saying we could go pro. They're saying we're naturals.' We both scored screamers on our debuts, we said, and had been assured by the manager that, from now on, we'd be considered the team's first choice strike partnership. We said I scored a hat-trick in game two and that one of them was 'a bicycle kick' and that all three had been set up by Harry. By January, I'd scored thirty-two goals in eight games. It was a good record and there was a brief craze of calling me 'Striker Nine'. Harry had been called 'the new Dalglish' by the manager, an Aberdonian known only by his first name, Archie.

'What about the other players?' we were asked, on Monday lunchtime. 'What do they think of you?'

'They worship us,' Harry said. 'Archie has to keep them separate from us.'

The truth was, we were substitutes and we'd stand with our sleeves pulled over our hands, getting lashed by rain, freezing on the touchline with jumpy fathers, unplugging our studs from the mud, the dead leaves and the dog shit. No one ever passed us the ball in the warm-up. Sometimes we'd kick the air between us like there was a ball there, while Archie ignored us and screamed 'Spread out!' at the boys on the pitch.

I requested the ball once in the warm-up, hoping to show some skill. 'Eee-are, Berky,' I said. He was our best player, Berky. His talent afforded him a rare placidity. Of all the boys at Kendal Under 11s, he was the one that Harry and I would, when we were alone, claim quite liked us. 'I think he thinks we're cool in a weird way,' I'd say.

'Eee-are,' Berky said, shaping to pass.

It took talent to kick a football into someone's face from the distance he did mine. Berky had talent; he could do endless keepy-ups. During games, girls gathered on the touchline opposite

Harry and me and shouted his name at sudden moments, as if they hadn't quite expected to. For months, I wondered whether he'd meant to get my face, or whether he'd have settled for my testicles or stomach. I went to stand with Harry and neither of us spoke, until the whistle blew and the match began.

'Wait till you get out there, Jim, eh?'

'It didn't actually hurt,' I said. 'It was the shock.'

We stood on a strip of grass that ran between two pitches. The games were always decided by the time Archie let us on. We used to muddy our legs by kneeling down in the goalmouth to prove to our parents we'd played.

Before that, aged nine, dressed as Gary Lineker, I practised keepy-ups in the backyard on the morning of the Ridley Summer Fair. My father was looking for me. I could hear him calling my name. 'He's in the Italian Courtyard,' Mum shouted, from somewhere high in the house. That was what she called our small backyard. It was full of hanging baskets that failed due to the low levels of sunlight. Dad came to the back door, holding a mug to his chest. I dropped the football onto my knee and attempted keepy-ups.

'Good, Jim. Nearly.' Dad gave me a side parting with his hand. 'Come on. You're good. I'm impressed.' Wind disturbed the tree above us, the hanging baskets turned and small bits of sunlight spiralled around the yard before settling on us in a fragile formation. Mum stood in the back doorway, wearing a colourful floral dress. 'Elizabeth's cutting the ribbon at midday. Why is he crying?'

An hour later, I stood beside a Batman and a clown. I dropped the ball onto my knee and my body sparked into action. I managed three keepy-ups. The third was the faintest of touches. A few minutes later, I was disqualified. Batman's mum said the contest was unjust on account of my aunt judging it. I picked up my ball and went to sit with Harry on the grass slope by the running track.

'Bad day,' I said. 'On a good day, I can do a thousand.'

'I've seen you do a thousand,' Harry said.

On a makeshift stage, Elizabeth Albright presented the clown with a tin of chocolates. After, she sang a song from *West Side Story*. Mum stood at the head of a crowd of villagers and patted her thigh in time.

'I don't get it,' Harry said. 'What is it with your family?'

Dad slipped in the Dads' Race. He sat in his lane, where he'd fallen, between the curving creosote lines, holding his eyes shut. He walked away without finishing. That night, I sat at the kitchen table watching Mum and Aunt Elizabeth drink champagne. They sang the songs that Charlie Albright had taught them, back in the sixties on the rug that was a stage, in the living room that was the Albert Hall. At one point, Mum tried to climb onto the table. My aunt gripped me. 'She's *so* talented,' she said. The mood swooned and Mum sank into a wicker chair.

'I didn't want to say earlier,' Elizabeth said. 'I didn't want to spoil things. But I die this year, OK, Milly.' Elizabeth emptied her champagne flute and held it to her eye like a telescope. 'I die of lung cancer during the Christmas special. I'm overjoyed about it actually.'

I looked at my mother. She was sleeping in the wicker chair. Her champagne flute leant in her loosening grip. It was about to spill.

On his tenth birthday, Harry hosted a sleepover and I was the only guest. At Harry's house, the slightest noise in the night would bring his dad marching down the corridor with the lined face and lost eyes of a woken adult. 'For Christ's sake, boys. *Sleep*,' he'd say, but in spite of this threat, on the night of his tenth birthday, Harry summoned me to his bedside and I saw he was shining a torch under his covers.

'What is it?'

'It's this.'

He pulled back the covers.

'I don't see anything.'

'*This.*'

He brought the torch beam close to his penis.

'Oh, I see,' I said.

'I know.'

The week we discovered Harry's pube, we also discovered table-tennis. We tried out for Ridley Table-tennis Club, and while it was true that we were the only two who did, it was also true that the head coach took us to one side afterwards for a special word.

'You've got the intellect, the reflexes . . . You're naturals.'

It was October 1992.

The day after our trial, we relayed the coach's praise in detail to the boys at Ridley Primary. 'Everyone's jealous,' Harry said, when the news failed to impress anyone. 'We're going to be the best two players in south Cumbria, Jim . . . It's scary.'

In conversation, I called Harry's pube 'your pube' and Harry called it 'my pube'. If one of us ever acquired some piece of information about penises and wished to conduct an experiment in order to see whether the information was true or not, we would always conduct the experiment on Harry, on account of him having a hair on one of his testicles and this seeming to us to be a mark of distinction. 'We should try it on yours,' I'd say, 'because of your pube.' And he would say, 'Yes, of course, my pube.'

When an acquaintance told us that his brother in the Marines had said that table-tennis was 'for complete gays' because no matter how hard the ball was hit you couldn't hurt your opponent, like, for instance, if you took a table-tennis ball point-blank to the testicles it wouldn't hurt a bit, Harry and I felt that we should investigate this and, since one of his had a hair, we should experiment on him.

'It sort of hurts, but you need to get a direct hit.'

'Just stay there.'

We were in Harry's garage. We lowered the roof of his dad's

Beetle and I stood on the driver's seat while Harry, wearing only his sky-blue underpants, spread himself against the garage door. I dare say we were both reminded of how, the previous year, Berky had kicked a football in my face and how, until he'd done so, we'd assumed he considered us cool in a weird way. But neither of us raised this and because I was a natural I was able to get a fair few balls on target. In the end, Harry concluded that, in a way, it hurt more than a football because it really stung, like a pinprick. 'And of course,' he said, 'the Marines aren't hard. *They're* complete gays.' The following month, his dad permanently removed the Beetle from the garage and replaced it with a second-hand table-tennis table.

My dad leant against the electric fire in the kitchen. Mum stood by the sink, holding a trumpet. It was winter and the windows were black. Spotlights lit the kitchen up pretty luridly and twinkled on the instrument's new brass. I stood in the doorway, my checked shirt tucked into blue cords and I had a little brown haircut on my head.

'You're going to be a natural. I just know it. And jazz, James, don't you think? I mean, it's like Sartre said, sitting in that Paris café, to be a note in a jazz tune is to be free. The French. You have to love the French.' Mum said Louis Armstrong was a great man, not just a great trumpeter, and then she left to play the piano in what she called the Music Room. Dad and I sat at the kitchen table, either side of the trumpet.

'Who's Sartre?'

'I can't answer that.'

'Who's Louis Armstrong?'

'A famous trumpet player.'

Julian Thorne taught physics and loved Dire Straits. He dyed his hair brown from 1990, from the age of forty, onwards. He listened to 'Money For Nothing' as he drove through the countryside to work. We were Thornes, Dad and I, and Elaine, not Albrights. Mum, like her sisters, refused to take her husband's surname. Sometimes letters would arrive for Mr and Mrs Thorne and Mum would drop them back onto the mat. 'I'm *Ms* Millicent Albright. How hard is that?'

Dad looked weary, sitting across from me. I touched the trumpet and asked what he thought. He sipped from his drink and said he didn't know. At Irene Albright's thirtieth, Dad twisted his ankle and wouldn't tell anyone how. The Christmas we went to Aunt Jayne's in LA, 1988, he lifted the lid of a wooden chest on the first landing and urinated into it during the night. He wore brown shoes. Each year, when an Albright sister did something sensational and we would travel, as a family, to the south or overseas to witness the sensational thing, Dad would wear his special Austin Reed suit, which included a white shirt and a crumpled green blazer. I couldn't help thinking that this was a bad suit, not a terrible one, but not a great one. Even when I'd watch him ironing the shirt and he'd bend down to me and, showing me the label, say, 'Look, Jim. Austin Reed.' I knew that it wasn't the best shirt. I sensed other people had better and, even if they didn't, there was something shameful about his devotion to the brand.

When I went to Queen's Secondary School the following year, I joined the jazz band, in which my sister Elaine already played sax. We practised on Tuesdays and were comprised of children whose parents connected freedom not with Dylan or the Beatles, but with the Jazz Age, with the very idea of the improvised jazz solo. None of us knew what circumstances in our parents' upbringing had given rise to our having to play jazz; we turned up after school on Tuesday and were given permission to remove our ties. Our status as jazz musicians made us hip at home and outcasts at school and that wasn't how you wanted it. In the song 'Moonlight Serenade', the bandleader would point at me and I'd stand and improvise. At my first concert, I played a b instead of a b flat and I went red. The week after, when we played at the Inter School Jazz Contest, I didn't hit one bad note. My solo had a free-and-easy, off-the-cuff feel. Elaine said it brought 'Moonlight Serenade' to life. On the bus back to school was a girl called Fiona Hohner. She was thin-lipped and her name rhymed. 'Good solo,' she said, and we sat together for a while in a road-sick silence. Our knees were close and they tapped when we turned corners. As the bus drove through the southern Lake District, past fog-hidden summits, paddocks of horses and meadows of sheep, Fiona Hohner, who was about my height, described male masturbation to me.

'What you do, see, is you rub it until it goes hard. That takes about a minute. Then you rub it really fast for two minutes and liquid comes out and it feels like a dream.'

I watched her right hand as she mimed the 'you rub it really fast for two minutes' part. I thought, That actually seems *too* fast. The issue of male masturbation wasn't entirely new. Elaine had made a few remarks that crushed my hopes. But also, as Fiona mimed that movement on the bus, I thought about Dilly.

On holiday in Cornwall in 1991, Elaine and I discussed our desire for inflatables; a lilo for her and a rubber ring for me. Elaine suggested that I ask Mum for money once we arrived at the beach. But before we'd even left our holiday cottage, she made this impossible. Elaine came downstairs dressed in a fashion that caused Mum to drop her spoon, choke on her muesli and swallow frantically so that a full expression of her disgust could begin. Elaine stood at the foot of the narrow staircase, wearing a flesh-coloured bikini, periodically widening her eyes as if to say, *What?*

'A one-piece swimming costume. Go upstairs and put on a one-piece swimming costume.'

'I'm getting a lilo then. Fact.'

Elaine turned to go upstairs.

'Oh, Jesus. It's a *thong*. Julian, look at this.'

Dad gave a small shake of his head. He stood in the kitchenette, loading a toast rack with buttered toast.

'Mum,' I said, stepping forwards. 'I feel that this year Elaine should have a lilo, whereas for me, I was thinking a rubber ring.'

'Lilos are for floating prostitutes, not twelve-year-old Albrights.'

'I'm a Thorne,' Elaine said. The gusset of her bikini had been swallowed by her buttocks. She looked naked. Later, at the beach, she laid her towel on the sand some distance away from us and sunbathed in a maroon one-piece swimming costume. Some older children set up their camp close to her and, for a while, my sister sat up on her elbows, staring out to sea and brushing sand from her pale thighs. A girl lit a cigarette and a boy said 'fuck'. Elaine stood, gathered up her towel and went to stand by the shore.

'Jim,' Dad said, 'let's take a walk.'

We went to a kiosk, where he bought two ice creams and a can of cider then poured the change into my hand.

'I'm going to take these back,' he said. 'Before they melt.'

I went to the beach shop, where a blond teenager with a pierced ear told me about rubber rings. He said I couldn't afford one. He talked about the different qualities of rubber and said that was what determined the difference in price. He pointed at a smiling inflatable dolphin. It hung from the roof, nodding in the breeze of a fan. 'That's cheap,' he said.

Harry was a very attacking table-tennis player. He could beat an opponent quickly if he got into a rhythm on his forehand. I was defensive. I would wear my opponent down with my backhand chop and what seemed to me to be my impossibly good reflexes. We played for Ridley C in a league that was largely made up of adults. *C! C! C!* In between matches we practised for hours in Harry's garage. We created databases on his dad's Nimbus and rated each player in the league. We travelled to village halls all round south Cumbria and found grown men waiting with packets of biscuits and the facilities for orange squash. We didn't just win; we destroyed our opponents. I think a lot of people instinctively consider themselves to be good at table-tennis. They underestimate the skill levels that can be achieved in the sport. Had the reader, if there is one, played me or Harry when we were eleven, it would have been a humiliation. I had eight serves, all disguised, all with cruel, unreadable spins.

'*C! C! C!*' Even when we'd spent the whole evening together, Harry would phone once we were home from the game. '*C! C! C!*'

'Can you believe it?' I'd sit on the bottom step with the old beige telephone, stretching the spiral wire till it straightened, then allowing it to slacken so it spiralled again.

'We're naturals, Jim.'

By Christmas, neither Harry nor I had lost a game and Ridley C were top of the Kendal and District Table-tennis League Division 3. We'd taken to writing detailed reports of the matches, which appeared, always heavily edited, in the *Ridley Month*. We referred to ourselves as 'The TT Princes of Ridley' and often ended our articles with wild speculation about our future in the game. We pooled our savings and had strips made at a printing shop in Lancaster. They were bright red and on the back of mine it said 'Thorne' and Harry's said 'King' and under each of our names was a large letter 'C'.

It was my skill on the trumpet that led to an experiment on Harry's penis in my bedroom, in December of that year, 1992. This occurred when I was yet to start at Queen's Secondary, and so was yet to improvise a solo in 'Moonlight Serenade' and yet to meet Fiona Hohner.

'I'm fairly sure that if I put my trumpet over your dick and play notes, Harry . . . well, I'm pretty sure you'll feel something.'

'What do girls truly understand about dicks, do you think?'

'I'm pretty sure it'll feel weird, Harry.'

'I'll need you to guarantee me you won't damage my pube.'

I pressed my trumpet onto his groin and played a few notes. He wore tracksuit bottoms, but, even so, when I blew a top G his eyes widened and his lips pursed. He felt something. And it would have been more sensational had I, as he was to later request, allowed Harry to remove his tracksuit bottoms and his underpants beforehand.

'It's agony,' he said.

'Is it?'

'It's absolute agony.'

'You do it to me.'

I handed the trumpet to Harry and steered it over my groin. Harry brought his pea-head to the mouthpiece and blew but, sadly, he couldn't manage even a low C, let alone one of the high notes that the experiment demanded. And so it became like all the other tests, insofar as we conducted it exclusively on Harry and his penis, distinguished as it was by a pube. Although unlike the other experiments, which were never repeated, this one could be done again and again. When Harry said things like, 'Jim, do you dare me to let you do that thing with your trumpet?' I'd play along with the idea that, for Harry, the experience was 'absolute agony' and I'd say things like, 'Well, if you're sure, Harry. If you think you can handle it.' And sometimes, I'd even say, 'I should warn you, Harold, I can go even higher these days.' He'd try to hide his excitement with a look of trepidation. Eventually, as I say, he said, 'Jim, do you dare me to let you do it without kecks?' And there I had to decline, but I did so politely and, to his credit, Harry didn't press the issue.

In March 1993, aged eleven, he and I walked into a small village hall in Staveley, near Kendal. We removed our anoraks to reveal our red strips. As I knelt to retie my shoelaces, Harry tapped my shoulder.

'Jim, look.'

Berky was warming up on a table at the end of the hall, beside which, on a trestle table, was a plastic jug of orange squash and a plate of digestive biscuits. He was playing with two other boys, Vinny and Calf-head. The three of them made up what Archie used to call the 'spine' of Kendal Under 11s Football Club. They were playing Round the Clock, running round the table, laughing and shouting. For people like Harry and me, games like Round the Clock were borderline offensive and contributed to a widely held belief in Western Europe that table-tennis isn't a real sport. Calf-head put a forehand into the net. Berky and Vinny descended on him. Vinny got him in a headlock while Berky rubbed a knuckle over his matted calf-like hair.

'It's OK,' I said.

'How do you know?'

Within a year, I'd be riding on a bus back from the Inter School Jazz Contest, watching as Fiona Hohner moved her hand 'really fast'. I'd be calling Harry to tell him with authority about the whole process she'd described, about how to rub it hard took about a minute and how the whole thing took about three minutes and culminated in liquid and a feeling like a dream. And after this, Harry would never request that high notes be played onto his penis again. When I was invited round for a sleepover he would no longer say, 'And, Jim, don't forget your trumpet.' And when more hairs grew from his testicles, we would not creep around in the dark shining torches onto them. When we talked till late and Stan King burst into the bedroom, hissing, 'For Christ's sake, boys – *sleep!*' it was usually because I'd been telling Harry stories about Elaine.

'She does it in the coal shed. To sixth-formers.'

'You're saying she genuinely *likes* dicks?'

'She must.'

Exchanges like this would get Harry up and out of bed, either angry, worried or deep in thought and, in this way, with him pacing in his pyjamas and his dad bursting into the room, time passed. I forgot about the summer I spent with the inflatable dolphin with the smile on its face; how I'd named him Dilly, how I'd swum out into the sea with him and climbed on his back. How I'd rubbed against him till it felt like a dream. I forgot about the times when I lay on the beach cleaning sand from Dilly's smile, telling myself that I must never take him out to sea again. I told myself never to search for that dream feeling again. I forgot, too, about the time I dishonoured that vow and swam with Dilly out into the Atlantic Ocean and made love to him with such conviction that he burst with a soft bang and vanished from between my legs and floated out to sea.

The unthinkable happened on that evening in Staveley Village Hall. Harry lost to Berky. He attacked too much and missed too many. He went red. He kicked a small metal bin across the hall and the umpire made him put it back. He was in tears. 'I'm just sweating,' he said. We sat on plastic chairs, drinking orange squash. Across the hall, Vinny, Berky and Calf-head grappled, legged each other up and looked to pin each other down.

'I'm sorry,' Harry said, without looking at me.

Berky and I warmed up by politely knocking the ball to each other. In the opening game, he landed a few big smashes, but often missed with the same shot. And the truth is, I was a sensational table-tennis player. I defended and defended till he missed and then, in the middle of the second game, I attacked. He retreated backwards as I hammered down forehand after forehand and he scrambled to get the ball back over the net. Eventually, Berky could do little else but send a return high into the air. I waited for the ball to bounce and smashed it. It leapt off his side of the table and hit him beneath his eye. 'Ouch.' Berky covered his handsome face with his hands and looked on the brink of tears.

Mum drove us home that night. Harry climbed from our silver Ford, said goodbye and closed the door. 'You like him, don't you?' Mum and I watched as Harry climbed the curved, gravel driveway leading to his parents' home. 'I admire how hard you've been teaching him the trumpet, James. But he's useless, isn't he? He's too – square.'

A year later, I was in the car with Mum again, only this time we were driving home from a jazz concert in Skipton. That night, the clarinettists were awed by the news that Elaine Thorne had been caught smoking and, because of this, she wouldn't get pointed out by the bandleader in 'Mack the Knife' and invited to stand up and improvise. Elaine herself was bored by the incident. She sat beside me on the back seat, not once turning from the window, even though outside it was dark.

'I thought your solo in "Moonlight Serenade" was wonderful.' Mum raised herself up in her seat to peep at me in the rear-view. I'd been doing the exact same solo for the past five or six concerts. I didn't improvise. I stood and played from memory.

I missed the final game of our first table-tennis season. I was in Paris watching Irene Albright perform in *Don Carlos*. The following month, at the end-of-season award ceremony, I won the prize for the Best New Player in Division 3. There's a beautiful aria in *Don Carlos*. It's about love. As always with Irene's operas, we watched as a family, sitting in a box on the first gallery, close to the stage. There were six curtain calls that night. By the end, my hands burned with each clap. Later, my cousin Jess and I sat in half-light beneath a large restaurant table, listening as the sisters celebrated. Towards the end of the evening, Elizabeth Albright's red high heels disappeared from view. 'We're getting bigger and bigger, aren't we? Listen, everybody.' She struck a champagne glass with a piece of cutlery. 'Shut up, Milly . . . I wasn't going to say this tonight, but I got the part. In fact, I got the lead part. I'm going to the West End!' The sisters cheered and there was applause. 'Can you believe I wasn't going to tell you? Can you? I was put on this earth for musical theatre!' I crawled over to Dad's feet and watched as they moved inside his brown shoes. They were clenching and unclenching like hands. 'Someone remind me,' I could hear Mum saying. She had to raise her voice to be heard. 'Everybody. *Everybody*. Why are we called the Albrights?'

3

I started at Queen's Secondary in September 1993. During our first lesson, an enormous boy named Bamber Law hummed subliminally to irritate our teacher. His charcoal-grey trousers were tight at the thigh and his jet-black nostril hair looked trimmed. He punctured my pencil-tin lid with his compass and ought to have been sent out really, but that would have gone against the spirit of the day.

We were told to line up in order of age and there was chaos as children turned in circles, pointing at each other, saying, 'I'm March.' 'I'm June.' 'I'm November, who else is November?' Bamber strode around the classroom, shouting, 'Bamber Law, May nineteenth. Bamber Law, May nineteenth.' I remained in my seat, scoring my palm with the curve of my protractor and wondering what it might mean to be born on the same day as someone as big as Bamber. Eventually, I returned my protractor to my pencil tin, which had a blue snail smiling on its lid, as well as the two small holes Bamber had made. Within the week, Harry would scratch lines at the rear of the snail's shell to imply that it had farted.

'I'm May nineteenth.' I stood beside Bamber. He smelt faintly of bacon and urine and his shirt, unlike most others, was not new.

'You're May nineteenth, too?'

I nodded.

I learnt about the Albright Gene in the autumn of 1994. Mum took a phone call in the hall while Elaine, Dad and I ate dinner. We sat and listened as she hung up, stood in silence for a while and then entered the kitchen with long, slow, Shakespearean strides.

'What is it?' Elaine asked.

'The BBC want to make a documentary about us.' Mum steadied herself on the dining table. 'We've made it . . . We've officially *made* it.'

The following month, my cousin Jess and I clung to the railings of the elevated terrace at the rear of her Surrey home and leant backwards towards the mown lawn. To the east was the clay tennis court and in the distance, secluded in a copse of tall firs, the outbuilding that housed the pool. Pitched on the lawn was a large yellow marquee.

'Mum says this is a mistake,' Jess said. 'She thinks people won't like us.'

When people used to talk about the next generation of Albrights, they meant Elaine, Jess and me. Jess was nine. Two years younger than me. She and I used to gather driftwood while on the beach in Devon. Once we'd gathered enough, we'd nail it together and exhibit the sculptures for our mums in the garden of our rented cottage. Mum once separated me from Jess and said, 'Yours is like professional art, James. The way the different planks of wood speak to each other is more subtle.' I told Jess this and she went red. Jess hasn't, to my knowledge, ever suffered from a sweat problem. In those days, she carried a grey toy mouse called Pooky with her at all times. Her mother, Irene, was the wealthiest Albright sister. A car was cloaked in black fabric in their double garage and was said to be a Rolls-Royce and to contain, according to Jess, four Albright brothers that the four sisters had murdered and hidden there. Jess once breathed on my Global Hypercolor T-shirt and, as was the case with those T-shirts, the section she breathed on changed colour. It turned pink and fell where I thought my heart was. My sister had one of those T-shirts, too. Before she wore a training bra, Elaine's breasts used to make hers change colour. It happened once on sports day. She blushed, but I think she was also quite proud.

'Jim, look.'

Jess pointed towards the conservatory. The four sisters walked out onto the lawn, their hair permed and huge, each of them in high heels and a summer dress. Behind them came a tall thin man in a smart blue suit, carrying a red notepad and some recording equipment.

Jess and I jumped down from the terrace and ran across the lawn. We pressed our faces against the window of the pool house; Elaine swam lengths wearing goggles and a peach-coloured cap. She spent most of her time in the pool house that week. Even if I went in and performed a bomb in the shallow end, my sister didn't break her stroke. I'd drain my lungs and lie on the tiles at the bottom of the deep end. Elaine would swim right over me in her goggles and black one-piece costume. It was still two years before she attended the raves at the Midland Hotel in Morecambe.

A thick hedge separated the garden from a small airfield. Jess and I crawled into it and paused. There, in the half-light, surrounded by brambles and wild berries, she told me she intended to become a vet, or, if not a vet, then the person who trained police dogs. She let a woodlouse climb onto her wrist and walk onto her hand. She twisted and turned her arm so that although the insect was moving quite fast, it appeared to go nowhere.

'The expectation is that you'll be an opera singer,' I said.

Jess half submerged her hand in the topsoil and allowed the woodlouse to climb down. I picked a red berry and crushed it with my thumb and forefinger. We crawled from the hedge and ran to the tall fence that surrounded the airfield. It was topped with coils of barbed wire. Jess lay on her back beneath it, looking at the sky without blinking.

'You'll be an opera singer,' I said. 'Elaine will be an artist.' I lay beside my cousin and removed a piece of broken leaf from her loose brown curls. I must have stung myself at some stage because I remember having to locate a dock-leaf and rub it against my forearm.

'What will you be, Jim?'

'I'll be sent to Europe to play professional table-tennis,' I said.

A small plane took off into the sky and I made some comment

about the Second World War, in which our great-uncle Godfrey bayoneted numerous Italians. The dock-leaf dyed my forearm pale green. I attempted to explain why the small plane made no sound as it rose. Through the trees we heard the Albright sisters laughing.

When Bamber Law came for tea we bought Rainbow Dust from the post office and lollies to lick and dip in it. He ran into my room, jumped onto my bed and broke two of its wooden brackets. 'Ah, a gay bed,' he said. He lifted the mattress with great ease and we assessed the damage. He said the bed was old fashioned and repeated that it was gay. 'It's quite new,' I said. Bamber let the mattress fall, causing a small gust of indoor wind.

'What have you got?' he said, planting the lolly in his dingy mouth.

I didn't have a Super NES, a Mega Drive, a Master System or an NES. Bamber sniffed around my bedroom like some kind of hog. He removed his school tie and whipped my wardrobe mirror. He cupped a fart he'd done deliberately and tried to make me smell it. Though his body was burly his head looked too big for it.

'My brother calls his willy Limp Denison,' Bamber said.

'I've got Lego.'

'Mine is Blanka.'

'Oh, right.'

There was a brick of Duplo nestling in the Lego box so I swallowed a plum stone of shame. Bamber grimaced and I considered playing high notes onto his penis, but the consequences of doing so seemed so uncertain. With both hands, he swept the Lego around the box, sorting through the bricks and making a neat pile of blue ones.

'It's real life,' he said. 'You don't have enough windows or white bricks to play the future.'

I can remember him sweeping the Lego round that box very clearly. I can remember the sound it made; it was like small waves breaking on a pebble beach at night.

★

I explained to Jess what gliders are and left her watching the sky. I crawled back through the hedge and went to check on Elaine. She was treading water in the deep end with her goggles lifted onto her forehead. In the house, I found Dad searching through his suitcase. As I entered his room, he abandoned the task without words and lay on the wooden floor, propping his head against the wall in a way that looked quite painful.

'Sorry,' he said.

In the corner of the room, his Austin Reed shirt was screwed up. He'd burnt a black triangle onto it with an iron. From where he was lying, he wouldn't have been able to see out of the window. His room looked down into the garden, where the sisters were gathered in the entrance of the yellow marquee, having their photo taken.

'Don't let people get to you, Jim.'

Dad removed his glasses because he needed to wipe his eyes. I went back out into the garden, to the marquee, where the sisters were seated now, at a circular table, caressing the stems of champagne flutes. The man in the blue suit held a microphone in one hand and made notes with the other.

'And the thing is —' this was Mum — 'we've all got this *gene*, all four of us. We call it the Albright Gene. We each put it to different uses. Although I'm a teacher, I also sing and write poetry . . . Oh, James, come, come and meet the BBC . . .'

The marquee was quite cold and smelt of sweating grass. 'James has it.' Mum gripped the man's forearm and steered the microphone close to her lips. 'He's destined to be a jazz trumpeter, like Louis Armstrong, who, like Daddy, I adore. I see him as the original cool guy.'

'Jess can already sing the aria from *La Bohème*,' Irene said.

'Elaine's thought processes are utterly unconventional.'

Jayne Albright yawned. It was an LA yawn; a combination of jet lag and a life spent in meetings more intense than this. Elizabeth Albright leant forwards to refill her glass. 'Should I talk about why Jayne and I *didn't* have children?'

'No, let me finish, Lizzie.' Mum stroked my cheek. 'Let me finish talking about the Gene.'

By pinching the top of his yellow head and bouncing him along the carpet, Bamber walked his Legoman from the front door of his blue home to the small, multicoloured building where my man lived.

'Hello in there.' Bamber's man was American. 'Time to go to work, buddy.'

I flicked my man through his front door, stood him up straight and bounced him over to Bamber's.

'Where do we work?'

'At the quarry, dummy.' Bamber gave me a frantic, wide-eyed look to indicate that the Lego box was the quarry.

'Oh, right,' I said.

'I'm having real trouble with my wife. Real trouble. I'll be glad to get to work.'

Bamber's man explained to mine how his wife and children were constantly asking for money and holidays and how, for him, going to the quarry was a relief from the stress of his home life. Mum poked her head round the door.

'Oh, hello. Is it Bamber?'

'Actually officially it's Barry, Mrs Thorne.'

Mum didn't correct Bamber's error with her surname. She was distracted by the spectacle of him jumping to his feet.

'My goodness, you're *huge*.'

'I'm exactly the same age as Jim. We're twins.'

Mum gave Bamber the same look she'd given Elaine's thong two years earlier in Cornwall.

'Well then. It's mung beans with lamb for tea.'

The BBC planned to use Mum's idea of the Albright Gene as the theoretical centrepiece for the documentary, which was due to be aired on Radio 4 in early winter, 1994.

'It's a kind of organising principle for the documentary as a whole.' This was over a breakfast of brown toast and honey. 'It makes sense of us. It answers the question, why are the Albrights all so special?'

'But is it actually real?'

'Of *course* it's real. This goes back generations, James. Daddy would have been a musician had it not been for poverty. He saw that art was the great healer. Godfrey was different. He couldn't be expected to entertain people after bayoneting numerous Italians.'

Neither Bamber nor I was able to cut our thumbs with Dad's penknife. In my bedroom, among the scattered Lego bricks, we took turns running its biggest blade across our skin. We weren't pressing hard enough. Bamber had set his heart on us being blood brothers on that first day at Queen's. I hadn't even wanted him to come round, but he kept demanding to.

'Let's leave it,' I said, folding the blade away and pocketing the knife.

'We can't give up,' Bamber said, stepping close to me, his half-smile dwarfed by his round, chubby face. 'There's another way.'

On his instruction, we went to the kitchen and poured two glasses of water. Bamber spat into one. I spat into the other. Bamber's spit involved tentacles of unswallowed lamb and half-chewed mung bean. It hung below the surface like a jellyfish.

'On three.' We each picked up the other's glass. 'One, two, *three*.'

I closed my eyes and drank. The spit slipped down my throat like a pill. I stopped drinking and thought I might be sick. Bamber was still looking into his glass at my small, silvery spittle. Out in the hall, Mum was speaking on the telephone. Bamber's jellyfish was inside my stomach. I felt pregnant.

'I mean honestly, Lizzie, two more different boys you couldn't imagine. It's like two different species, like little and large . . . And they've got such different destinies . . . yes . . . uh-huh . . . well, *exactly*. . .'

Bamber concentrated on my floating spit as he listened. 'Let's go,' he said, emptying the glass into the sink. He ran out of the kitchen and up the stairs, eliciting a squeal from Mum as he rushed past her.

This time, our men didn't go to work at the quarry, but I think it was real life. The Legomen went on adventures round my bedroom, climbing over my bed, my desk and my bookshelves. Bamber kept saying, 'Come on, Private Thorne. Keep going,' in a voice that sounded like he was straining to be heard against a howling wind or a sandstorm. 'Follow me, Private Thorne. Hang on in there.'

The following day at school, we didn't speak, and that's how it went between us. It wasn't hostile, it was just the way it was. Years passed, and it became clear that Bamber wasn't any kind of bully. In fact, he got seriously bullied himself later on because of his weight and because his voice slowed once it broke and because he cried, aged fifteen, when he lost his Tamagotchi on a trip to Harrogate. In our third year at Queen's, it rained heavily during the annual cross-country run and we were forced to take showers. I saw Bamber's penis through the steam and the noise. It was hairier than my dad's. It was longer, too, but Bamber's body was so fat it made his penis appear small. He was trying to hide from everyone, washing himself with one hand clasped over it.

In 2004, I met Bamber in Manchester, where he was working as a bouncer at a nightclub called Romp.

'Eee-are, Jim . . . It's me, Barry.'

He wore a black bandanna with a silver, oriental pattern on it. It was fastened so tightly that it squeezed and bloated his face. He wore the collar of his trench coat up, but there was a nervousness about him, despite his appearance. He didn't really look at me. I was taller than him. In between checking students' bags for drugs and miniature vodka bottles, he told me that he'd twice been out to Afghanistan and expected to go to Iraq.

'Everyone's impressed, Jim. I showed Mother your picture on

the Net. You and Harry King sitting on a bench.' I hadn't heard one of those slow, deep Cumbrian accents in years. 'I always tell people we're blood brothers,' Bamber said. 'I say I went round your house.'

He died at a roadblock near Basra in 2005, a month after our twenty-third birthday. His accent sounded so Cumbrian that night in Manchester. The students looked so much younger than him. Many wore wild clothes that I associated with the eighties.

Dad went to bed early the evening *In Search of the Albrights* was aired on Radio 4. I listened to it in the kitchen with Mum and Elaine. The story I remember most clearly was told by Jayne Albright.

'It wasn't all ice cream and sing-songs,' Jayne said. 'I think it's important to realise our father was bipolar. That's how he'd be diagnosed now. He felt he was less of a man than his brother, Godfrey, the war hero. Daddy loved entertainment, but he could be brutal, sitting in his armchair smoking his pipe while the four of us stood there, singing.'

The programme focused on the careers of Irene and Elizabeth and, to a lesser extent, on Jayne's success in Hollywood. Mum spoke once to describe what it was like growing up with her sisters. Her intonation was strange; you could tell that they'd edited a fragment out of something that, in reality, had flowed and lasted longer. There was no mention of the Albright Gene, or how my mum sang and wrote poems.

'Don't answer that,' she said, when the programme ended and the telephone rang in the hall. 'Don't, Elaine. Let it ring.'

Backstage at the Queen's Christmas Fair 1995, I blew saliva from the pipes of my trumpet. Fiona Hohner balanced her flute on the floor, took her hands away and caught it before it fell. Across the classroom, Elaine and the other saxophonists shared a two-litre bottle of Fanta. I hadn't really spoken to Fiona since that time on the bus. In the meantime, Dilly had burst and so I'd swapped dolphins for pillows. Each night, when I went to bed, I'd rub against one and I even spoke to the pillow and kissed the slip as if a lady's lips were there. I said, 'Oh, darling, I love you, I *love* you.' Shivering at the bus stop that winter, Harry made off-the-cuff remarks about tossing himself off. Once, he stroked his penis through his school trousers with the lid of my pencil tin, which, by then, was entirely silver on account of my having scratched away the smiling snail and all the other paint using a compass point. Harry said he couldn't help himself.

I was thirteen. We played a jazzy version of 'O Little Town of Bethlehem' and I got the solo. I stood and started playing this low C in a shabby, jazzy style, C, C, then in one simple climb I found F, and I held it on, increased the volume and dropped with a relaxed, confident slur down, on the offbeat, to D sharp. D sharp, high F, high F. The solo was going so well that I glanced out into the audience. Mum stood with her eyes shut and her perm moving to our music. To my left, Fiona watched me, holding her flute across her lap.

I took a deep breath and began alternating quickly between top C and top G. Having performed this trick for six or seven seconds, the audience applauded me. Mum nodded and shot at the ceiling with a finger pistol. I remembered how much she loved Louis Armstrong, not just as a musician, but as a man. I remembered how whenever we saw him singing or playing the trumpet on television, she'd say, 'Isn't he beautiful?' I continued to alternate quickly between top C and top G and the audience kept clapping. I caught Fiona's eye and she smiled.

Perhaps it was because I repeated the trick for too long, or perhaps it was because I began to run out of breath, whatever it was, the audience stopped applauding. I think they call it a 'trill'. The audience stopped applauding my trill. Mum opened her eyes, holstered her finger pistol, grimaced and shook her head. I had eight bars to fill before the saxophones returned with the main melody. I played the low C again. It sounded terrible, so I stopped. The drummer's brushes scraped the snare and the trombones plodded the bass line. It was looking like a low point for me until Elaine stood up and improvised over my silence on her saxophone.

'I thought you were good,' Fiona told me afterwards. We were alone backstage.

'I feel unbelievably miserable,' I said.

Fiona pulled a violet scrunchie from her hair. 'So, are you coming to the gym?' She was going through a greasy stage, maybe, because her hair pretty much stayed as it was. She bent herself double and shook it with both hands. Her face was flushed when she stood up straight. 'No?' She dismantled her flute into three bits and placed each into the blue velvet case. 'See you then,' she said.

I blew the fresh saliva from the pipes of my trumpet. Fiona had left behind her scrunchie; I picked it up, put it round my wrist and left the classroom. Instead of walking to the gym, where the disco was, or to the assembly hall, where the Young Enterprise stalls were, I walked into the dark part of the school. One of the chemistry laboratories was open; I sat at the teacher's desk. The blinds were down, it smelt of iodine and was silent. All the chairs were stacked on the tables. I twisted on the teacher's gas tap and its soft hiss was all there was. I twisted it off.

I arrived in the gym in time to watch the last dance. The song was called 'Love Is All Around'. Boys who had play-fought through the evening's upbeat songs and had legged each other up rather than dance, were leaning against the wall now, disgraced. I found a place among them and watched the people on the dance floor.

It was part of a soundtrack to a film, the song. *Four Weddings And A Funeral*. We saw it at the cinema as a family. Elaine described it as 'utter cack', but I enjoyed it. Afterwards, we'd stood in the cinema car park in Lancaster. Mum placed a hand on the cold roof of our silver Ford. 'He's remembered. Hugh Grant has remembered what it *is* to be English.'

I leant against the gym wall, beside climbing ropes that

ponytailed from the ceiling. When a girl shrieked and pushed her dance partner to the ground, I didn't take much notice. But then the song ended and the same girl staggered towards me, arms outstretched, knees buckling. And I knew with the first flicker of the lights in the rafters that the girl was my sister. She hugged me as the gymnasium illuminated.

'You saved me,' I said. 'Earlier.'

Elaine hung almost all her weight from my shoulders and whispered that she loved Dad.

'What a start,' Mum said of my solo, as we drove home. She gripped the steering wheel tight. Beside her, in the passenger seat, Dad burped and let his eyelids flicker, as he drifted in and out of shallow sleep, occasionally sniffing or letting a soft chuckle slip. Elaine worked her way across the back seat and whispered into my ear, touching it, too, with her tongue. 'I did it, Jim,' she whispered. 'Tonight. Guess who with.' I didn't guess. 'I did it in the coal shed with Nathan Lustard. He doesn't even go to school.'

In her diary, Elaine doesn't mention standing up to cover my solo. When we got back home, she rushed from the car but could only crawl along the floor of the hallway like a crooked cat, vomiting Fanta and vodka onto the floorboards.

'I'm sorry,' she said quietly, between retches.

'You're experimenting.'

Dad went upstairs and made the hinges of the spare-room door whimper.

I pulled my pillow under the duvet and I mounted it and kissed it in the dark.

'Oh, Fiona, I love you. I *love* you.'

A cactus of adolescence flowered inside Elaine. Her moods and language became tropical. When our parents went to the Lake District to try to rescue their marriage, she threw a party at our house, filling the kitchen with farmhands and boys from the years above. I mingled as best I could. In the hall, I asked a boy what the music was and he made me smell his index finger and told me it was happy hardcore. His finger smelt of seaweed in a Cornish cove. He and his girlfriend laughed when I told them that. I know now where his finger had been and these days, from time to time, I remember the shriek of delight the girl gave as I tentatively sniffed. The boy threw up in the Italian Courtyard shortly after. He somehow succeeded in permanently staining a flagstone. As the night went on, more and more Vauxhall Novas were parked at ever more unsettling angles around the old lamp post in front of our house. Boys and girls danced on the kitchen table, pointing rhythmically at the air in front of their faces. Two lads came downstairs dressed as my parents and performed a comic double act, miming doggy-style sex. My sister climbed the stairs with Nathan Lustard and my heart broke a bit. The following day, when my parents returned, Dad went straight upstairs and made the spare-room door squeal and slam. Mum stood in the kitchen doorway, holding her suitcase, sniffing the air.

'Fuck off,' Elaine said. She had wrapped herself in a duvet and was sitting on the window seat, looking out into the Italian Courtyard.

'Marijuana,' Mum said.

'*Fuck off.*'

Mum fell slowly to her knees and sobbed for a surprisingly short time. She made a cup of tea and sat with Elaine and me. For a while, we watched as she silently pointed out the various cigarette burns on the tabletop. One of her shoes was in a hanging basket out in the Italian Courtyard. As if to cheer her up, Elaine predicted that she and Dad were getting divorced.

'No, Elaine. We aren't.'

The note read, 'Will you go out with me?' It was delivered by two girls with threadbare, Tipp-Ex-stained ties who smelt of perfume and packed lunch. I met them by the tennis courts the following day.

'Well, will you?'

Beyond the tennis courts was the football pitch, where a group of boys were gathering. Beyond that, Fiona Hohner sat on a damp bench, staring nervously at her lap. The green sleeves of her school jumper were pulled over her fists. I walked over and we sat in silence, watching the boys form a line so that two captains could pick teams. When the game began, Fiona and I followed it carefully and when something funny happened, like when Bamber Law went in to a tackle and hurt a first year, I would laugh and Fiona would, too.

We kissed in the school's old coal shed. We kissed in a fast, repetitive way and I thought, We aren't doing this right. This is too fast. I felt a twinge of guilt for Dilly, too, who was floating somewhere at sea, maybe halfway to America or in a whale's stomach. But the guilt wasn't major because Dilly was an inflatable dolphin, after all. The following morning, I signed my name in the condensation of the kitchen window.

4

The ball sat in Harry's palm. I adopted the 'ready stance' and gestured for him to serve. He did so and it was a topspin, forehand serve which I countered with a backhand chop. I stepped back in anticipation of a fast, attacking shot. It came, but it missed and bounced towards the back of the garage. I knelt down to retrieve the ball from under a rusting pile of Stan King's gardening tools and when I finally spotted it, it was quite a way away. I had to close one eye and really reach for it and I almost pulled a muscle. When I stood up, Harry was gone. I was standing alone clutching a table-tennis ball.

The sound of music led me out of the garage and across Harry's driveway. Harry, my pea-headed friend, sat on a bench at the bottom of his lush, sloping lawn, sheltered by the low limbs of a lime tree. His legs were crossed in what I considered at the time to be the woman's way and he was playing an acoustic guitar and singing. His fingertips stumbled on the fret board and he smiled at his error, looked into the sky and re-sang a word to the corrected, firmly strummed chord. I returned to the garage and stored the ball on the table under Harry's slanted bat.

There are many shots to master in table-tennis and you've got to master them all really, or most of them. You've got to execute offensive forehands with stacks of side as well as topspin and all the power you can generate. You're looking for a vanishing point with those attacking strokes; a beat of what feels like invisibility as the bat hits the ball. It's all about reading the spin. You decode the language of your opponent's body, the angle of their wrist, the shape of their torso, the invisible line drawn in the air by the tip of their bat. The ball arrives as your patient, but leaves as your victim. You diagnose its nausea. You prepare a cure and a novel disease.

★

'The thing is, Jim.' Dad and I lay on the bed in the spare room. He crossed his bare feet. 'Teaching was never for me. I always loved science. Do you know what I wanted to be when I was a kid?'

On a desk by the window was our family's first computer. On the bedside table was a book called *How to Taste: A Guide to Scotch Whisky*, and a copy of a book by Richard Branson. There was also a piece of printer paper on which Dad had typed the word 'Ideas'. The word was emboldened and underlined.

'An astronaut.'

'Oh, right.'

Dad had quit his teaching job and bought the computer shortly after the weekend in the Lake District with Mum. He stopped smoking and the computer relaxed him. If I walked past the spare room, he'd often invite me in and show me something he'd created on Microsoft Paint, or how he'd incorporated a piece of clip art into a Word document.

'I'm too old to be an astronaut, so it's plan B.'

'What's plan B?'

He reached for the sheet of paper marked 'Ideas', held it out in front of us and flicked it.

'I want to be a businessman.'

The biggest shock I received in 1995 wasn't Dad's career change, it was the news that Charlie Albright, my grandfather, was still alive.

'He didn't *want* us to visit,' Mum said. She drove Elaine and I south on the M6. Outside, it was bright, but the car was cold. 'After the diagnosis, he made that clear – *no visiting me here*. Those were his exact words.'

Charlie Albright lay in a bed with his eyes closed, in a dust-smelling psychiatric care home near Stroud. There was a free-standing heater that was switched off. On the bedside table was a lamp with an orange shade and, in its light, bluebells peeped over the rim of a Manchester United mug. In the corner, by the window, was a double bass.

'Still asleep?' A nurse arrived with a tray of biscuits and some beakers of orange. I asked about the origins of the mug.

'We give all the men football things,' the nurse said. 'If they can't remember who it was they supported, we choose Man United.'

Charlie Albright woke not long before we had to leave. His lips were dry and his brown eyes were bloodshot. He was musical and too young to fight in the war. Mum cried and he said, 'No, no, no.' She bit her lower lip. When she couldn't contain her feelings any more, the words 'Don't worry' came from her mouth with a sob and I thought she might say art is a great healer, but, instead, she said, 'We'll entertain.' She put her arms round Elaine and me. Her father looked up at her and tried to speak.

His coffin was made of Somerset willow. His double bass was leant against the pulpit. At the back of the church, a row of old men sat together in silence with pale faces and Manchester United bobble hats. Irene Albright sang 'Ave Maria'. Elizabeth Albright spoke. She described how adamant her father had been that he be left alone, having been diagnosed with dementia. He had asked her, she said, to communicate simply with newspaper cuttings.

'It brought me great happiness,' Elizabeth said. 'Cutting round reviews and other articles. I kissed each one before putting it in the envelope. I'm sure my sisters did the same.'

Of the four, only Irene, the eldest, cried. The sisters formed a tight embrace in the car park. When they separated, Mum was left, ashen-faced, watching the priest unlock his bike from the graveyard railings and the group of Manchester United fans climb into their blue minibus.

'I sent him letters,' she said, as we sat in traffic, south of Birmingham. 'I sent him letters about you two.'

I spent the journey giving secret waves to children in passing cars. Though most waved back, few smiled; the majority flashed their palms in acknowledgement then looked away. Occasionally cars drove adjacent to us for minutes on end, seemingly travelling at the precise speed we were. Such was the case with a ginger-haired girl in a beige baseball cap. She replied to my wave by flicking a V and pressing it against her window. She then tapped her father's shoulder and requested, I assume, that he accelerate away.

At Hilton Park service station, Mum, Elaine and me shared a steel pot of stewed tea intended for two not three. Elaine lobbied for *Just Seventeen* but wasn't successful. When we rejoined the motorway, Mum put on a Miles Davis tape; it sounded so abrasive she switched it off almost immediately. We came off at Junction 35, north of Lancaster, just as the sun slipped below a horizon of dark crags. Elaine removed her headphones and asked where we were. Streetlight rhythmically illuminated us. As we joined the road to Ridley, Mum said Dad's full name quietly to herself.

At a barbecue once, when we lived in the south, Dad and I played on the lawn. We played a game called Combat Bombastic. It was all to do with how he was about to explode and I had to escape. He chased me, counting down from ten, and then, once he got to zero and he had me in his arms, he said, 'Combat Bombastic,' in a robotic voice and he detonated. We rolled over and his glasses broke at the bridge. For months he sellotaped them together in the morning before work.

When we got back home after Charlie Albright's funeral, we found Dad beneath the piano in the Music Room. He looked like a man asleep against the trunk of a tree. Elaine and I waited by the door as Mum approached him. The innards of his computer lay dismantled on the rug, beside a diagram of a motherboard, half a banana and our cat, Pop, who sat very neatly, cleaning her ear with a licked paw. Mum touched Dad's shoulder lightly, then shook it a little, then held him with both hands and shouted his name.

'Julian, you fool. Oh, Julian, you *fool*.'

It was awkward watching her put him into the recovery position. It was like watching big children wrestle on wet winter grass. She dragged him away from the piano and laid him down among the bits of dismantled computer. She checked his pulse and listened to his breathing. She stroked his cheek while Elaine called an ambulance.

Mum once told me that she stopped taking Dad seriously after he dyed his hair one evening in 1990. We ate tuna pasta and no one mentioned what he'd done until Mum asked Elaine, 'Do you like your father's hair?' Dad sat at the head of the table, his hair the colour of milk chocolate and still damp from the dying process.

On that afternoon in 1995, paramedics carried him from the Music Room on a stretcher. He was taken to the intensive care unit of the hospital in Lancaster. Mum, Elaine and I followed in the car, listening to the Miles Davis tape. Elaine and I waited in the canteen, where I tried to eat chips and a sausage roll, but it felt like it was all getting stuck near my Adam's apple. 'He's a dick,' Elaine said, under her breath. 'Fact. If he dies, I'm leaving home. Fact.'

When we went to see him, he had happy eyes and a bloodless face. He patted the hospital bed and showed a pride in his surroundings. After resetting his smile several times, his energy levels dipped and he slept. When he woke, Elaine had returned to the canteen and he and I were alone.

'I was flying over the Lake District, Jim.' Dad laid his hand across my wrist but didn't grip. 'I was flying over the mountains, over teaching, over your mum and her sisters. They were all down on the ground looking up at me and Richard Branson. Richard was with me, holding onto my hand because he couldn't fly.' Dad blinked several times and very nearly fell asleep. 'We landed on the summit of Scafell Pike. Richard put his arm round me and said how good I was, how he wished he could hire me.' Dad inhaled cautiously, turned my hand and looked at my palm. 'We flew to the moon, Jim. We saw a Golden Eagle.'

Later, I wrapped my legs round my pillow and said to it, 'Oh darling, I love you . . .' and I kissed the slip as if lips were there. 'Oh, Fiona, I *love* you.'

'Jim.' I turned and dismounted the pillow in one movement. Elaine stood in my bedroom doorway, eating some bread. 'You do know that's not what it's like.'

'I'm tired,' I said.

'Sex isn't like that.' My sister's tongue emerged to lick her lips and, when it did, it caught the light of my bedside lamp and glistened. 'All that "oh, darling, I love you" stuff. That doesn't happen.' She turned to leave, then paused. 'He drank an entire bottle of whisky, Jim. He's diabetic. So he *is* a dick. Fact.'

Red-faced girls in turquoise T-shirts jogged the curves of the running track. Cricketers practised in the nets. Four boys trained for the relay, passing a glittery baton to each other over and over. It was a sunny day and this was before my sweat problem, though only just. In the middle of the field, the head groundsman, whose name I forget, was mowing the cricket pitch. The whine of his mower seemed to come and go, amplifying when he turned away from the school and began to mow towards us.

'I've quit the table-tennis team,' I said.

'I'm not a big fan of fizzy drinks, you know,' Fiona said, pushing a small twig into the soil. 'The sixth-formers are getting a can-machine.'

'I've retired. It isn't a real sport.'

Fiona tightened her ponytail and neatened the two strands of hair that spiralled down the sides of her face. This was one of the first occasions we'd spent any time together since I'd agreed to be her boyfriend, unless you count kissing in the coal shed, which I don't.

'We play it on holiday sometimes,' she said. 'I'm really good.'

Harry didn't wear his red strip in his last days as a Ridley C player. He wore a beaded necklace, a bright yellow T-shirt and long Bermuda shorts. He didn't seem to care when our coach said, 'Get some proper kit, this isn't Miami Beach.' At home, he had a television in his bedroom. He used his mum's rowing machine on a daily basis and became strong. His only moment of weakness occurred when he was accused, apparently correctly, of having a sperm stain on the crotch of his jeans. 'It's yogurt,' he'd argued, with confidence. But then he went red, licked his finger and began scraping rather frantically at the stain.

A roar came from the cricket nets and a ball flew high into the sky, eventually landing near a group of girls, who grabbed each other, looked at it and shrieked.

'Jim. We're over, OK?' Fiona said.

'I love you.'

'I like someone else.'

'Who?'

'Open your eyes, Jim. Who do you think?'

Mr Shep. That's what we used to call the groundsman at Queen's. He was so tall his limbs were all out of proportion and he walked with a huge limp and I suspected one of his thighs was twice the size of the other. He paused in the middle of the cricket field, removed his hands from the mower and wiped his forehead with a rag he took from the pocket of his maroon dungarees. He stepped to one side and seemed to be checking that the lines were straight. They were.

A week later, at the summer disco, I walked into the gymnasium wearing a red Next shirt, blue jeans and my school shoes. I watched boys sliding across the floor on their knees and, towards the back, I saw others leant against the walls, their hair gelled, their faces straight. When the last song came on, I did a stupid thing. I stood in the corner of the gym and I embraced myself. It was that old joke – when you make your own hands roam around your back and feel your own bottom so it looks like you're passionately kissing someone. I did it so well a teacher grabbed my shoulder and said, 'That's too far, you two.' When he saw it was an illusion, he took a step back and red and white lights flashed on his frown.

It came out that Harry had gone to the coal shed with Fiona

before she'd dumped me. They call that cheating. It seemed a strange word to use. Harry and I never spoke about it, as we never spoke about the end of Ridley C. I don't know why Harry stopped loving the game, but maybe, as I say, it was because, on an instinctive level, many Westerners don't consider table-tennis to be a real sport. They see it as a miniature version of something grander and that's not the case in China.

I sat on a crash mat at the edge of the dance floor. Fiona and Harry held each other and slow-danced in a beam of pink light. I watched the adult techniques Fiona used when touching my friend's bottom. Where had she learnt them? Harry guided her slowly from side to side; their foreheads touched. When the song ended, they kissed in a slow, cautious way, as the lights in the rafters flickered and then came on.

REAL LIFE

5

I've covered Peta's morning shift twice this week after she texted in the middle of the night and begged me to. Peta still texts in block capitals, though the lower case has been available since 1999. She meets men online, goes on dates and tends to stay the night with them. I prepared a 'Top of the Morning!' for when she got in today. She sipped it between yawns, sitting on the stainless-steel workstation, still in the black jeans and knee-high boots she wears for these dates.

'How was he?'

'Not so nice, but I clung to him all night.'

I sliced mango in silence. Sex is important in life. You probably have your own attitude to it. Childhood left me with a desire to love. I'm going to write about Kate Reynolds. The story begins in January 1996, when Irene Albright signed a lucrative record deal. It's funny how I can write sentences like *The story begins in January 1996* . . . I truly feel my writing's improving. I recently bought a smaller notepad in addition to this one in which I record my passing thoughts, for example, 'I lived inside Mum for eight months – quite happily.' Or, 'When Elaine fell from the dead apple tree in the garden back in Ridley, it was the gooseberry bush that broke her fall. She tore some culottes that Mum had sewn and I've been adding extra gooseberries to "Top of the Morning!" to intensify its sourness!'

The story begins in January 1996. However, on 13 February that year, the boy band Take That split up and a telephone helpline was put in place to console distraught fans. I called it as a joke, with the intention of saying I was glad. I did this when the house was empty and my call was answered by a Liverpudlian lady, who possessed the out of tune, crystal-bell version of that city's accent.

'I know this is hard, love, but you're going to be all right.'

I sat at the bottom of the stairs, spooling the telephone's wire on my thumb and all of a sudden feeling silly. I opened my mouth to speak, but gasped instead. My Adam's apple felt pierced and I fought off the tears with a frown.

'You've still got your CDs,' the lady said. 'And there'll be some boss solo albums.'

'Sorry,' I said.

Before the woman could reply, I hung up.

The story begins in January 1996. In February 1996, Harry requested permission to perform in assembly and it was granted. While some people liked to imagine their funeral, others, such as Harry, liked to imagine the social benefits of doing something cool in assembly. Harry didn't just imagine it; he combed his blond hair over his ears, picked up his acoustic guitar and walked out in front of the whole school. He performed 'Wonderwall' and, by so doing, he unleashed love, the love of an entire school, which is no small amount. In the aftermath of his performance, the young, newly hired IT teachers started borrowing CDs off him and lending him their own. By singing in assembly, Harry had put himself under threat – the threat was social failure and public humiliation. He'd put his entire adolescence on the line. But as he strummed the final chord and stood up, you wouldn't have known. He looked blasé. He glanced up to acknowledge, with a confused half-smile, that the entire assembly hall was applauding. Around me, everyone stood up. Girls supported themselves on the shoulders of boys and jumped to get a look at Harry. And I knew, sitting there with my legs crossed, that our friendship was probably done for. By lunchtime, the name of his band had gone all round school. It was Monkey Eats Man.

The story begins in January 1996, when Mum took a phone call in the hall. 'Really, Irene? . . . And you've signed it? . . . Bellissimo!' Irene Albright's performance in *Aida*, opposite Luciano Pavarotti at La Scala, Milan, would be recorded and released worldwide on double CD and quadruple vinyl. Mum drank half a bottle of red wine and sang to herself the aria concerning love from *Don Carlos*. Then she ate a chocolate mousse. Her joy vanished as swiftly as it arrived. She sat down, shelved her breasts on the kitchen table and reflected in a hoarse voice and with a thin mousse-moustache that 'It's hard to stay at the top, James. It's *so* hard up here.'

I visited the spare room, where the curtains were drawn and the only light came from Dad's television, which illuminated his pale face. His eyes looked incapable of closing and he was playing on the Super Nintendo he'd bought following his first trip to Kendal AA. 'Do you like Mario, Jim?' he asked me, without taking his eyes off the screen or altering his expression at all. Down in the hallway, Mum sang the words, 'Made it,' into the phone in an operatic style. Dad gritted his teeth and cut a corner on Mario Kart, steering Mario off-road and driving him slowly across a patch of nuclear green grass.

'Irene's singing with Pavarotti,' I said.

'Hang on a second.'

'Mario's cool.'

'He is, Jim!' Having rejoined the road, Dad hit a banana skin and spun to a stop. Yoshi drove past, followed by the Princess. 'Mario's got it right,' Dad said, building up speed again. 'A good job. A reliable colleague in Luigi. And then think about Sonic the Hedgehog! Always going too quickly, acting over the top. I can see Sonic enjoying opera.'

'Mario's Italian.'

'I can really picture Sonic at the opera, Jim.'

One evening, some days later, Mum sat in the wicker chair, obscured by a broadsheet newspaper. Dad cooked spaghetti bolognaise and, for some time, I'd been aware that he was humming softly, as Mum argued that Robin Hood was a Marxist. '. . . and so England *does* have a tradition of wealth distribution . . .' I write this because it was the first time I remember anyone mentioning Tony Blair. 'He's a *late* baby boomer, too, like me.' This, in turn, reminds me of the time a few years later, in 1999, when Mum first watched *The Osbournes*. 'So this is it, is it? We just watch them live, rather than living ourselves? He's my age, this retard. In fact, he's older. He's an *actual* baby boomer.'

Mum collapsed her newspaper and took a seat at the kitchen table, where Dad was now serving his bolognaise.

'Was that Nirvana I heard coming from your bedroom earlier, Elaine?'

My sister was slumped at the head of the table. 'I need them to make a new album,' she said. She wore a shabby purple smock that had tiny circular mirrors stitched into the fabric. 'I've only got one and it's on tape.'

Each plate of spaghetti released an odourless steam. Mum put her cutlery down and looked at her daughter with great curiosity.

'You do know their singer's dead, don't you?'

'Sorry?'

'You do know their singer *killed* himself.'

'Whose?'

'Nirvana's.'

Elaine focused on her plate of food. Mum smiled. 'Oh, come on now. You knew. You *must* have known.' And it was as she said this, as she said that Elaine *must* have known, that we all became sure that she hadn't. There was something about the way Elaine observed the small movements of her fork as she idly coiled a sauceless strand of spaghetti.

'Kurt Cobain isn't dead.'

'You liked happy hardcore,' I said. 'You wouldn't have known.'

Kurt Cobain received a bullet to the head over two years before this family meal, in April 1994. It was a year that began with a number one for D:Ream and their song 'Things Can Only Get Better'.

'Kurt's not dead.' The cuff of Elaine's smock was resting in her bolognaise. 'He's *not dead.*'

'He is,' Dad said, pushing his chair out from under the table.

'He's definitely dead.' He removed Elaine's wrist from the sauce and gripped it.

We followed Dad to the spare room and waited in silence as he booted up his PC, which whirred and groaned while Elaine sniffed and tutted and a modem bleeped and glinged and Dad leant over the keyboard and typed 'kurt cobain dead body' into AltaVista. Bit by bit and very slowly, a black-and-white photograph appeared on the screen. We saw a trainer. A leg. A man crouched down holding a notepad. An oddly short arm. It was grainy and, I thought, fairly inconclusive. But when it was finally all there, Dad pressed his fingertip right onto the screen and said, 'There.' Elaine nodded and left the room. The next thing I heard were her fast footsteps on the stairs and Mum attacking Dad, telling him that he was sick, profoundly sick, and perverted, too, in a way, because this was the most twisted and insensitive thing she'd ever witnessed. 'I loathe you, Julian,' she said. 'Listen to what I'm saying. I *loathe* you.' It was the first time we used the Internet as a family.

I found Elaine fashioning a shrine in the corner of her bedroom, near the window. She knelt in front of it in a haze of joss stick smoke, clutching her Nirvana cassette in both hands.

'Are you OK?'

'Get out.'

'But are you OK?'

'Get out.'

At the 1996 Brit Awards, Michael Jackson performs his single 'Earth Song'. As he begins the third verse, people dressed in rags assemble on a white slope at the back of the stage. After the key change, during the extended climax of the song, Jackson hovers above the stage on a crane and the camera cuts to the people in rags and finds them weeping, anguished, shaking their fists and wringing their hands. When the music settles and returns to the original piano refrain, Michael Jackson removes his black clothes to reveal bright white ones. The people behind him remove their rags to reveal colourful outfits. Jackson stands in a spotlight and assumes the position of Jesus on the Cross. One by one, the people embrace him and kiss his hands. Jackson is embraced by representatives of different faiths and races. He kisses the forehead of an elderly Orthodox Jew. At the end of his performance, he quotes statistics on the destruction of the rainforest and the death of children through hunger. He says he loves and believes in the members of the audience. Beside him, a girl in a yellow T-shirt translates his words into sign language. Halfway through this performance, Jarvis Cocker, the frontman of the Sheffield band Pulp, climbs onto the stage from the audience, bends over and uses his hands to imply the breeze of a fart. One of Jackson's dancers, an African tribesman, tries to force Cocker from the stage. Cocker evades him long enough to lift up his cardigan to reveal his black T-shirt. The protest, Cocker says afterwards, is designed to deflate the American's performance, which the Englishman considers overblown.

During Euro '96, Dad shot me with an invisible machine gun. 'I can't watch the game, Jim. I'm working.' It was an automatic weapon. He shot me twice and ran upstairs. On the half-landing, he stooped, bit the ring from a hand grenade and tossed it towards me. He faked its explosion from the upstairs landing. I went to see my sister.

Someone once told me that youth's a love affair with newness. For Elaine, it was a whirlwind romance. She was by her bedroom window, sticking a Jamie Redknapp poster to the wall. Beside me, in a bin bag, were the remains of the Kurt Cobain shrine, which had expanded in the week it existed to include pencil sketches, candles stuck in wine bottles and scraps of paper on which Elaine had written out Nirvana lyrics in neat. 'You're binning this?' I said. She'd taken down a poster of a baby sea lion, too, that had hung by her bed since 1990.

'Grunge ended,' she said. 'So did rave.'

She wore a pair of fitted red hot pants and a white crop top.

On her midriff, painted in red lipstick and Tipp-Ex, was a flag of St George. She had the same flag on both cheeks. She danced, raising up alternate knees and pointing at the ceiling with alternate hands. She let her tongue dangle slightly from her mouth. Having stuck up the poster of the England footballer, Elaine danced into her en-suite bathroom with her tongue still dangling, and when she returned, she was sipping, slightly self-consciously, from a bottle of yellow liquid. It was Hooch. She came close and took rather a large swig and wiped her mouth with the back of her hand. 'What?' she said. And I said, 'Nothing.' Elaine approached her stereo, turned the music down and told me to leave because she had things to do. 'I've got to shave before the England game, Jim. Get it?'

Kate Reynolds was in my year at Queen's Secondary, but had remained well camouflaged due to good marks, brown hair, invisible parents, adequate friends, no netball, competent hockey, cello skills, a remote home and a look in her hazel eye that said that somewhere beyond Queen's, somewhere beyond her doomed peers and beyond the north of England, an actual life was waiting for her. One afternoon in Textiles, a teacher ran a yellow tape measure around Kate's chest and looked down to read the measurement.

'Crikey.'

I pierced the index finger of my left hand with a sewing pin.

'Crikey. Kate Reynolds. You've got a magnificent bust.'

I looked across the room with a finger in my mouth, sucking my blood. Kate appeared flustered and quite depressed. I wanted to lie face down on my stomach until the 1990s ended. Kate Reynolds. Her trousers weren't fitted fashion trousers but were charcoal-grey boy's trousers, which was very refreshing. I got the tightening – a blocked throat and tense testicles. I was barely breathing when a second teacher arrived to divide us into Young Enterprise groups.

'OK, listen, everyone . . . Everyone, be quiet and listen. Harry

King . . . Kate Reynolds . . . and Jim Thorne. That's team one. You need an idea for your business. Next, it's . . .'

Our first meeting took place in a classroom attached to the Home Economics kitchen. Thirty or so first years were learning to cook full English breakfasts. The air smelt of pork and Lynx Atlantis. 'I'll tell you what people want,' Harry said. He wore a green-and-yellow Adidas jacket. I'd seen him in it already while on my lunchtime laps of the school. The members of Monkey Eats Man occupied the stoop of a disused entrance to the physics labs. It proved a good location for Harry to perform impromptu concerts, which I always hurried past rather than attend.

'Go on,' Kate said.

'Badges,' Harry said. 'People really need badges.'

The *Sun* splashed onto our doormat in the summer of 1996. 'What a grotesque error.' Mum dangled the newspaper from the tips of her fingers. 'I hate to even hold it. I can feel myself becoming stupid. Jim, quick, open the bin. In fact, get a fresh bin liner.'

Having called the newsagent, she learnt that Dad had added the *Sun* to our normal order. Rather than confront him, she put the newspaper in its own private bin liner and took it straight outside. She did this every day for a week and Dad never once complained. Nor did he ever come down and fish it out of the bin. Soon, Mum stopped bothering with the bin-liner ritual and stopped sniffing it and recoiling and saying, 'Uh, it *reeks* of hate.' Instead, what happened was, after three weeks or so, the *Sun* found its way onto the breakfast table each morning and Elaine and I started to read it.

The second strange arrival of that summer came the day England played Scotland in the European Championship. Paul Gascoigne scores what's generally regarded as a wondergoal. He flicks the ball over Colin Hendry's head with his left foot and volleys it into the air of the goal with his right. The other England players spray water into his mouth to celebrate. It's a reference to the binge drinking they've been doing in the week before the tournament. Soon after Gascoigne scored, our doorbell rang. I went out into the hall and noticed Dad swaying on the stairs, gripping the banister.

On our doorstep, reaching up to ring the doorbell once more, was my cousin, Jess Albright. A black Jaguar XJS was parked beside the old lamp post and Irene Albright, dressed in white fur coat, shades and black headscarf, was retrieving a large suitcase from its boot.

'Aren't you supposed to be in Milan?' I said.

'Absolutely,' Jess replied.

Irene squeezed past her daughter, passed me, and walked down the hall without saying hello. She set down her suitcase at the foot of the stairs and looked at Dad, who was still gripping the banister with both hands and turning more pale by the second. Mum appeared on the half-landing; she performed several slightly ambiguous joy-hoots as she descended the stairs, passing Dad, and entering her sister's embrace. 'Oh, God,' she said. 'What are you *doing* here?'

Irene searched through her handbag and handed a piece of paper to Mum. She then went into the kitchen, sat at the table and bowed her head.

'"Dear Milly. Disaster – Irene has lost her voice."' Mum read the note aloud. It was written not by Irene but by her husband, Edmund Lyle. '"She kept complaining that a snake was living in her throat. She claimed it was the snake from the garden of Eden, which of course is the Devil in disguise. The deal's off. She needs to hide somewhere out of the way, away from the stress, at least until she can speak. Call me as soon as she makes a sound."'

Dad fainted in the hall, where he'd been listening at the door. He fell into the kitchen and spread himself out on the floor. Mum made me run for his insulin needles and she calmly brought him round with an injection, while continuing to read Edmund's letter. '"We're telling the press she's got cancer. We'll say pancreatic. If you could see about getting Jess in at James's school, that would be lovely. She has to be with Irene to continue her singing tuition. Hope you and Julian are well. Very grateful. Sad days. Edmund."'

In the corner of the kitchen, Jess stood in a navy-blue dress. She was twelve now. Her brown eyes were zealous but sullen. There were two ruby spots on her forehead. She looked round the kitchen, squinting slightly, sympathetic but unimpressed. She'd abandoned the name Lyle in favour of Albright. Of our generation, such as it was, Jess was the brightest hope.

Irene sat with her face closed and largely covered by her wild curls. Dad slumped in the wicker chair. Mum, at the kitchen table, was only just beginning to count the cost of her sister's presence. There would be no double CD, no quadruple vinyl, no dinner with Pavarotti, no night out for the Albrights. 'Pancreatic cancer,' she said. The doorbell rang again.

'I'll go,' I said.

On the doorstep, looking at me through quarter-closed eyes, was Nathan Lustard. He was carrying Elaine. Her body looked very small as he brought it into the hall. The flags of St George on her cheeks were both smudged and there was an aromatic orange smear near her lips. Her hot pants had slipped down her bottom a little and one white bra strap fell from her shoulder.

Nathan carefully lowered Elaine onto the sofa in the Music Room. Mum muted the television and Jess Albright sat at the piano and began playing a piece of classical music, Handel, I think. Irene stroked Elaine's hair while Mum went in search of water. He was a tall, thin man, Nathan. He wore brogues with tracksuit bottoms and a woollen Fila jumper. He gave the impression that even bumping into him might hurt, might be like colliding with a brass statue in the dark. He was rumoured to possess a large Ying-Yang coffee table, which people, including myself, very much liked the idea of. 'We were drinking,' he said. He had the same deep, dumb Cumbrian accent as Bamber. 'She was drinking lager. England scored.' On the muted television,

Gascoigne's goal replayed in slow motion. Mum returned with a washing-up bowl and quickly wiped the flags of St George from my sister's cheeks and the sick from her lips. Elaine's eyes opened and, waving Mum away, she declared herself absolutely fine. 'I had five pints, Jim,' she told me, as if I was the only person in the room, before she retched fruitfully into the bowl.

Jess Albright slept on a mattress beside my bed and this made it tricky to mount my pillow and say, 'Oh, Kate, darling, I love you. I *love* you.' I hoped, in those days, that the ability to talk candidly about my penis might make Harry and me friends again. Three times a week, in the steam of the shower, I spluttered things like, 'Magnificent bust, Kate Reynolds, bras,' and generally did my best to bring about the feeling that I had only experienced with pillows and an inflatable dolphin. But the truth is, I struggled to.

'Jim?'

'Yeh?'

'How long do you think before my mum speaks?'

We talked in the dark before sleep, Jess and I. She made friends quickly at Queen's. She played in every orchestra and sang in the choir. She got the piss taken out of her a bit, too, because she was southern and appeared not to use hairspray. At home, she followed a strict programme of schoolwork, singing, piano practice, dancing and reading, all of it done under the watchful eye of her mute mother, who, it turned out, loved the *Sun* and read it each day without showing any of the disdain that made Mum describe it as 'a long and boring love letter from the Devil'. Irene even took time to read the articles that surrounded the Page 3 Girl, which I didn't dare do on account of the debilitating tightening.

Jess slept in a pair of white pyjamas decorated with violet flowers, and even though, since she'd arrived, I could no longer tell my pillow how much I loved it, I actually enjoyed talking to Jess about things. She'd ask me questions about my life, I'd talk about Kate, she'd turn out the light and sometimes, in the darkness, she'd say my name and, when I replied, she'd say, 'Nothing.'

One night, the bedroom ceiling creaked. The old wooden floorboards were rubbing against each other. We lay there listening; our eyes open in the dark. And even though Jess was twelve and I was naive, I think we both knew that the strange creaks above us could mean only one thing; that Nathan Lustard, who stank of sheep, fags and minty aftershave, whose green Nissan Bluebird was parked outside and who slept over most weekend nights, was upstairs doing it with Elaine, in one of the positions, doing it fairly frantically, causing the ginger floorboards to rub and speak. The performance peaked with a rush of creaks and concluded with some staccato afterthoughts. The ceiling went quiet and Jess fluffed her pillow. In the darkness, she was looking at me; I could tell by the mood of the room.

'Jim?'

'Yeh?'

'Nothing.'

At Queen's, for a while, you were teased for saying 'Hey' instead of 'Hi'. You were accused of trying to be American. But this changed gradually and, in fact, I became addicted to saying 'Hey' to Kate Reynolds. After Double Maths on Tuesday, I'd pass her in the glass corridor that linked the old part of the school to the new. I'd clutch the strap of my rucksack and say, 'Hey.' And she'd say, 'Hey,' and I could have kept on like this for years – just saying 'Hey'. Then one day I said 'Hey' and she said, 'Jim, wait.' She pulled me to one side of the glass corridor. 'We need to have a meeting about badge designs. You and Harry could come to mine one night next week. Maybe Wednesday, after his band practice?'

Kate's house was called Sea View. She made me remove my shoes at the door. I followed her up the wide staircase and got a pretty miserable tightening. I was a perv, I think, in those days.

Yes, I was a perv. I untightened slightly as we entered her bedroom. My big toe poked out of a hole in my sock and I gave myself unsevere friction burns by rubbing it against the thick beige carpet.

'Sorry about this.' Kate nodded at the bedroom walls, taking a seat at her cluttered desk. 'My stepdad won't let me redecorate because of uni and leaving home.'

A blue-sky mural covered every inch of the walls and ceiling. White clouds had been painted using a sponge and there was the occasional bird in flight, distant jumbo jet and green hot-air balloon. Standing in Kate's bedroom felt like flying.

'That's four years away,' I said.

'It'll go fast, he says.'

Kate touched her CD player and piano music played, only quietly at first. 'I love this,' she said. Cellos circled slowly round a low melody. 'It's Rachmaninov.' She leant back against the sky wall and closed her eyes. She tilted her head and allowed a smile to slowly melt. I knew not to mention the music I admired. Ini Kamoze, Whitney Houston, Skee-lo, Scatman John. We brainstormed for a while and by the time Harry arrived from his band practice, Kate and I had settled on two badge designs.

'We're doing one with a picture of Simone de Beauvoir on it,' Kate said, as Harry removed his Kangol beret, leant his guitar against the bookcase and smirked at the contents of Kate's inflatable CD rack. 'She's a feminist,' Kate continued. 'I'm going to write a leaflet about her life and work, so people know exactly what she stood for. And then for the second one we're using the slogan "Women Are Manufactured", which is a paraphrase of something Simone de Beauvoir said. But we like the way it's *Man*ufactured on our badge, because it hints at men being in charge. That's what we thought, isn't it, Jim?'

'Yes,' I said. 'It's gender politics.'

'Great.' Harry lay on Kate's single bed, resting his head on her pillow. 'Well, I'm doing one with the Union Jack on it, one with the word "SMEG" written in big letters, and one with "Oasis Suck" on it, which obviously isn't true, but cool people will wear it.'

Later, we ate lamb stew with Walter, the man who looked after Kate. We ate in the candlelit gloom of his dining room, where the walls were filled with framed photographs of serious men with beards and guns. Walter conducted his thoughts with a forked morsel of lamb that dripped. His eyes were glazed and his hairline was high up on his yellow head, as if it were retreating from reality.

'Improving life is like bailing out a dinghy in a storm. The world is always full of new humans.' Walter filled his glass with more red wine and did the same for Harry. Before we'd sat down he'd insisted we should drink. 'All over the animal kingdom parents are guarding their young. Frogs are guarding tadpoles. Man, meanwhile, continues to reel from the invention of the screen and the camera.' I wanted to ask Kate where her mum was. 'There is newness, everywhere, like mould,' Walter announced. He lectured at Lancaster University. His thoughts rose on waves of wine and concentration, then drowned or were washed away, saddened and soaking wet.

'No one understands you, Walter,' Kate said.

The old man dropped his fork, spat out some lamb and brought his head crashing down, so his forehead was pressed against the face of his wristwatch and his small shoulders were hunching and unhunching quickly.

'What is it?' Kate asked.

Walter laughed until his lungs gave in.

'What's so funny?'

'I'm laughing, Kate.' He lifted his head. 'I'm laughing because when I was twenty-six I wrote a poem.' He hummed to calm himself and sat up straight. 'And I sent this poem to a publishing house in an envelope along with a typed letter. And they sent me a letter saying they thought it was good, but not quite there. I was living in South Kensington, before it became posh. Your mother used to visit me most days and she did so on the day of the rejection. It was raining. She walked in and there I was, standing by my mantelpiece. I screwed up the letter and threw it in the fire – so dramatic! Your mother sat me down and do you know what she did? She brushed my hair with a hairbrush that belonged to *my* mother. Her hair dripped rain onto mine as she did this, and she said, "No one understands you, Walter."'

'That doesn't sound like Mum,' Kate said.

Walter directed Harry to a small drawer in a mahogany corner cabinet and Harry returned with a packet of cigarettes. The four of us laid our cutlery over the remains of the stew and we each lit one on a Zippo that Walter passed round. 'The poem was about me, aged five, going to see downed Messerschmitts exhibited in Trafalgar Square.' He went to get another bottle of wine and, in his absence, the three of us blew smoke and looked at each other. It was Walter who told me youth is a love affair with newness. His moods arrived with the intensity of adverts and then left like pop songs fading. He stubbed out his first cigarette in the stew and attacked Kate incoherently, saying, 'I teach your mother about feminism, don't I? I give her the right ideas. That's freedom, isn't it? Be*lief*. We were happy.' But his mood would soften quickly and quite beautifully and he would light a cigarette, exhale the first lungful of smoke into the gloom, watch it drift and say, 'Well, the important thing is that we're here. That's the most important thing, boys. It's an immense pity. But we have to be somewhere. And we are. We're here.'

And so the evening drifted on until Walter lost his temper with a dying candle and began claiming that contemporary culture was petty and of no consequence, and death, death was the most pitiful idea he'd ever heard, 'like some drably elaborate undergraduate thesis'.

'Eee-are, Walter,' Harry said. 'Hold on. What are you talking about?'

'Harry's in a band,' Kate said. 'Called Monkey Eats Man.'

Walter snorted. A speck of saliva arced through the candlelight and landed in my lap. 'That's right, I am in a band,' Harry said. It was that night at Sea View, I think, that I first noticed his capacity for altering his voice. Harry acquired new accents and tones like other people acquire new coats or shoes. It dawned on me that evening, as he and Walter discussed popular music, that he had begun to speak with an unmistakably Mancunian accent.

'Every band fails,' Walter said.

'What?'

'Every band fails.'

'In what possible way did the Beatles fail?'

'It's not just them. It's all bands. You're twelve years old. You don't know.'

'We're fourteen,' Kate said.

Harry placed a fag in his mouth, flicked open the lid of the Zippo and raised it with both hands to the cigarette's unlit tip. He flicked the metal wheel with his thumb but no flame came. The wheel turned a little but it made an awful metal-on-metal scratching sound that made me wince.

'You're talking rubbish.' Harry tried the lighter twice more but again got no flame, only the scrape. 'I'm telling you. This is a great time. Pop is dead. Oasis are . . . We're real . . . We're –'

'There's no flint,' Walter interrupted. 'You'll not get it working. The flint's worn away.'

Harry fed his fag to the flame of a shrinking candle and sucked. The following night, the lights in the assembly hall dimmed and the stage lit up. Parents sat at the back on classroom chairs. Pupils gathered in their own clothes at the foot of the stage. Harry lifted a red electric guitar onto his shoulder and shrugged. He strummed the strings and twisted the volume on his amplifier, causing a deep, fizzing hum. He bounced on the spot before leaning into the microphone. The song was the football anthem, 'Three Lions'. Harry's voice was echoing all around the hall. It had broken. His balls had dropped and mine had not. I wore

Y-fronts, he wore boxers – I'd spotted their waistband at Kate's. It was impossible to know how many pubes his underwear contained.

I walked from the bathroom to my bedroom, dripping. Jess was already tucked up on her mattress. Elaine sat with her, wearing a pale denim miniskirt. When she saw me, my sister reclined on the bed and smiled.

'You do know Nathan deals drugs, don't you, Jim?'

Jess and I shared a glance and I tried to appear calm for her sake. The silence was brief and it creaked like the ceiling at weekends.

'I'm not interested.'

'God,' Elaine said. 'He sells to *everyone*.'

'Good.'

'Even people in your year. Weed, Ecstasy. What are you going to do?'

'Go to bed.'

'Are you gonna dob me in to Mum?'

I shook my head and Elaine seemed miffed. She straightened the hem of her skirt and sat up.

'You know that girl you fancy?'

'Elaine, why are you here?'

'Kate something-or-other.'

'Kate Reynolds,' Jess said.

'*Yes*. Do you want to know something about Kate Reynolds, Jim?' I was wearing baby blue Y-fronts. I was sucking in my stomach. 'She's got a ridiculously hairy beaver!'

This time the silence was lush and unfurled in the air like ivy. Jess bowed her head and I let my stomach sag. 'Girls talk,' Elaine said, adopting an oddly sensitive tone. 'She doesn't shave it like you should.'

'Get out, Elaine.'

'Er, *no*.'

'Get *out* of my room.'

I kicked my sister's lower spine with my bare foot. I jumped on her back and began squashing her down and rapping her scalp with my knuckles. 'Kate hasn't got a mum,' I said. 'No one told her.' Elaine grabbed some skin on my neck and twisted and pinched it very hard. For the short duration of the pain, I scratched and punched her with all my strength. I didn't stop until I could hear her saying my name and I noticed that inside her voice there was no anger at all and no hatred either, but simply a fantastic shame.

'You *perv*, Jim. You complete fucking *perv.*'

Elaine's nipple, I remember, was vulnerable, smooth and far bigger than I imagined. She pushed me off her, covered herself and left the room.

The rumour that Kate Reynolds had a ridiculously hairy beaver was widespread. I'd heard it confirmed by more than one person. It hurt to hear people talk about her that way. But school was a nightmare. I heard Kate's pubes were so long she could make a ponytail with them and it looked like she had a hair-penis. At Queen's Summer Fair, 1996, she and I stood behind a table of badges, some of which carried a picture of Simone de Beauvoir, some of which read 'Women Are Manufactured', and others that carried a Union Jack or read 'SMEG' or 'Oasis Suck'. Kate straightened the stack of leaflets she'd made about the life and work of Simone de Beauvoir. She'd made them on a computer, using clip art; a stick man held his finger to his lip and a large question mark hung in the air above his head.

'These are amazing,' I said.

The school hall was busy with parents and children and our rival stalls were doing a good trade. On the stage, Harry's guitar and amp stood beside a kick drum that had 'Monkey Eats Man' written on it. They were due to perform, which was the reason Harry couldn't help us with the stall. There was the usual disco in the gymnasium, too. Kate wore a black beret and a tartan skirt with a large safety pin attached to it.

'I hate school,' she said. 'I really don't think anyone hates school as much as I do.'

Our first customer was Walter. He slalomed over with a glass of wine and picked up a leaflet. 'Brilliant,' he shouted. '*Genius.*' He took a 'Women Are Manufactured' badge and, having tried to fasten it to the lapel of his tweed blazer, he held it aloft. 'This is great!' He stumbled behind the trestle table and began shouting, 'Come on. Come and buy badges!' And people did. A queue grew and Kate and I had to spring into action.

Harry joined us, briefly. His hair looked somehow feathered. It covered his ears and made his entire head look bigger. His thick sideburns shamed my silken moustache. I shaved once every six weeks or so, using Elaine's Lady Shave, which I'd stolen from the bin in her bathroom and stored in our old Lego box.

'Are you nervous about playing?' I asked.

'Hell no,' he said.

Harry took one 'SMEG' and one 'Oasis Suck' badge and put a pound in my biscuit tin. He pinned the badges to his jacket and walked away from our stall.

'It's dying down,' Walter said. 'I must sit.'

'You take a break, too, Jim.'

'What about these?'

We'd sold none of the Simone de Beauvoir badge. The only badge to sell out that day was the one with 'SMEG' written on it. I took a leaflet from the untouched pile and walked into the crowd of parents. Later, I found Kate sitting alone, cross-legged, in an alcove off the main corridor. I was holding her leaflet.

Simone de Beauvoir never married, but she did share a long and stimulating relationship with fellow philosopher Jean-Paul Sartre. They would frequently work together in the same room. Both would smoke cigarettes. Sartre's nickname for Simone was 'Beaver' and he would always . . .

Kate's head was bowed; her hair fell to form russet curtains either side of her face. To this day, I enjoy imagining the mood inside that shelter of hair. Were her eyes closed? Did she sigh? Or was she simply looking down at her hands that were clasped and resting on the red-and-black tartan of her skirt? Was she thinking about school and what a cold start it is, how wild and formal? I cleaned my front teeth with the tip of my tongue. *Sartre's nickname for Simone was 'Beaver'.*

'Kate?'

'Oh, hey. I've closed the stall.'

'Kate, I've read your leaflet and –'

'I'm thinking about burning down the music block.'

'I've read your leaflet, Kate, and I feel –'

'Oh, please, Jim, don't.'

'I feel you could be my Beaver.'

'I beg your pardon.'

'Please. Beaver.'

Monkey Eats Man were playing 'Wonderwall' in the hall. It was being played by the DJ in the gymnasium, too. We were alone, Kate and I. Only we would know that two versions of the same song mingled once, out of sync, in the main corridor at our school.

'Kate, will you go out with me?'

Later, by the banks of the River Lune, I pulled down my jeans and took a quick, controlled crap. It was peaceful. I felt poached and nowhere, my hands gripping the cold stones, listening as the river ran in the dark. I weed on my trousers, sadly. I'd been so focused on the other issue that I'd neglected to steer the obligatory piss away from my jeans, which were gathered in front of me, around my ankles. I wiped my arse with a dock-leaf, pulled up my damp trousers and walked away.

Above me, in a field overlooking the riverbank, Harry smoked weed with a small group, including his bandmates and one or two lower-school girls. I'd been standing alone in the coal shed when I'd heard their voices. I'd followed them, from a distance, to the river. But once there, I sat in moonshadow, among the oak trees, on the cooling grass, listening for the occasional burst of laughter.

Maybe I should have climbed up the riverbank and sat with Harry. Instead, I found my way back to the road and walked until the low light of a phonebox appeared. I paid 10p to call Mum.

I don't know what the England players did after losing to Germany in the semi-final of Euro '96. Centre back Tony Adams says he started drinking in the dressing room and barely sobered up for the next seven weeks. The following day, defenders Stuart Pearce and Gareth Southgate went to a Sex Pistols concert and even introduced the band. I wonder if any of them would have been consoled by the news that, as they walked off the pitch at Wembley watching Germans celebrate, somewhere in the north, a middle-aged diabetic was on his knees, raising his fists to his closed eyes and tilting his head to the ceiling. 'Doom,' Dad said, drawing out the word and reaching for the box that the game came in. 'I've completed Doom 2, Jim. Doom 2: Hell on Earth.'

I stood in the doorway of our spare room. It was his fuggy and dingy lair. His pink duvet was crumpled at the bottom of his bed and night sweat had left a gold stain on the sheet.

'Does the *Sun get* to your mother?' he said. 'I used to enjoy reading it. It used to drive her mad. In the seventies.'

Dad stood beside his desk, where a piece of paper that carried the word 'Ideas' was blank except for one bullet-pointed sentence.

- A computer game about real life.

He held his invisible machine gun just above waist height and adjusted his hands so it was pointing at me. Hours of concentration had left his forehead in bad shape, crease-wise, and his eyes had defaulted to a puzzled but determined squint. 'Still,' he said, in response to a fresh, creeping thought. I stepped backwards towards the door and he seemed to forget about his machine gun altogether. He held his hands by his sides and nodded as I left.

6

Following the break-up of Take That, Gary Barlow, the band's principle songwriter, releases a debut solo single called 'Forever Love'. I purchased batteries from the newsagents and put them in Elaine's radio. I sat in a deckchair down the garden, drinking blackcurrant juice. The radio lay half submerged in the uncut grass. The hinge of the garden gate whimpered and Harry walked down the lawn wearing circular sunglasses and his beret. As boys, we'd shared the secret that we knew nothing. He shone a torch beam onto his first pube. It wasn't a secret we cared to share any more. By 1996, Harry's confidence made IT teachers timid. He tore photographs from music magazines to inspire his hairdresser. He'd entered the world of entertainment. He lay down in the sunshine, on the lawn, beside my deckchair. The algae-stained greenhouse was crammed with weeds and half-dead tomato plants. The charts counted down with enthusiasm, forming a structure. Harry picked a daisy, twirled its stem, plucked its petals and rubbed its yellow stigma to dust.

'There's something I want you to know, Jim.'

I still saw Kate Reynolds in the corridors at Queen's, but I no longer said 'Hey' to her. I wanted to, of course, but I didn't. In our English Language SAT I ended up sitting quite near her, towards the back of the gymnasium. On my desk, someone had written 'I can see tanned tits from here', and though this graffiti gave me a maddening tightening, mostly I looked at Kate. Her oversized green jumper hung loose, as did her charcoal-grey trousers. She wrote, wide-eyed, biting half of her lower lip, filling the pages of her answer booklet and calmly raising her hand to request a second. She wasn't a swot. Her quietness wasn't meekness. She was escaping.

Harry tore a clump of grass from the earth and sifted through the blades, arranging them according to some mystery criteria. We sat in silence, visited by an occasional breeze and surveyed by small garden birds. Harry turned the radio right down, but if I really concentrated, I could faintly hear the raised voice of the DJ. Harry took a Bounty from his satchel and handed me half. I liked coconut in those days. We ate, looking at each other. He licked his finger, pocketed the wrapper and stood up.

'I'm bored, Jim,' he said.

Looking back, it's clear it was something he needed me to know. It was important to him. Before he left, he looked down at me and I saw myself in the opaque, circular lenses of his sunglasses. I saw the way I looked at him.

'Gary Barlow won't go to number one, Jim. Pop is dead.'

Harry turned and walked up the lawn towards the gate. It was the walk of someone who had thought about walking.

The following Sunday, Jess sang 'Ave Maria' in Lancaster Cathedral. Edmund Lyle drove up from London to watch her perform. It was the day we all realised how gifted Jess was. She wore shiny, dark blue shoes with silver buckles. The white collar of her dress rose to her chin. Jess unleashed love; she was the first of our generation to do so. As she sang, her father leant to me, and instead of saying all the usual stuff, like how she'd be big in America and could expect to do concerts at the Albert Hall, he said, 'My daughter.' The silence that followed her performance longed for applause. Jess stood still, looking calm and slightly bored. The bishop stumbled on his ascent to his pulpit and stuttered some words of thanks to Jess and, additionally, to God. Jess and I sat on the back seat together on the drive home. 'It's really no big deal,' she said. 'Step on it, Auntie Milly. I'm in a rush.' Harry, of course, was wrong about Gary Barlow's 'Forever Love'. It went straight to number one. But as we drove towards Ridley on that Sunday afternoon, Jess predicted its immediate demise. It's a hierarchy of hope, the pop chart, if buying stuff is akin to prayer. We gathered round the radio in our bedroom and Jess had her hope rewarded. The new number one had been number two the previous week, but Barlow could only keep it from the top spot for seven days. When it played, Jess improvised a centre parting and danced with real abandon. She'd purchased the single on her lunch hour, the previous day, after rehearsing 'Ave Maria' at the cathedral. The song was called 'Wannabe', by a group called the Spice Girls.

Once we'd eaten dinner and said goodbye to her dad, Jess and I lay together in my bed. She kissed Pooky, her grey mouse, on his nose and then dropped him onto the floor and turned out the bedside lamp. 'Work tomorrow, darling,' she said, and in the darkness our hands touched. 'We'll muddle through, Jim, OK? I promise we will.' Jess cupped her hands over my ear; her words were a lukewarm whisper. 'Would you like to make love?'

It was a game she'd played at boarding school. The girls would climb into bed together and say the things adults say before they go to sleep. Then they'd say the things adults say before they make children.

'Yes,' I said.

It began with small movements and heat in her fingertips. Our legs entwined and we rubbed against each other, saying the word 'love', softly, so no one heard. A week later, we did it again.

'Work tomorrow, darling. We'll muddle through, Jess, I promise.'

She wore a T-shirt that she'd made herself. She'd painted the words 'Girl Power' on it in big pink letters.

'Would you like to make a baby?' she said.

Underneath the covers it smelt of fabric paint.

I stood in front of my wardrobe mirror and I sang to a love song that was playing on the radio and imagined that I was unleashing the love of a packed assembly hall. I imagined the long-limbed, sulky, non-virgins of the upper school uncrossing their legs and sitting up on their knees. I imagined the lush-eyebrowed, high-achieving Jane Bennets, watching me with solemn eyes and flushed cheeks, questioning the wisdom of their sexual ambivalence and, after brief consideration, choosing to reject all the nauseas of high-puberty in favour of cheap, multi-tooled make-up kits, long horrendous silences and, who knew, maybe even some tender dry-sex on the made-beds of lenient parents. Above all, I imagined Kate Reynolds, who would be somewhere in the assembly hall, straight-faced, her arms folded, repressing a yawn and deciding that she actually quite liked me. When the song ended, I relaxed my grip on the invisible microphone and smiled bashfully, as Harry had done. It was then that Mum came into my bedroom and shame rattled inside me like the treat inside an Easter egg.

'Singing,' she said.

Mum switched the radio off and we sat together on my bed. She wore a beige trouser suit with a white shirt and red bow tie. Her perm rose four inches above her forehead and flowed down as far as her shoulders. 'It must be annoying for you,' she said, indicating the mattress on the floor. 'Having Jess in here.' The curtains were drawn and rain tapped on the window. I was still a little out of breath from singing. They were so real, my fantasies of unleashing love. Sometimes, I dreamt that I'd died and I was singing at my own funeral and that all kinds of people were coming forwards to reappraise my schooldays.

'This is history, James,' Mum told me. She'd come to say goodbye. She was leaving for Blackpool to attend the Labour Party Conference ahead of the election that was due the following year. 'This could be momentous,' she said. 'Truly.'

While she was away, we made an effort to watch the news. The joke was to say, 'There she is,' when they cut to wide shots of the conference audience. Irene still wasn't speaking. When we were alone with her, Elaine, Jess and I would often speak *for* her. For example, Jess might ask, 'Mum, do you like the Spice Girls?' And then she'd speak in a posh voice with her mouth half closed and say, 'Oh yes, darling, I love the Spice Girls. I think they're the best thing since Placido Domingo.' Irene couldn't even laugh, such was her muteness. She'd frown. Elaine took it further. 'Do you like Ecstasy, Auntie Irene? Oh yes, Lainey, I absolutely *adore* Ecstasy. Sometimes I put it in my tea, but normally up my arsey-warsey.' No matter what they said, nothing could make the Soprano speak or even draw her eyes from the television. On the Sunday evening, as we watched the news, the phone rang in the hall. It was Jayne Albright. Since attaching her bra to a pillow, all those years ago, and kissing the cups and straps, Jayne had been my favourite aunt.

'Mum's not here,' I told her.

'I'm actually with your mum now, James . . . I need you to listen carefully . . .'

I stood beside the television in the Music Room. Tony Blair spoke at a podium, gesturing to his audience with his loose fist. I lowered the volume and reported the news that Mum wasn't there. She had not attended the conference in Blackpool. She had never intended to. She was in hospital, having an operation I referred to as a 'double vasectomy'. No one acknowledged my mistake. Everyone knew what breast cancer was.

It was the news of my mum's illness that drew the first noise from Irene Albright. Perhaps it was guilt about her fake pancreatic cancer, I don't know. She climbed off the sofa and approached the television. She held out her index finger, all set to turn it off. Then her head dropped and her finger recoiled; she basically howled.

Jayne Albright arrived in Ridley the following morning in time to help me load the dishwasher. I scraped milky cornflakes into the bin and passed Jayne the bowls. Her hair was cropped and bleached blonde and it caused a slight heart-twist, seeing an Albright sister without huge hair.

'James, I'm taking you out this afternoon. Think of it as our first date.'

A decade in Los Angeles had left Aunt Jayne's voice mirror-plated and monotonous. Her meanings were fugitive and the ambiguity made me swallow. We left Ridley at 6 p.m. and drove to Morecambe. Jayne was a terrible driver. She handled the gearstick crudely and several times she blundered the clutch. 'Sorry about this.' She stalled at a green light. 'I'm used to automatic.' It was dusk. Children played on the practice green at the golf course on the outskirts of Morecambe. To the west was the bay. The tide was out and a mile of fudge-coloured sand separated Morecambe's promenade from the Grange coast. Beyond Grange were the mountains of the southern Lake District and the setting sun made the jagged horizon glow.

'The moment I get here, I miss LA,' Jayne said. 'Then the moment I'm back in LA, I miss here.' I smiled and Jayne reset her chin, lifting it and angling it towards me. 'How are you feeling about all this, James?'

I looked out of the window. Cars were pulling in to park so that their passengers could walk the entire promenade. Strings of colourful bulbs dangled between the lamp posts and seagulls hovered in the grey sky. We stopped at a red light and Aunt Jayne turned to me.

'Action or comedy?'

The lights turned green. We passed a row of yellow guest houses, a second-hand bookshop, an amusement arcade, a Woolworths. The Midland Hotel stood on the seashore, separated from the other buildings by the road. Its white deco curve traced the coastline. Behind it was the narrow shingle beach, where, the previous year, Elaine had delivered her blow job, although I did not know that then. Jayne indicated late and turned down a side street lined with parked cars and houses with small doors.

'Action.'

'No one does it like Hollywood.'

'No.'

We entered the car park of the Apollo. It was large, empty and dotted with pools of orange street light. There were so many free spaces it seemed odd to have to choose one. I wasn't sure on what criteria you could base the choice. We slowed for a moment and Jayne tapped the steering wheel, appearing to evaluate the hundreds of identical bays. She chose one close to the entrance, beside the spaces for the disabled. She killed the engine and we sat in silence, studying a row of illuminated film posters.

'I didn't work on any of them,' Jayne said.

She retrieved her handbag from the back seat.

'I worked on this,' she said, in the foyer, where several cardboard cut-outs advertised forthcoming films. Jayne flicked a cut-out on which a man and woman, circa 1950, clasped each other's forearms, contemplating one another. Her flick didn't tear the cardboard, but it did leave a mark. 'It's lousy. Avoid.'

The name badge of the girl who sold us our tickets told us that her favourite film was *Se7en*. Her 'Hiya' was harsh and it jarred a bit with her sassy red shirt with its white collar and buttons.

'Two for *Independence Day*,' Jayne said.

I went and stood by the concessions stand, where 'Rock Around the Clock' was distorting slightly on speakers installed in the ceiling. Two large white screws stirred red and blue Slush Puppy in two plastic tanks. Two slopes of popcorn lay in glass cabinets under bright lights. Two girls stood hunched in 1950s uniforms, whispering by an old-fashioned Coke advert.

'Doesn't this look weird?' I said, as Jayne approached with our tickets. I tapped the red Slush Puppy container and one of the girls stepped forward to the counter. Her favourite film was *Beaches*.

'Where would you like to sit?' Jayne asked.

The light of the cinema screen flickered on a rake of empty burgundy seats.

'Don't the tickets say?'

'Come on. Don't be wet.'

Jayne lost patience and chose two in the middle, several rows up from the front. I threaded my hand through the drinks-holder.

A Pepsi advert ended and the houselights died. The double-doors to the foyer closed. We were completely alone. The screen showed that the film was a 12 certificate. I was fourteen. Jayne sank into her seat, spreading her legs so her knee fell into view.

Independence Day begins with a large shadow creeping across the moon, over the American flag, over an abandoned lunar module. Down on earth, the first alien spaceship is sighted over Iraq's 'Northern Desert'. The second is sighted over Russia. Next, the Manhattan skyline, including the two towers of the World Trade Centre, as viewed from Brooklyn, beneath the bridge, is entirely bathed in shadow.

The screen's light shone gold on Jayne's nylon-stockinged knee. She asked if I was OK and I nodded. I couldn't see her face because she was slumped so low and the seats were large and their headrests winged. I watched her knee, not because north of it were knickers and maybe they were tight, made of silk and emitted an alien odour, or because south of it was a foot that sometimes stepped into the footwells of LA taxis or was rubbed by Beverly Hills masseurs. I watched her knee because I wanted to grab it and press my forehead to its cap and perform grunting noises for it. I watched it because I wanted to put a table-tennis bat in a toy pram and push it round wherever I went.

In *Independence Day*, diplomacy is impossible because the aliens are so indiscreet and aggressive. Millions of people die when they simultaneously destroy some of the world's major cities. Americans retaliate with fighter jets, but it's futile, until the end, when a middle-aged man named Russell Casse, in accordance with Norman Mailer's 1957 portrait of 'The White Negro', suddenly becomes cool. Russell Casse displays calmness in the face of oppression. As he flies towards the alien's huge grey spacecraft, his missile fails to launch; it jams. But rather than panic, Casse steers his plane into the core of the enemy's ship. He smiles as the eye of death widens for him. He and his plane explode in the heart of the alien craft, causing it to fall from the sky.

Afterwards, Jayne and I blinked in the bright lights of the foyer. It was busier now. A line of kids, the odd adult, queued for tickets. Two men played air hockey, but only one took it seriously. In quiet corners, new teenage couples linked arms with each other and bowed their heads. Outside, the sky was splintering into the darkest blues. Jayne and I sat in her hire car in silence. She tossed her handbag onto the back seat then held my headrest as she ground the gearbox and reversed, twisting her neck to see through the rear window.

I knew what suicide was. A teacher had committed it the previous year and, by so doing, she had earned a remembrance moment in a September assembly. The rumour was she had hanged herself using one of the climbing ropes in the gymnasium.

We paused at the exit of the Apollo's car park, waiting for a lull in the traffic on the coast road.

'Did you enjoy that?' Jayne said.

'Yes,' I said.

We pulled out. The Midland Hotel came instantly into view; its white walls shone under the street light. Beyond it, the lid of the day had closed completely. Jayne indicated, turned in and joined a car queue for a drive-thru. She looked at me and smiled. In the gloom of the hire car, her bleached hair glowed. The warm, dashboard lights made shadows of her eyes. She turned on the overhead and looked for her purse.

'Don't tell anyone I took you here,' Jayne said, smiling. She edged the hire car forwards so we were alongside the intercom and she wound down her window. The speaker was situated in the smile of Ronald McDonald. His white face was entirely raised. His eyebrows were arched and positioned just below the hairline of his red bouffant. With a yellow-gloved hand he gestured to the menu. A female voice with a thick Morecambe accent greeted us and asked if she could take our order.

'I'll take a Medium Quarter Pounder Meal with Coke and also a . . .' Jayne returned her head to the car and looked at me. 'Jim?'

'A Hamburger Happy Meal with Coke.'

'A Happy Meal? Really?'

I nodded. She leant out of the window.

'And a Hamburger Happy Meal, please. With Coke. And that's it.'

The voice repeated our order. Jayne confirmed it, wound up her window and sighed. I drummed softly on my knees. The next time the window came down there was a burst of voices coming from a hatch. A quite fat girl in a headset handed Jayne the paper bag and wished us a good evening. Jayne swung the car into the car park, turned off the engine and handed me my drink and the small box containing my meal. I ate a fry and sunk a little in my seat. In the box, between the hamburger and the fries, a Muppets figurine lay sealed in plastic. I removed it covertly and dropped it into the footwell. Jayne lay her Quarter Pounder on her lap and lifted its lid with care.

Mum had intended to keep her breast cancer a secret from everyone. The Labour Party Conference had seemed like the perfect cover story. But then a week before she was due to have the operation she called Jayne and confessed. She said it was easier to tell a sister who was sitting in an office in Beverly Hills than it was to tell a husband who was playing on a computer upstairs. Mum didn't want any fuss, Jayne told me, any build-up. She wanted to bear the burden alone. I held a fry for a moment and it went cold. I let the idea of the hamburger build in my head.

'The guy died at the end, didn't he?' I said.

Aunt Jayne chewed her Quarter Pounder with her mouth open. 'Excuse me,' she said. 'Yum, *yes*. It wasn't kamikaze though. His missile jammed. It was self-sacrifice. The humour was what made the film work.'

She crushed her burger box and ate the last of her fries quickly. She turned the headlights on. They illuminated a new brick wall that we'd parked in front of. She flicked the lights off and turned to me.

'I'm no good at this, OK, Jim.'

'I'll help look after her.'

'Do you know what a mastectomy is?'

My aunt gripped the steering wheel with both hands. Her second sob involved a gesture of despair; her hand fell, caught the light lever and illuminated the brick wall once again. 'After you were born,' she said, following a deep and stuttered inhalation, 'Milly sat by your incubator, reminding you to breathe.'

I remembered how the hardest thing about being English in Los Angeles was the dating. I remembered how Aunt Jayne didn't know how to fuck an American. As we drove home, I couldn't help thinking that the whole evening had been like a date. I couldn't help thinking that dates, if I ever went on one, would be noticeably similar.

When we got back to Ridley, Elaine led me upstairs to where a bedside lamp cast a pink light onto Mum's sleep-frown. She looked like she was thawing, having been frozen. Elaine explained how Mum was vulnerable to infection, how we'd have to wash our hands meticulously and stick to a personal towel. Aunt Jayne returned to Los Angeles two days later. Someone new would hire that car. The company would have to freshen the air because it smelt of McDonald's and under the passenger seat a Miss Piggy was wrapped in plastic.

Long strands of permed hair fell from Mum's scalp in the first month of her chemotherapy. I was sad to find them clinging to my clothes, or curled up in the plughole in the bathtub. Of the four Albright sisters, only Elizabeth and Irene maintained perms.

Wearing a short skirt and knee-high leather boots, my cousin Jess performed 'Wannabe' at Queen's Christmas Fair, 1996. She embraced a column of air, closed her eyes and thrusted and rubbed against it, spanking an imagined bottom. It reminded me of when Fiona Hohner mimed masturbation, all those years ago, except that Jess was miming standing-up sex. It caused a sensation among the teachers. One or two parents left.

'How could they?' Irene said, in the weak voice she possessed in the months that followed her silence. 'How could the school allow a twelve-year-old girl to dress like that and to *sing that song*? And what's the point in having that voice, Jessica, if all you're going to sing is pop? The Spice Girls mime. They don't sing live. They're completely manufactured.'

Jess leant against the kitchen sink and folded her arms over her red boob tube. In the wicker chair, Mum sat, grey-faced, wearing a yellow bandanna. 'It's true,' she said, quietly. 'And they're not beautiful. They look like sluts. I mean, they look like *actual* prostitutes.'

'I'm going to be a pop star,' Jess said. 'I *hate* classical music. I mean, hel*lo*, it's *shit*.'

Irene was wounded by her daughter's swear word, whereas Mum seemed galvanised by it. 'As I understand it –' she shuffled up in her seat and her bandanna went wonky – 'girl power is the subjugation of men by women using previously discouraged modes of sexual temptation. Women become sexy. Men become horny. The world becomes peaceful. Is that it?'

Later that night, I turned out the light and shuffled to the side of my bed. Jess climbed in beside me. A double mastectomy is when they remove your breasts completely. I know that now. In the days after a dose of chemotherapy, Mum lay still and silent in her bed. I found her one night, eyebrow-less, being sick onto the blue carpet on the landing. Her bandanna had fallen off; her scalp glowed like a weak light bulb. She pulled at the neckline of her nightie and in the moonlight I saw the two twisted, asterisk-like scars where her breasts had been cut from her.

'I like classical music,' I said to Jess.

'I'm going to be a pop star,' she whispered.

'We've got work in the morning.'

'Don't worry, OK. We'll muddle through.'

'I know we will. We'll manage, money-wise.'

Having said these things, we rubbed against one another, still wearing our underwear. We quietly said the word 'love' and I recalled the passion with which, earlier on that evening, Jess had embraced the column of air and thrusted into it, singing 'Wannabe' in the colourful stage lights at Queen's.

'Shall we try this standing up?' I whispered.

'Try what standing up?' Jess said.

Our legs were entwined but we'd stopped moving. I thought about it, but I didn't know the answer to her question.

'Nothing,' I said. 'Love.' I tried to recommence the normal thing that she and I did, the rubbing. I raised the tempo. 'Love . . . *love*.' Very calmly, Jess slid down from my bed and onto her mattress. She fluffed her pillow, whispered hello to Pooky, and dragged her duvet over her. I lay and listened as her breathing deepened.

'Jess?' I said.

There was no 'Yeh?'

No 'Nothing.'

After storming the stage during Michael Jackson's performance at the Brit Awards, Jarvis Cocker is arrested and subsequently released. He gives a number of press conferences and interviews, including a long one to Chris Evans on *TFI Friday*. He talks about the eagerness of Michael Jackson's LA lawyers to press charges against him. They accuse him of abusing the children on the stage. The event highlights the vastly different scales on which the two men, both singers, are famous. Cocker is at the height of his fame in England, but even so, during the interviews and the press conferences, though he maintains his good humour and his critique of Jackson's 'Earth Song' performance, a dwarfing effect has taken place. The Englishman looks small, strangely unfamous and chilled by his encounter with Jackson. 'It would be good for him,' Cocker says in a press conference, smoking a cigarette, 'to get a bit of reality into his life.'

In February 1997, a year after Cocker invades the stage at the Brit Awards, Geri Halliwell appears on the front page of the *Sun* wearing a Union Jack vest as a dress, black knickers and bright red platform boots. I picked the newspaper off the mat and took it to Elaine's bedroom, which was empty, on account of her relationship with Nathan Lustard. She stayed with him often, in Cowan Bridge, in his house with the Ying-Yang coffee table.

Sitting on my sister's bed, I removed the front page of the *Sun* and pushed it into my mouth, like magicians conceal handkerchiefs in their fists. I chewed it till it was pulp.

'I wanted to read that.' Jess stood in the doorway. The Spice Girls' second single was a ballad called '2 Become 1'. What a straightforward image that was. I chewed a moment longer and then, holding Jess's eye, allowed the grey pebble of mushed newspaper to drop into my waiting palm. I tossed it into the corner where the Jamie Redknapp poster had been, and, before that, the Kurt Cobain shrine. It made a sloppy sound as it landed on the floor beneath Elaine's computer.

'I'm hungry,' I said.

After performing 'Wannabe' so well, Jess switched social groups. She was promoted. Rumour said she'd downed three bottles of Metz in quick succession at a gathering held in a concrete tube at a local rec, and, in the dizzying moments that followed, she had kissed a boy in the buzzing air and seclusion of a Milnthorpe Substation.

'Would you fuck Geri Halliwell, Jim,' she said. 'If she told you you could?'

I aired my tongue to try to lose the taste of ink. I said nothing. Jess took the remainder of the newspaper from me. She left the room and walked into the brown meadow of puberty, with its fungus, its thistles, its toadstools and rabbits. She went without me, as Harry did. She spent Saturdays in town by the fountain or downstairs in Topshop, where she bought a red bra that Irene forbade her to wear. It lived in a bag with its receipt beneath my bed. At night, sometimes, I thought I heard it crying. Jess would return from the outside world fatigued and quiet. I found her in Elaine's bedroom once, rummaging through the box where my sister kept her diary.

'What are you looking for?'

'I'm not looking for anything.'

Our house was silent. Dad played computer games. Mum lay in bed, chalk-faced, buried deep under duvets. I fastened the red bra to my pillow, of course. I only meant to do it once, but I did it so many times. I filled the cups with as many pairs of my Y-fronts as I could. I made them brim. I planted kisses on the pillow's midriff, rising slowly towards the bra, which I stroked tenderly before rubbing my own nipples against it.

The day they left, Irene and Jess sang loud arpeggios in the Music Room. I sat on the stairs, amazed by the strength of their voices. A few months later, I found what Jess had been looking for at the back of Elaine's underwear drawer. It was pink and involved beads. I brought its tip to my nose and sniffed.

7

I would never play football professionally because of the inevitable prank culture. I hate the thought that on a training retreat in somewhere like Dubai, my teammates might shave my eyebrows off, or that I might be complicit in the shaving of another. I get the feeling Peta enjoys prank cultures. At work, she flicks lemon juice in my face quite regularly. She loves slapstick. It's refreshing. She leaves banana skins on the floor of the smoothie stand.

I was co-emperor of an empire once with a new boy who came to Queen's from the YTS scheme at Manchester United. He arrived on a winter morning, during PE. He walked across a frozen football pitch, dressed in a full United strip. Me and some other boys stood still as he approached, all of us soaked in March rain. On higher ground, on the rugby pitch, a teacher was losing control. One boy swept his wet, black fringe from his forehead and, indicating the new boy, said, 'What the fuck is this?' I pulled my silky sleeves over my fists, unplugged my studs from the mud and replanted them.

Later, once the rain stopped, I gave the boy a tour of Queen's. I showed him the coal shed, where Elaine lost her virginity and where Harry betrayed me with Fiona Hohner. I explained these things to him. He didn't laugh. His eyes moved timidly as though their sockets weren't their own. He looked at me till I looked away.

'I was born with it,' he said.

'Oh, right.'

'It's a port wine stain.'

'Were you friends with Beckham?'

'No.'

'Can you get rid of it?'

The boy shook his head.

'This place isn't just for sex and kissing. The stoners get stoned in here. Some people sumo-wrestle.'

Daniel Parker had a slight Afro. It lacked the definition of Afros I'd seen on television. It looked like springs bursting from a damaged machine. 'Listen,' he said, as we walked through the teachers' car park. 'Everyone's talking about Beckham, right, because he's in the first team. But it's not like that when you're at Carrington. No one cares about him that much. It's Roy Keane and Cantona, they're the main people. If you want to know a player to look out for at United, then look out for a lad called Ben Thornley. He's better than Beckham. He's not quite got it right yet, but he will do, trust me. And listen because here it is, right.' A group of year eights kicked a tennis ball around among the teachers' hatchbacks. 'Beckham's seen as a bit flash at Carrington,' Daniel continued. 'He's seen as a bit fancy, so he won't be able to be a proper leader. But do you want to know who *will* lead?'

'Sure.'

Daniel described a young Manchester United centre back named Chris Casper. 'He'll be playing in the first team soon. No one doubts that. And here it is, right, he's tough, Chrissy Casper, he's a proper lad. He's going to be England captain.'

When the year eights shouted insults at Daniel, he didn't respond. They called him 'Gorbachev'. When they threw the tennis ball at him, they wouldn't have known he came from Manchester United's Carrington training complex. Daniel cushioned the ball on his chest and did keepy-ups. Years earlier, dressed as Gary Lineker, I'd managed only three, in a fancy-dress line-up. Daniel could've gone on all day. I turned away to hide my happiness. Daniel volleyed the tennis ball over the school wall onto a road where year eights weren't allowed.

'Where are the toilets?' he said. 'Show me them.'

'You're really good,' I said. 'You'll be the best here.'

'It's just skills.' Daniel leant against an old green car and shook his head. 'You've got to be a man, Jim, all right? Show me where the toilets are. You've got to ask yourself, what would Chrissy Casper do?'

The year eights dispersed and the rain came again. On the back seat of the green car there was a rusting dumbbell and a half-eaten apple. Wind electrified Daniel's Afro. The fact his face was purple meant I'd hardly registered he was black.

When he came for tea, I cooked him a frozen pizza. We ate in my bedroom, where Daniel produced a copy of *FHM*, which obviously gave me a quick, nervous tightening – not just the woman on the cover, who wore a bikini, but the whole situation, the fact that a black boy was in my bedroom, the fact he had a skin disease, the fact he was an amazing footballer, the fact he could calmly remove rude magazines from his rucksack. I burnt the roof of my mouth on the pizza slice.

'There's a poster in there, Jim. Stick it up. Chrissy Casper reads *FHM*. He's got actual porn in his locker.'

Daniel unpacked a series of unlabelled videotapes from his bag. I lifted the corner of *FHM* and saw a woman's skin. Her complexion reminded me of the lid of my McDonald's hamburger.

'Here it is, right, Jim. Shut the door.'

'Do you think someone like Kate Reynolds would go for this?'

'For what?'

'Pornos.'

'*FHM* isn't a porno, Jim.'

'But even so, it's got big tits in it.'

'Jim,' Daniel said, quite tenderly. 'Chrissy Casper does exactly what Chrissy Casper wants, non-stop, and if someone like Beckham's not pulling his weight on the pitch you can be damn sure, right, that Chrissy Casper'll let him know. Look at these.' He held a videotape in each hand. 'I know how this whole thing works. You don't. I've made mistakes. And I don't mean my stain. I had shyness. I never earned respect. So here it is, right.' He handed me one of the tapes. 'This is what we're gonna give to the world. And the world is gonna give us some respect and some money. If there's one thing they say at Carrington it's that you *earn* respect. Chris Casper, Keane, Cantona, even Ben Thornley, they've *earned* respect. That's what we're gonna do.'

'So, what are they?'

'They're pornos.'

'Oh, right.'

'We're gonna make some money, Jim.'

That night, I stayed up watching television long after everyone had gone to bed. I watched *Eurotrash* and learned about a lady called Lolo Ferrari, who had the biggest breasts in the world. Turquoise veins forked beneath their stretched skin. When it was over, I put one of Daniel's videos into the player and sat in our antique armchair. I didn't watch much of it. Halfway through the first scene, I ejected the tape and went upstairs. That night, I didn't hug or kiss or attach a bra to my pillow or say to it, 'Oh, darling, Kate, I *love* you.' It was like Elaine had said years ago, 'That's not what it's like.'

On the Friday of Daniel Parker's first week, he and I lunched together in the dinner hall. I struggled to get used to his face. I often went through entire conversations without looking directly at him. Not that my own face was particularly good; I still scraped hairs from it with Elaine's Lady Shave and often decapitated spots in the process. I used my mum's antique hand mirror to monitor the hairs growing around my anus. They grew back after I burnt them away with a match flame and I remember once I resolved to kill myself if they continued to do so.

'We'll sell them for a fiver each,' Daniel said. He ate chips and gravy. I ate pasta bake. We sat alone on a grey, hexagon table, not far from where, the previous year, Harry had sung 'Wonderwall'.

'What is porn, Daniel? I mean what exactly is it?'

'My brother gets them off his foster dad. It's entertainment.'

'What I mean is, what will we say if we get caught?'

'There's a risk, right, obviously. But ask yourself, Jim —'

'Can we say it's educational?'

'Ask yourself what would Chrissy Casper do in a situation like this?'

'What would he do?'

'No one respects you, Jim. You know that, right?'

I nodded.

Two weeks later, Daniel and I stood by the fountain in Lancaster, as calm as spies as boys handed over fivers. We wore silky tracksuit bottoms. On Daniel's recommendation, I'd bought a lime green Ben Sherman shirt with white buttons. He explained that it was time to 'Forget Next. Here it is, right, sports shops, *this* is where lads shop. Buy these, Jim, seriously.' He wore white Kappa trousers and a black Ben Sherman. No one called him Gorbachev. We were known round Queen's as the Video Guys.

I woke one night to the sound of the door knocker, a brass lion's head as loud as a gunshot. Mum and Elaine stood on the landing in their dressing gowns. Downstairs, the letter box gave a metallic flap, as a man groaned through it.

'It's Nathan,' Elaine whispered.

Mum leant against the frame of her bedroom door. She wore the blue bobble hat that she slept in that winter.

'I've dumped him, Jim.'

For her A-level art essay, Elaine wrote about Damien Hirst. ('People think Hirst's shark is just called *The Shark*. But it isn't, Jim. It's called *The Physical Impossibility of Death in the Mind of Someone Living*.')

'Put Mum to bed, OK. I'll go and get rid of him.'

I guided Mum back into her bedroom, where it smelt of sweat and tea tree. She was asleep already, really, but was able to climb into bed without too much help. I tucked the duvet under her chin. On the bedside table was a leaflet entitled 'What Are My Options? A Guide to Breast Reconstruction'. She snored softly, her mouth slightly ajar. I thought about closing it and kissing it, but instead I went to my own bed and lay awake listening.

Two sets of footsteps climbed the stairs.

I had never heard the ceiling creak so quickly.

On 1 May 1997, election day, we were shown a video on the Peterloo Massacre and Tolpuddle Martyrs, but the lesson fell apart because Harry had a digital watch that could operate any video player in existence. He kept stopping the video at key moments. When the teacher went over to figure out the problem, Harry would start it up again. And so on. We watched the struggle for democracy in fast-forward and rewind. It felt like the pinnacle of technological achievement that day, Harry's watch.

Around five, I opened the front door to see Kate Reynolds standing there looking weary and urgent, wearing a red headband, a German army shirt and a purple sash slung diagonally across her chest. It read 'New Labour'. Beyond her, the old lamp post was unlit.

'Oh.' She took a step back. 'I'm sorry, Jim. I didn't know you lived here.'

'How's it going?'

'Are your parents in?'

'What are you doing here?'

'I should go.'

'Oh, right.'

Walter's knackered blue Fiat Regatta was parked by the War Memorial. I recognised it from the driveway at Sea View.

'Have they voted, Jim, your parents?'

'I could cook you a pizza.'

Kate shook her head. 'I can't.' She looked over her shoulder and then at the evening sky. For a moment, all we did was breathe. There was no wind and I don't think any cars drove through the square.

'The Video Guys. I know what that is, Jim.'

'I don't watch them.'

'Tell your parents to vote Labour.'

'I don't watch them, Kate.'

She turned, walked towards the lamp post and disappeared down Main Street. I stood on the doorstep, feeling a little like a snail's head, peeping out of its shell, its tentacles lengthening then contracting. I closed the front door. I could hear the faint sound of Dad hitting Enter over and over in the spare room. I used to pretend that I was only a lodger. I used to imagine school was my dead-end job and that my parents were strangers who rented in the same building as me. Elaine was a friend who worked nights. Pop was a stray cat, and if I came across her, I'd say, in quite a high voice, 'Hello there. Hello. Where did you come from, eh?'

The poster that came free with the April '97 issue of *FHM* carried a photograph of a lady called Gail Porter. She was smiling and clutching her bosoms. It was stuck to my bedroom wall for less than ten seconds because it felt insensitive, putting her there. My privates were my privates. Gail Porter's privates were Gail Porter's. I didn't want anyone coming in and assuming I needed nude women on my wall. It seemed like a sombre, pretty pitiful admission, so I stuck her on the inside of my wardrobe door. When Elaine was at Nathan's and my parents were safely shut in their rooms, I'd open it and there, in front of all the new tracksuits and bright shirts that Daniel had chosen for me, I'd kneel down.

Each time a Tory MP lost their seat on election night, Mum released the weakest cheers I'd ever heard. Grey hair grew from her scalp in the first months of New Labour's government. She refused to dye it and kept it short. 'The socialists are back.' She came back to life. 'I look like Jean Seberg, don't I? She married a Black Panther. *Why* didn't I marry a Black Panther?'

Dad volunteered at an old people's home in Silverdale. He used to cycle over and play computer games for the pensioners in their huge lounge. The residents were too weak or out of touch to play themselves, but they enjoyed watching Dad, as he sat cross-legged beneath their television, hitting the joypad. It wasn't a business, as such. The work was unpaid. But they did value him. They used to laugh when he punched the floral carpet in anger or celebrated a success by rolling onto his back and waving his legs in the air. And Dad did his best to involve the elderly residents in the games, saying, 'Shall I go through here, Connie? What do you think, Wilfred, is that a zombie? Should I shoot it?' Pale faces creased into intrigued, slightly disgusted stares and one particular man, a Second World War veteran named Howard, always asked, 'Is it real, Mr Thorne? Can we clarify this? Is it real?' His intonation rose elegantly. 'Are they human? Is it real?' Howard and the others frequently requested Resident Evil 2, the zombie-killing game, when Dad asked everyone what they'd prefer him to play. ('Actua Ice Hockey? Mortal Kombat 4?') They sat motionless in dusty chairs, watching Dad shoot his way through room after room of groaning zombies, before the excruciating, Zimmer-framed trudge to the dining room for a lunch of a dry ham sandwich and a bowl of pea soup. The residents would die, of course, fairly regularly, and so Dad would come in to see an empty seat or, perhaps, a new person altogether, to whom he'd explain the situation. ('Right, so I'm a rookie police officer in the Midwestern town of Raccoon City. It's full of zombies because of an outbreak of the T-virus, a new type of biological weapon secretly developed by . . .)

In July 1997, Nathan Lustard drove Mum and me to Queen's for the opening night of Elaine's A-level art exhibition. It was the first time Mum went out without her headscarf. Nathan looked like a real dapper drug dealer. He wore a blue suit, a white shirt and a grey leather tie. As he parked in the teachers' car park, he said, 'Positive thoughts, people. All right?'

Parents gathered in the foyer of the art block, waiting to view their children's work. A woman sipped red wine and I remember she said that, 'If you put a Monet in a dark room, it lights it up.' Nathan and I passed through the crowd and into an artificial corridor created by two lines of easels. It steered off to the right and, through the wooden legs of the easels, shoes moved to the rhythm of an argument.

Someone had painted a brown horse. It had noticeable testicles and had been awarded an A. Someone else had painted a countryside scene, but instead of the sheep being white, they were purple. That got a B. Elaine wore a red dress with a thin, shiny, black belt. She was in discussion with two teachers.

'Of course, we can't control what you do in private, Elaine, but this is *our* exhibition. You're representing the school.'

Displayed across two easels was the largest work of art in the room. My sister's. She'd been given a D.

'It stinks,' said the second teacher. 'We need to get some fresh air in here.'

Elaine's art was comprised of a large piece of chipboard, painted white, into which Elaine had hammered over a hundred long, silver nails. Nathan stooped to read the title of the piece, which was printed in the bottom corner. Personally, I'd never seen a condom before. It was difficult to suddenly see so many, all of them used and dangling from nails. Some were clearly old and I suppose the first, the blackest, might have dated from the Christmas Fair of 1995, the night Elaine rescued me as my solo faltered.

'*Christ*,' Nathan said, stepping backwards. 'Christ, Elaine . . .' He loosened his tie, looked at my sister as if he might cry, and walked away, past the purple sheep and the horse, through the small crowd of parents and out into the summer evening. The teachers followed. They went to pacify the parents. Elaine put her arm round me and sipped from her wine.

'What do you think, brother?'

'It's good.'

'I didn't have enough. I had to go back out with him.'

'Oh, right.'

'He always made me do stuff too soon.'

The teachers returned and together we shrouded Elaine's art in black fabric. It wasn't easy, but we managed it in the end.

Only the bottom corner of the piece was left uncovered, the corner where the title was painted in gold.

I Never Loved You.

Mum admired her daughter's ambition and, to some extent, her bravery. 'But.' We walked down the hall, having arranged a taxi home. 'Anyone could do it, Elaine. Couldn't they?' She'd said the same of the Spice Girls to Jess the previous summer. 'I'm right though, aren't I? Anyone *could* do what you did, sweetheart. If they wanted to. Couldn't they?'

Mum decided against breast reconstruction. 'I'd be Pamela Anderson, wouldn't I? Who needs boobs? I don't especially *want* to be sexy. I want to be sophisticated, stylish, mysterious. A woman with a boob job is like a man with a comb-over, don't you think, James, *you* understand, don't you?'

She and Dad had their longest conversation of the 1990s on 1 September 1997.

'What are you doing, Julian?'

'Buttering toast.'

'You don't butter the toast *before* you put it in the toast rack.'

'Leave me to it.'

'You let *them* butter the toast. That's the whole point in *having* a toast rack.'

'Please, Mill, leave me to it.'

'How can I?'

'It's a case of either/or. There's two ways, OK. Leave me to it.'

'If you're buttering the toast you might as well serve it on a plate. What if she doesn't want butter?'

'Why wouldn't she want butter?'

'Jayne lives in LA, Julian. She's dieting.'

'It's either/or, Milly, OK. Really. Leave me to it.'

'Can you see what's happening here?'

'Jesus.'

'All the butter is drifting down the toast slice.'

'Jesus Christ.'

'Julian, it *is*. Look at how it's gathering at the bottom of the slice and try and imagine how buttery those bites will be.'

'Jim, would you tell Jayne breakfast's ready.'

'And see here. See how it's turning this colour? It's sort of curdling, isn't it?'

'Please, Mill, could we just –'

'It's basically *cooking*, Julian. That's why it's crystallising. It's literally *cooking* in the heat of the toast.'

'Look. What I imagine is, she'll choose between jam, marmalade and so on. But you assume butter. No one likes dry toast.'

'You've made a mistake.'

'And anyway Jayne won't care. She'll be too upset.'

'Don't do that, Julian.'

'What?'

'Don't use Princess Diana as an excuse for your toast.'

'I'm *not*.'

'Julian?'

'*What?*'

'Your eggs are on fire.'

'Oh my God. Milly, why . . . why didn't you –'

'The thing is, Julian. Careful . . . Do it slowly . . . The thing is, Julian, it's a wonderful toast rack. It's a day for a toast rack. It's beguiling.'

I used to think a lot about the corner of Stryd Fawr and Friars Road, where my parents met. I hoped, one day, to be there, too, talking to a girl about serious things. I could really see myself, slouched and pretty troubled, talking to a girl who was smoking and quite seriously troubled, too, but with big breasts that she was utterly indifferent to, and I could hear myself talking about what I was doing, not what I was doing there, on the corner of Stryd Fawr and Friars Road in Bangor, but what I was doing in my life, now I'd left home and met her.

The day Diana died, BBC1 showed pictures of beautiful

landscapes and played Beethoven over them. Shortly after calling the toast rack beguiling, Mum said Princess Diana was, too. That happened with words and her. Certain words rained down on certain days.

'I've always enjoyed *looking* at Diana. And that's the word for her, isn't it? – *beguiling*?'

Kate Reynolds was caught smoking weed in the old coal shed at the start of the sixth form. The rumour was she didn't flinch when the teacher entered. The rumour was she finished her joint, picked up her rucksack and walked straight off the premises. She never came back and there was no magic after that and none of the tension that schooldays need; I was lovelorn and got tightenings over crude stuff. I got up and went to school because I couldn't think of anything else to do.

In the autumn of 1998, Daniel handed me a video with the letters 'PA' on its spine. I sat in our antique chair one night and watched it. An orange orchid grew inside me. Its roots somewhere near my bowels, its flower sprouting out of my mouth. The picture was crappy. It had been filmed off a computer screen. I adjusted the tracking and out of the static came Pamela Anderson. It was a home video. It was amateur. It sold well. Even girls bought it, and lads who hadn't shown interest before. We'd all grown up with Pamela Anderson running along the shoreline of our youth. And now there she was, in her natural habitat, sucking on her husband's privates.

One Sunday night in May 1999, a Ford Transit is parked half way across Westminster Bridge. Three people climb out and set up an electricity generator and a projector with a lens as long as a cannon. They project a 60ft image of a naked Gail Porter across the Thames and onto the honey-coloured walls of the Palace of Westminster. Porter is facing away and glancing over her shoulder. Half of her right breast is in shot though any trace of her nipple has been airbrushed away. The people work for a guerilla marketing company. Gail Porter's image shines on the palace wall for thirty minutes, until a policeman slowly crosses the bridge on foot and reports that Betty Boothroyd, the Speaker of the House of Commons, has complained that her bedroom is flooded with light. Pictures of the stunt are printed in all the newspapers the following morning.

The Gail Porter stunt is financed by *FHM*. They subsequently superimpose the words 'Vote Gail' onto the image to publicise their annual list of the hundred sexiest women on earth. I no longer kept a poster of her stuck to the inside of my wardrobe door. The day-to-day process of removing and replacing tracksuits had damaged it. I'd taken it down and binned it.

'Who would vote for something like that?' Mum argued that throwing eggs at Parliament was absolutely fine. 'Even trying to blow it up is understandable. But this is the world of soft porn, James. It's juvenile.'

Daniel Parker voted for the actress Sarah Michelle Gellar. She won.

Elaine's early letters home from art school described how her D grade was like a badge of honour. ('It means I'm good!') Elaine was popular in London. Her tutors invited her to gallery openings. She met the Chapman brothers and Gilbert and George and said that in their presence she could barely breathe. She met Tracey Emin. ('Tracey's exactly the same in private as she is in public – *amazing*.')

We never saw Nathan Lustard again after the exhibition. Just before Christmas 1997, the police raided his house in Cowan Bridge. They laid out all his possessions on the pavement. A crowd gathered under umbrellas. Children giggled as his private stash of pornographic magazines was piled carefully beside a gurgling drain. Nathan went mental, I heard, dancing around his belongings on the pavement, wearing handcuffs and an old yellow dressing gown. They brought out his CDs, CD racks, clothes, his dumbbells, his stereo and the huge Ying-Yang coffee table, which turned out to be something he'd made himself, quite badly, using some black and white paint and a rough circle of chipboard. Finally, a policeman appeared holding a brown A4 envelope. Nathan stood still, his robe flapping in the wind, his hair flattened by rain; the policeman removed a sandwich bag of Ecstasy pills from the envelope and, rumour had it, Nathan just looked at the sky. His mistake was buying an electronic pager. The people who worked in the call centre reported messages about 'skunk' and 'E'. He was sentenced to three years in Lancaster prison.

In 1998, you used to get the piss taken out of you at Queen's if you admitted to using chat rooms sincerely. You could use them as a joke, I remember, but if you took them seriously you were seen as a loner. But this wasn't the case for the lower school. Rumours went round that kids in year eight had built websites that humiliated teachers. Of course, the journey from the chat rooms of AOL to porn sites was only a click. Mine and Daniel's tracksuits bobbled and there's not much you can do when that happens.

We didn't attend the first sixth-form ball because we couldn't get dates. In 1998, you didn't have to rent a limousine or even speak to your date, but you did need one – it was symbolic. It's different now, I hear; you do rent a limo and you get a special photo taken and you sit on the same round table along with two or three other couples and you all eat the three-course meal and dance together. All Daniel and I needed was for two girls to say yes to us.

Twelve days before the start of the 1998 World Cup, David Beckham stays at Elton John's mansion near Nice with his girl-friend, Victoria Adams. They are driven in Elton's Bentley to the Hotel Eze. Victoria drinks a glass of orange juice and eats a green salad. David eats a prawn starter and a main course that includes a chicken breast. The meal costs six hundred francs. David pays on card. Within three weeks, he will walk from a French football field, pulling his England shirt from his shorts, having been red-carded for kicking. But, on this occasion, he walks down a gravel path with his girlfriend, both of them staring into the lenses of paparazzi cameras. David is wearing sandals and a black sarong. He is engaged to a Spice Girl.

In 1980, before I was born, an eighteen-year-old black guy, the product of a Barnados home, like Daniel, scores a wondergoal for Norwich City against Liverpool. He receives the ball with his back to goal, twenty-five yards out. He flicks it up, turns and volleys it in one motion. BBC1 broadcasts the game. Barry Davies shouts, 'Oh, what a goal! Oh! That's a magnificent goal!'

The ball is yet to settle in the air of the goal, but the man who kicked it is already famous. His name is Justin Fashanu. Over the next two decades, he will struggle through a football career that includes nineteen clubs. In 1981, his transfer to Nottingham Forest makes him Britain's first million-pound black footballer. In 1988, he has a short spell at Los Angeles Heat.

Justin Fashanu will not live up to the promise of the wonder-goal against Liverpool. He struggles with fame. It becomes a maddening obsession. He dresses flamboyantly and this makes him unpopular in the dour world of 1980s football. In 1982, he releases a single, 'Do It Cos You Like It', but it fails to chart.

The thing is, Justin Fashanu is gay. He comes out in a 1990 exclusive for the *Sun*. Less than three weeks before David Beckham eats at the Hotel Eze wearing a black sarong, Justin Fashanu hangs himself in a garage in Shoreditch, east London.

'I actually *like* your stain,' I told Daniel. 'It's cool, in a weird way.' We shared a pepperoni pizza in the Music Room. Daniel turned onto his stomach and enclosed a triangle of carpet with his index fingers and thumbs.

'You know why I left Carrington, Jim?'

'Bullying.'

'That's right.'

Daniel went quiet and lowered the tip of his nose onto the carpet and said, quietly and without moving, 'It wasn't to do with my stain.' He described how four boys wrestled him down onto the tiled floor of the communal shower. 'I'd no confidence,' Daniel said. They held down his splayed arms and legs. No one wanted to punch him directly in his face so they queued to punch his nuts. Daniel described the ringleader as an 'old-fashioned-style centre back with no pace at all'.

There's a prank culture in football. That's the truth. Daniel pressed his face into the carpet and made funny noises to disguise the fact that he was crying. When he finally lifted his head, carpet fluff clung to his port wine stain.

'I will make it as a footballer, you know,' he said.

Neither Chris Casper nor Ben Thornley succeeds in breaking into the Manchester United first team. Thornley makes a total of nine appearances, but suffers a serious injury in a match against Blackburn Rovers. He has spells at Huddersfield and Aberdeen between 1996 and 2002 when he does, on occasions, hint at the form that gave Sir Alex Ferguson such high hopes. His career fades away.

Chris Casper plays for the Manchester United first team only once. He is sent out on loan to play for Bournemouth, Swindon Town and Reading, before signing officially to Reading in 1998. He breaks his tibia and his fibia competing for the ball with Cardiff City's Richard Carpenter on Boxing Day 1999. Casper is given oxygen while still on the pitch. Players around him from both sides can see the injury is serious. Some walk in circles while treatment is administered, holding their shirts over their noses and mouths. As he is carried from the pitch on a stretcher, Chris Casper is still able to raise an arm and point an accusatory finger at Richard Carpenter. The game stops for five minutes. Chris Casper never plays football again. He and Ben Thornley feature heavily in chapter 2 of David Beckham's 2003 autobiography *My Side*.

8

Dear All,

Big news! I've met a man. I expect you'll all laugh at this. It's love! He's beautiful and he *has* to come to Crete with us. Art is going well. London is liberating. It makes me wonder why we live in the north. Why do we?

Much love,

Elaine

'There they are, look. Elaine. *Elaine!*'

We met in a square near the cathedral in Iraklion, Crete. Elaine stood in a sea of tables, chairs and sunlit, white parasols. Beside her, reclined elegantly in his chair, was a very handsome man wearing navy blue shorts, aviators and a white linen shirt. His hair was a burnt blond, parted sideways with wax and a casual hand. As we approached, dragging our suitcases and sweating, he lit a cigarette and lifted a bottle of rosé from an ice bucket. 'Well, he*ll*o there.' Elaine wore small white shorts, a salmon vest and shades. She stole the cigarette from the young man's pout and planted it in her own. She threw her arms round Mum and, locked in the embrace, she removed the cigarette, exhaled smoke and smiled at me.

'OK, so, Mum, this is Benny. Benny, this is my mum, that's my dad, and this is Jim.'

A year in London had stolen the Cumbrian from Elaine's voice. She had developed a self-consciously confused intonation and began most sentences with 'OK, so . . .' Mum approached Benny, said her name and offered him her hand. Rather than stand up, Benny held her fingers lightly as if he was assessing the cleanliness of their tips.

'Elaine's told me all about you, Millicent. I've been dreading meeting you.'

There was a brief silence in which the sun's heat seemed to intensify.

'OK, so he's *joking*, Mum!' As soon as Elaine had uttered the 'jo' of 'joking', Mum dropped her suitcase in hysterics, laughing harder than she ever had. 'I love that. Oh, I *love* that, don't I? Deadpan.' Her laughter drew the attention of surrounding tables. As it subsided, she scrutinised the label of Benny's wine. 'Julian, this is great; come on,' she said. 'The holiday starts here.' And though my dad, standing there in the midday heat, wearing jeans and a grey anorak, gestured at the huge amounts of luggage we had, Mum waved him away and hailed a waiter with a flamenco click.

'You should know that I adore your daughter, Millicent,' Benny said. 'I mean her art's dreadful and she's phenomenally ugly but she just, like, *kills* me somehow, you know?'

Such remarks would cause Mum to snort into her wine and say, 'Oh, I *love* this. Elaine, where did you *find* this man? Can *I* go out with him?'

'Didn't she say? She found me selling crack cocaine to newborn babies on Spitalfields Market.'

'Oh, you can't − *say* that!'

'I'm sorry. Forgive me. I was selling flick knives to chimpan*zees* when I met Elaine. How could I have forgotten?'

Raised in Devon by 'a closet poof and a divine angel' Benny Giles took two years out in India before RADA. He claimed that the begging lepers in Mumbai prepared him for the desperation of aspiring actors. 'It was hell, of course, RADA, full of wannabes, but, you know, I got out, I got what I needed and that's what matters.' What he needed wasn't clear, but what he got was a number of parts in some Young Vic productions in London, playing suave young men or tortured homosexuals. In a review of his most recent performance in Noël Coward's *The Vortex*, the *Evening Standard* praised Benny's effortless gravitas and dignity: 'When Benny Giles matures and makes the transition to film, we might have a white Morgan Freeman on our hands.'

'I find myself doing a lot of, like, Joe Orton. But I don't want to be typecast, so I'm turning a lot of parts down. I hate the trivial. Let me make that clear.'

You only had to look at his tanned, sandalled feet to know that Benny Giles was a success. After an hour in that Cretan square, he had all of us charmed. The only thing that broke his flow was Dad passing out and sliding from a chair onto the hot cobbles. At which point, Benny ordered water in accented Greek and saw about hiring taxis.

'He's fantastic,' Mum said, as we ascended a mountain on a winding road. The colour drained from her face. 'He's an Albright,' she whispered. 'Oh God, stop the car. Jim, wind your window down . . . open the door . . .' Rosé-soaked plane food pooled on the roadside. Mum laughed between retches, clenching my hand and cursing herself.

In the fortnight we spent in Crete, Benny Giles's humour made a neat transition from spiky and controversial to self-deprecating and charming. On day two, he wandered into the kitchen, wearing a pair of very tight white trunks. 'Try to resist me, Millicent. Try to resist me, though I accept it won't be easy.' He spent his days serving the women cocktails and sandwiches by the pool, occasionally instigating quick and hilarious competitions with Elaine, like diving in the style of a disabled person or of Superman, or seeing how far they could each run across the surface of the water before sinking. I watched it all from the shade of the veranda, which, owing to our paleness, Dad and I had to drag our sunloungers under. At twenty-six, Benny was a boy disguised as a man. When Elaine suggested they walk to the nearest town to 'stock up on fags and get wrecked', Benny made it clear that 'I can't. I've gotta roast the vegetables, sweetheart. The Mediterranean vegetables. And then there's the sangria, the couscous, I won't have time, baby.' At least once a day he would lift himself out of the pool and, with muscles rippling and water pouring off him, he'd declare, 'I have to sort out my taxes for this year.' And no one knew quite what to say.

On the penultimate day of the holiday, he invited Dad to take a walk through the groves of crooked olive trees that surrounded the villa. The air ached with the slow tick of cicadas. Mum and Elaine drank beer on the veranda. 'A decent man,' Mum said, raising her bottle for a non-contact cheers. 'He reminds me of Chandler from *Friends*. Don't you think, Elaine? I mean, he's not derivative, but he's similar.'

After dinner, during which Mum referred to Benny as 'son', I took a bottle of beer from the fridge and went to the rear of the villa to sit alone. It wasn't long before hushed voices broke the silence on the balcony above.

'Oh my God, Elaine, it was awful, seriously, it was too much, too fucking much. Pass me the fags, will you?'

I took a sip of beer, folded up my body so my chin rested between my knees and I embraced my legs. The tone of Benny's speech altered in private; what was ironic became sincere and what was warm became vicious.

'Your dad is so fucking old-fashioned. And I mean, I was only joking, really, you know, like, asking his permission. I wasn't even all that serious . . . . I mean, come on, I just thought because he and I haven't really had a chance to talk because he's so, well, he's so *passive*, isn't he? He's like a corpse, isn't he? I bet he loved it, me asking his permission . . . Julian Thorne, lying on his sunbed all day with his Richard Branson biog. He really ummed and aahhed. He asked me who I preferred out of Sonic and Mario. Can you believe that? He said Mario because Mario's got a trade to fall back on. I disagreed, of course. I used to *love* Sonic.'

'Ben, he's ill, remember. He's depressed.'

'Do you know what he said at one point, Elaine?'

'I don't want to know.'

'Warning. This is gonna make you piss your pants. He said that he and I had something in common because we've both done charity work. He was comparing his old people's home gig with the two years I spent in India. Can you believe that? Elaine, seriously, can you be*lieve* that?'

'You can be a dick, you know.'

'*I* can be a dick? Come on, Elaine. Your mum is mad. Your dad is borderline brain-dead.'

'You don't have to be so full of it though. You don't have to say it even.'

'Do you want me to do the monkey dance?'

'*No.*'

'Yes, you do. You want me to do the monkey dance –'

'I honestly don't.'

'You honestly do.'

'Do not!'

'Doo doo doo, doo doo doo, I'm a little monkey, I'm a little monkey –'

'Please stop it!'

'Monkey is funky tiddley tunky. Monkey is hunky biddley bunky –'

'Oh God, stop, Benny, please.'

'Will you marry the little monkey, will you, will you, will you? Your daddy says it's your call.'

I cannot describe the monkey dance because I did not see it. They went quiet after this exchange. A chair leg scraped against the flagstones. I filled my empty beer bottle with Cretan dust and gravel. I heard Benny whispering, 'Marry me, marry me.' I stared out across dry fields of anguished trees. It was dusk.

Eight months later, Elaine wore a black dress for the wedding. Benny wore a pink poncho with yellow feathers in his hair. At the reception, in a pub off Curtain Road, east London, Mum made a speech welcoming Benny to the Albrights. She described the moment when we'd first seen them, sitting together in that beautiful square in Iraklion, the previous summer. 'Two amazing people,' she said. She balanced on a wooden chair in a pub that was pretty grotty and proud of being so. 'I'd like to announce that, as of yesterday, I am a published poet. That is, I will be, when my debut collection, *Lady Beast*, is published next year. And so . . . oh, thank you, you're too kind . . . and so gone are the days of teaching! To the new millennium, to Benny Giles and Elaine Albright, the hippest couple in England!'

Earlier in her speech, Mum told the story of how she'd first met my dad on the corner of Stryd Fawr and Friars Road, Bangor. She described how energised by the moon landing he had been on that day.

Normally, it's seventeen-year-olds who die in crashes on the narrow roads round Ridley. They'd get an assembly of remembrance at Queen's, where you got equal kudos for crying or not crying when their friends made speeches. The seventeen-year-olds that died got called 'teen angels' at school. They died but they also unleashed love and that wasn't the case with my dad.

A few months after the holiday in Crete, he cycled to the old people's home in Silverdale. He carried a Nintendo 64 under one arm and winter was setting in. The driver of the car that hit him was able to call the ambulance. When it arrived, Dad's hand was resting on a joypad that had spilled from the box and he wasn't breathing. He wasn't a teen angel because he was forty-eight. He'd died a lot of virtual deaths, that's for sure, but they don't prepare you.

When I went back for my final year at Queen's in 1999, Daniel Parker wasn't there. A week went by and then, unannounced, he rang the doorbell one evening. He lifted himself off the low wall. You could still see where it had been repaired, having been broken by the removal van. Daniel, as he had when I'd first met him, wore a Manchester United shirt. He had been invited to return to Carrington, to the United youth academy.

'I've found my biological nana,' he said.

'Oh, right.'

'She's in Stockport.'

'I like your hair,' I said. 'Are you wearing a necklace?'

The car waiting for Daniel beside the lamp post sounded its horn.

'These are just basic braids, right, Jim. It's nothing fancy. This is a crucifix.'

'OK.'

'I heard about your dad.'

Daniel's braids ran in meticulous lines from the front to the back of his scalp. They contained red and black beads.

I nodded.

My dad spent a lot of time playing computer games, it's true, but I can see why. It was downhill from the moon landing, I think, for him. The following year, when I left home and went to university, I took his computer keyboard with me. Dust had gathered on the keys that weren't needed for playing Final Doom on the PC. He'd worn the word 'Enter' off its pad.

It had been Daniel Parker I'd first told about Benny Giles. He listened carefully to my description. He considered the matter for a short time before saying, 'He'll do well, Jim; a lad like that.'

As we said goodbye on the doorstep, we talked about the Video Guys. I had to hold my breath as we looked at each other. Our empire had completely crumbled. Daniel placed his hand on the back of his head and exhaled.

'I never watched them, Jim,' he said.

He turned and walked to the car. The light in the old lamp post came on. 'See you,' I called, and I wanted to add, *You're good enough*. But I didn't. And he didn't turn round or wave. On the back of his shirt, printed in capital letters, was the word 'Beckham'.

A quiet-voiced, grey-suited woman sat in our antique chair and said that fewer and fewer people were opting for hymns. People were opting for classic rock and pop songs. She praised the crematorium's sound system. 'But with a family like this perhaps Julian would have wanted someone to sing, or read a poem, or a *play*.'

'You didn't know my husband,' Mum said, taking a deep breath, before adding, in the wash of these words, 'He hated art.'

I heard the clink of cup and saucer. Mum enjoyed the words 'my husband' in the period after Dad's death. The words, combined with the past tense, gave her marriage an air of nostalgia that pleased her. 'I'm very sorry but my husband is dead,' she told cold-callers, who telephoned to try and sell him something.

The meeting with the funeral director lasted nearly an hour. Each suggestion she made was met with the same pitying smile. 'You didn't know my husband.' Those words were like the flames that burned the coffin.

'I'd like to sing "Money For Nothing", Mum,' I said.

'What kind of a funeral is this?'

'He liked it.'

'Is this wise, James?'

'He really liked it.'

Once the funeral director was gone, Mum kissed my eyebrow and we lay on the settee together. 'Do you know, when I was little −' she said, slowly stroking my forehead − 'I had a horse called Santa Carlo Mist that I kept in a stable at the foot of my bed with a magical dragon called Ingrid. There was a field near our house and we'd ride there after school. Jayne and Irene rode side-saddle and Elizabeth, naturally, was a cowgirl and used to pretend to fall off and roll around. I liked to think that Santa Carlo Mist was different to my sisters' horses. I would whisper in his ear and he would rear up on his hind legs and neigh. I galloped round and round the field until Daddy appeared at the gate to call us in for tea.'

Mum sat up and held me firmly by the shoulders.

'Have sex, James,' she said. 'Once you're old enough, if you want to, have sex. I haven't given you any Catholicism by accident, have I? My parents really con*demned* it. Daddy told us pubic hair was a sign of evil thoughts. He said it when we were young, thinking we'd forget. But we didn't. It was very hard − four young women in a small house. Irene was the first to make love. She might tell you the story if you ask. She did it in the field with the son of a local judge. She crept into the house afterwards and found Daddy waiting at the top of the stairs. She tells it better than I do. He beat her.'

Mum slumped down into the settee, squinting into the middle distance.

'Every now and then there were real horses in the field. They'd meet us at the gate and we'd stroke their noses and let them blow on our hands. But whenever I galloped over to them on Santa Carlo Mist, they bolted.'

Britney Spears's first single, 'Baby One More Time', is a global hit in 1999. In the video, she dresses as a schoolgirl and sucks the red rubber on the end of a pencil. In the video for her third single, 'I Was Born To Make You Happy', Britney lies asleep in a bed, dreaming. She dreams that she is singing in a room in which one wall is coated in silver foil. She is wearing a silver top and her breasts have enlarged. They look fake, but they also look computerised. In the press, Britney is accused of having had breast augmentation. The issue cuts to the heart of her authenticity. Is she real or fake?

'They *are* fake. And she's not even finished developing yet.'

Each morning, Mum pushed triangular pads into specially designed bras. I went to her room once and took two pads from her underwear drawer. I stood in front of her wardrobe mirror and held them over my eyes.

On the last day of school, we signed each other's shirts with marker pens. My shirt was stolen by a group of girls, and when it was returned to me, someone had sketched a vagina on the back of it. They'd sketched it in detail using a thin-tipped marker pen.

A rumour went round that three expelled year nines had pissed in a Super Soaker and were somewhere on the premises. I spent the day wandering round on my own. I went to the old coal shed. I'd never kissed Kate Reynolds there and, the truth is, that made my schooldays feel a bit hollow. I don't know what it's like elsewhere, but in the rural north, we longed for love. As I left the coal shed, the sun blazed and the three year nine boys formed a triangle around me. Two came and held my arms while the other charged the gun. I don't think they were looking for me specifically. I honestly believe that. The vagina on my back didn't help. It was like a target. I struggled, but they got me. It all seemed to last so long. School in general. Pupils that drew swastikas on each other's shirts got letters home, even though they weren't coming back. Bamber got very badly egged in the teachers' car park. He left the school covered in flour, totally white.

Dad received a note from Richard Branson's secretary, thanking him on Richard's behalf for his 'kind letter' and clarifying that 'I'm afraid you will have to apply for jobs in the conventional manner. Mr Branson doesn't intervene personally.'

Mum sat at the kitchen table reading the *Sun*. I placed the letter across the spine where page 2 meets page 3. She picked it up and considered it for a minute, before folding it in half three times. She returned to the article that was printed beside the breasts of the topless girl, whose name was Jordan. When Mum finally looked up, she held my eyes and widened her own with a tiny shake of her head, as if to say, *What?*

'Nothing,' I said.

'They don't know he's dead.'

'I know.'

In 1999, the former child star Dustin Diamond, famous for playing the part of Screech in *Saved by the Bell*, is informed that an ex-lover is threatening to publicly release video footage of him and her having sex. His advisers suggest that he take out an injunction against the woman to prevent the tape damaging his reputation. Rather than do this, Diamond decides to endorse the release of the sex tape in the hope that it will enhance his status and lead to a resurgence of his career. A small wave of publicity is caused by his decision. It breaks to nothing.

A woman named Jill in baggy jeans and a semi-transparent

blouse played the chords from 'Money For Nothing' using the 'Viola' voice on her Roland keyboard. During our brief rehearsal, she insisted that we perform the song without percussion. 'We'll make a hymm of it,' she said. 'Have faith in the words.' And the truth is I was too anxious and depressed to argue.

The priest announced me and I went to the lectern, looking down at the coffin and out over the small congregation. Without drums and without electric guitar it became a lead-footed and unwise rendition of 'Money For Nothing.' On the front row, Mum half-stood and encouraged everyone to clap along, but they were such slow claps and so hesitant and haphazard and, frankly, the consensus Mum built around the clapping was so weak it collapsed before I'd even sung the second verse. I felt selfconscious and extremely foolish after that. Jill backtracked on her no percussion policy and introduced a thin beat to keep me from drifting out of time, but it came in far too fast and so she frantically slowed its tempo by repeatedly pressing a button until the different elements – kick drum, high-hat, cymbal, snare – all sounded stranded and estranged from each other. Jill told me at the wake that the beat was called 'Rave 3'. By then she was tipsy, kept talking about Fleetwood Mac and red wine had left a tide-mark on her lower lip.

The wake was held at the old people's home in Silverdale so that the residents could attend. I filled a paper plate with dry sandwiches and perched on a row of interlocked Zimmer frames. A resident, Sidney, cornered me and lectured me about the things he'd seen Dad do. He described the swarms of groaning humans he'd witnessed Dad murder. 'I knew your father during the war,' he said. 'We flew together.' Sidney, who had swollen ankles and muggy eyes and who was deep into his long life's last year, took some angel cake from his paper plate. Before taking a bite, he said, 'Thank you for singing.'

WORK LIFE

9

Peta's latest smoothie combines pineapple, parsley, carrot and mint. She calls it 'The Sexy Katowice!'. We're really using our imaginations when it comes to naming our drinks. Tangerine, lemon and ginger is called 'Kiss on the Lips!'. Blueberries, blackberries and raspberries is called 'I Love Leonardo DiCaprio!'. Mango, papaya and Cantaloupe melon is 'Jesus Internet Dates!'. Nothing is as popular as my 'Top of the Morning!'. We've had to order extra gooseberries to meet the demand. Each morning, I brim the steel sink with them and wash their prickly skins. Once I've prepared the stand, there's an hour of quiet. I pull down the shutter, lie on the counter, take out my phone and play solitaire.

The fruit is delivered at five on Friday mornings. I wait on high street in the cold and watch the mannequins in the lit windows of Primark. I hear hi-tech sex dolls are getting popular. I hear Japanese businessmen rent houses for their dolls and hold funerals when they upgrade. I googled 'coffins' recently, having heard a story about a man on his deathbed who listened as a friend read him a comprehensive list of all the Internet searches and online contributions the man had made during his life. He died in tears, I heard. I think I dreamt this. I can't have heard it, I don't think. I clear my history instinctively after every session online. I don't think twice about it. It's like flushing a toilet.

In the cold of the morning, I banter with the fishmongers. Mostly they're Czech. They heave crates of North Sea cod and Spanish sea bass off the backs of freezer trucks and spill smashed ice at my feet. I lift wooden boxes of gooseberries and watermelons from the pavement and stagger back to the stand.

For clients for whom cost is an issue or for those who are simply looking
for a practical yet inexpensive coffin our Simple Basic Coffin may be the

answer. It is constructed of MDF over which is laid a foil veneer in a wood grain design. Available without handles, as illustrated, or with four handles at no additional cost.

I'm yet to write down my thoughts on the acting career of Macaulay Culkin. I need to write about how I became friends with Harry King again, how the two of us wrote a song called 'Inside the Explosion'. Somewhere along the way, this took the form of a novel, not a memoir. Even if that is the case, it's all true. For example, peas, cauliflower, apple and new potato is called 'The Career of Take That!'. Mango, Conference pear and watermelon is called 'Love Unlimited!'. Passion fruit, peach, vanilla bean and apple is 'Please Attempt to Forget the Past!'.

At the height of Benny Giles's celebrity, in 2005, the Albrights gathered in London to hear Irene sing Violetta in *La Traviata*. Such was the commotion Benny caused in public places at the time, Mum negotiated a private room in a Covent Garden pizzeria, near to the Royal Opera House. She told the waiter that, in truth, we were all famous, not just Benny. She told him about her poetry, about Irene's comeback and about the recent success of Jess and me in the music industry. And though the sleek, bored waiter was in another world, he smiled and nodded. He showed Mum and me into the private room, where the air was a little stale and it was gloomy and the walls were lined with vintage pasta advertisements made from tin, as well as portraits of opera singers and dried sunflowers.

The previous evening, we had attended the launch of Ladylike, the girl band Jess joined after graduating from stage school. Aside from a hangover, I had woken to two new photographs on my phone. The first was a self-portrait by Benny. The second captured two people making love and, frankly, I found that photo upsetting. I stared at it a great deal that day. I tried to delete it, even getting as far as the 'Are you sure? Yes/No' screen. But although it made me feel very down indeed, I couldn't delete it. In fact, I couldn't stop looking at it.

'Have you even slept, James?' Mum said. She stood at the private room's only window. 'You look my age.'

By 2005, all four Albright sisters were single. The previous year, when her comeback began in Stuttgart, Irene Albright returned to her dressing room to see two shocked faces, one behind the other, reflected in her mirror. Edmund, her husband, and a Norwegian soprano, her understudy. The mirror was framed by bright light bulbs and several broke during the fight that ensued. Edmund told the solicitor he'd been banking on a longer encore. 'If she'd sung better, would we be separating? That's a serious question.' Elizabeth Albright, meanwhile, remained wedded to her career while Jayne, who had given up trying to find love with Americans, had left Los Angeles and returned to England to live in Pimlico and to work at the British Film Institute.

Mum pressed her cheek to the window and peered down into the Covent Garden streets. Raindrops rippled on the pane; she stepped back and sighed as silver trickles were lit by a burst of sunlight. 'It seems silly to have a private room,' she said, returning to me and squeezing my shoulder. 'You're like me, aren't you? I never *wanted* to be famous. It just . . . well, it just sort of happened.'

In 2000, the *Poetry Review* said Mum's debut collection, *Lady Beast*, was 'swimming in cliché'. In the months that followed, *Lady Beast* did what few poetry collections do. It sold thousands of copies. Magazines ran features. Reader's Digest awarded it a prize and, that Christmas, Mum leant towards a microphone on Radio 4's *Woman's Hour* and recited her poem 'Autograph' to people all over Great Britain.

'"On a cold morning in January, our night's exhalations cloud the pane."' Her reading voice was low and tender. '"You, with one finger, write your name. And tears fall . . ." That one's about my son,' she said, playing midwife to the pregnant pause. 'He's here in Manchester. They're more talented than their mothers, his generation. There's Jessica, she's at stage school. My daughter, Elaine, she's at the Slade and has Saatchi chasing after her. The Albright Gene lives on.'

And, of course, Martha Kearney wanted to know all about that. 'The Albright Gene? What is that?' Mum talked at length about where the gene came from, who had it and how it shaped the destiny of the Albright family. She recounted the family joke. '. . . and then we shout, *Because we're all stars!* We're only joking, Martha, of course. Goodness, it's so naff!' Later that day, she and I drank coffee and ate Caesar salads at the Cornerhouse. She had the sombre glow of a published poet. She took a book called *No Logo* from her scarlet soft-leather handbag and called it the bible of anti-capitalism. 'I *loathe* Starbucks.' She struck the rim of her coffee cup with the neck of her teaspoon and rose in her seat. 'All the world's the same, and all the men and women simply . . . *Il faut resister.*' She took a box from a carrier bag and placed it on the table. 'I bought you a mobile phone.'

On the corner of Whitworth Street, an eight-storey apartment block was under construction. The sound of drilling drowned the sound of Mum crunching a crouton. Further down Whitworth Street, the Hacienda, Manchester's legendary dance club, was entering its fourth year without an entertainment licence. It was less than ten years since rave, the end of which had seen songs like 'No Limit' top the singles chart.

'I've bought myself the same model,' Mum said. 'Nokia. There's a silly little address book where you can type the names of your friends. I'm working on a poem about how carrying round a phone is like carrying around one's own little mobile reality. It's like carrying around *proof* of yourself. Actions still speak louder than words and fear of fear is fear of life, James, and fear of life is spreading. What do you think?'

'I'm grateful for this.'

It was my first. A midnight-blue Nokia 3210 with lower-case, predictive texting and a game called Snake II, where you played a snake that ate small dots and animals. The more you ate, the longer you became and the harder it was to avoid bumping into your own body. If you did that, you died. I could get myself so big my body filled the screen and I had to coil myself tight. A month after those salads, the Hacienda was bought by a property development firm and the process to convert it into residential flats began.

The five years that followed brought five new phones. The fifth, a flip phone, a Samsung, had a primitive car-racing game. You steered left or right, the horizon scrolled, but you never got any closer to it. When you rear-ended an oncoming car you lost all speed and the frustration made my heart twitch. It had a camera, too, of course, the flip phone. In fact, it had two, one on the back for general use and one on the front for self-portraits. It was ringing in 2005, as Mum and I waited for the others in the private room.

'Answer it. Who is it?'

'It's Harry.'

'What happened to the phone I got you? Mine's still working.'

A middle-class woman born before 1970 can make a mobile phone last many years. They show almost no interest in upgrades and it's mesmerising, the ease with which they limit the gush of progress to a drip. To watch Mum text was tense and painful. She treated the predictive function like a witless secretary. 'I don't want to write that. Why would I want to write that?' There was a bluntness to her text messages. Even when they were tender they sounded like barks from an electronic dog. 'Very proud. You deserve. Go son!' she sent, when I signed a record deal in 2003. In the subtext, there's a funeral for the meaning she abbreviated. The trick is to avoid that. The trick is to make the abbreviation a celebration; good texters do that.

I silenced Harry's call. The waiter returned and lit five candles with one match. Mum touched her palm with the tip of her knife and talked about her second poetry collection, the follow-up to *Lady Beast*. 'It won't just be about breast cancer,' she said. 'It will be *about* poetry. I'm calling it *Cucumber Sandwiches*. It's about being like this.' Mum indicated her padded chest with both hands. 'But it's also about the effect of self-consciousness on humans. When you and Harry wrote "Inside the Explosion" you didn't know anything about song writing. You simply wrote on instinct and –'

My phone was ringing again.

'Poor Harry,' she said. 'I remember Harry King when he blushed whenever I spoke. He was *so square*. How has he become so hip?'

I went to the window. Outside, it was still raining lightly. A street clown coiled a string of Union Jack bunting. Two men in tuxedos looped arms and walked towards the Royal Opera House, sheltering beneath a golfing umbrella. I turned to find Mum arranging her cutlery with extreme care, bringing her face level with the tabletop and making tiny adjustments to the location of each piece. She did this. She play-acted the neuroses she wished she suffered from. 'Did you hear, James? *Cucumber Sandwiches* is not just about breast cancer.' She adjusted the position of her fork a fraction. 'It's *about* poetry.'

Mum once claimed in an interview for the *Daily Telegraph* that, for her, all words were like brain-damaged adults. 'Or like fish heads,' she said. 'Like fallen leaves. Some days, I don't even understand simple ones like "sunshine". Each one has a frightening echo. Can you hear?'

Conversely, she once brandished a massive dictionary and told me everything I needed to know was in it. 'They should give every ten-year-old *this*. To hell with *everything* except words. Back to basics. Words. Are. Everything, James. Here, look, one at random . . . *labia* . . . there it is!'

Really, she was fine with the meanings of words. At the height of her fame, in 2002, she got tipsy after seeing Benny in *Peer Gynt* at the National. 'I wish I was more . . . more . . .' We lay in twin beds in a Bayswater hotel. Our room looked out over

Hyde Park. 'I wish I was more in*sane*, James, you know, like Van Gogh? I sometimes wish I was genuinely insane.'

I went to a house party on Millennium Eve and ended up in the parents' bedroom with a girl. By mistake, I spent quite a while licking her pubes. I thought the vagina was located at the bottom of a woman's midriff, sort of facing out, if you can imagine that. The girl, who I remember was known by the nickname Lotti, pushed my mouth down between her legs and I was overcome by what seemed to be a moist, boiling chaos. I could hear people shouting the countdown downstairs. '*Three . . . two . . . one . . .*' The rumour the mistake generated ruined my last two terms at Queen's. It led to a vagina being sketched on my leaving shirt.

I studied History at Manchester and there, in my first year, in my halls of residence, I met Leanne Childe, a loud, quite wonderful, happy girl with natural blonde hair, whose childhood, from what she told me, was all mood rings and Judy Blume, cider and mild bulimia. Long before losing her virginity, she cut drawings of sexual positions out of teenage magazines. She abandoned Take That when Robbie did and got into Guns N' Roses. On a family holiday to Knossos in 1996, while dancing on a dance floor, a man in his forties put his fingertip in her anus. I met her in October 2000. Leanne said she was 'praying' for a second series of *Big Brother*. She made a rota for cleaning the social area and made us all chip in, weekly, for a big carton of milk. All except Mohammed contributed. He was an Algerian who wore tracksuits, had a sparse moustache and didn't drink milk. Leanne Childe dumped her boyfriend on the shared phone at the end of the first week. She called him 'working class', in a tone that was more revelatory than insulting. She bought a George Foreman Grill with her first student loan. She managed to seduce someone virtually every time she went out. It was my first encounter with a highly sexual young woman who wasn't Elaine. Most days I'd enter the kitchen to find some man making Leanne breakfast. 'How does she like her eggs?' he'd ask. 'How do you get this grill to work?' In those first few months in Manchester, Leanne Childe slept with jocks, goths, posh boys, indie kids, hippies, rough lads, gym freaks, black guys, Asians, gamers, geeks, shy guys, comedians, older men, women, schoolboys, lecturers, foreigners, brick layers. I'd see them nervously tapping the hotplate of the George Foreman Grill to check if it was warming up. Leanne would sing Britney through her morning shower and slink into the kitchen smelling beautiful, eat a little and leave for a lecture while the guy washed up. At Christmas time, she insisted she and I have a roast dinner to celebrate our first term.

Mohammed had walnut-brown eyes and a Muhammad Ali poster on his bedroom door, facing outwards. He came to my bedroom one evening looking for twenty-pence pieces for the washing machine. He stood by the bookcase holding a bulging bin liner. Through the window, there were trees without leaves. Through them, I could make out the lights of bars and takeaways on Fallowfield's main road. Mohammed had a way of silently surveying a room that made you feel raw. My chubby, grey Toshiba laptop became visibly dated as he tapped its space bar and woke it. I was half way through a game of intermediate level Minesweeper. Mohammed correctly diffused three or four mines before accidentally detonating one and ending the game.

'Sorry,' he said.

'Don't worry about it.'

He closed the laptop and took a Charles de Gaulle biography from my bookcase.

'Why this?'

I sighed, slumped in my seat and let both arms hang dead-weight so my knuckles brushed the carpet. 'De Gaulle kept the European dream alive,' I said. 'During the war. He's like the French Winston Churchill.'

'Have you got any twenties?'

'He *did*.'

'I believe you.'

'You've got to love the French, Mo.'

'Fuck them. Fuck the French.'

Mohammed laughed and I laughed, too, because it was funny, the way he'd said it. He stood there in his silky Puma tracksuit with his bin liner over his shoulder full of dirty ones. He and I used to listen to hip hop in his room and play Grand Theft Auto II together. It was in the days when Grand Theft Auto offered a bird's-eye view of Liberty City, when it was difficult to shoot with any accuracy. I tended to just watch Mohammed play. If his phone rang, he answered it in Arabic and I played until his conversation ended.

In 1960, two independent groups construct prototype video cameras light enough to be carried by a single human being. There is a group in Paris and another in New York. To test their inventions, the American group follows a young politician who's competing in the Wisconsin Primary. Meanwhile, the French group chronicles the summer of 1960 in Paris. They stop people in the street and ask them if they are happy. Back in America, John F. Kennedy is filmed from behind and slightly above as he walks through a crowd of his adoring supporters. For the first time in history, video cameras are light enough to respond to the instincts and decisions of their human subjects. If someone runs away, someone else can pursue them with a video camera.

Once she was sure her cutlery was straight, Mum picked up the soup spoon, beat her palm with its bowl and said, 'Point in case. Why am I never late? I can't imagine Van Gogh arriving early. I'm obedient. I depress the hell out of myself.'

Not so long after, Elaine and Benny arrived. Benny stepped into the room and frowned at its lowish ceiling. 'At least it's private,' he said. 'Jim. My great gay friend. Two days in a row. What a treat.' He sank into a chair at the head of the table. He ordered champagne so briskly that Elaine looked at her palms for several seconds. Benny, too, was hung-over from the Ladylike launch. He had the dimming eyes of a man who'd shown potential and largely fulfilled it, but who was, nonetheless, thirty-two, moody, mortal and slightly anxious, having seen his innocence buried beneath a blizzard of cash and praise. 'Not going to say hello, Jim? No? Well, can I say something? You look like a clothed piece of shit this evening. It's the opera, dude. You wear a suit.' Benny found fame in 2002 by starring in an advertising campaign for an early mass-market camera phone. At certain times of the year, his adverts appeared on television so regularly that, when they did, no one said anything. In the ads, Benny's character would approach a celebrity in public and request that they pose for a photograph with him. The celebrity would agree and Benny would embrace them, holding his phone above their heads. He then sent the photo to friends along with the message 'Look who I bumped into!' The adverts proved popular. There was something about Benny's handsome insanity that made him likeable. So much so that the writers developed his character. They wrote an advert in which he met a black girl in an Internet cafe and, although she wasn't famous, only beautiful, he asked her for a photo and their tricky romance began. By 2003, Benny would frequently be recognised in streets and in clubs. People would recreate the scene from the early adverts with him. The only difference was, on these occasions, Benny was the celebrity.

'So, Benny,' Mum said, 'what's your verdict on Ladylike?'

'Let me see . . .' As he considered the issue, Benny's eyebrows rose and his lower lip bloomed. 'I'd have to say . . . utter shite.'

'*Non*sense. Elaine, what about you? Ladylike. You can imagine it in magazines, can't you? *Ladylike!*'

Elaine ran her fingers slowly through a candle flame.

'I need to tell you two about *Cucumber Sandwiches*. I've just been telling James. It's big. We're talking breast amputation here, guys. But it's also *about* poetry.'

Elaine smiled at our mother, but said nothing, so Mum returned to the task of repositioning her soup spoon with even more wired tenacity. Elaine wore a pale denim jacket and a red checked shirt. She was only twenty-six, and yet her early marriage and five years spent with Benny as 'the hippest couple in England' had left an unfocused look in her eye and had almost halved the volume of her voice. In 2001, Charles Saatchi sent scouts to her graduation exhibition at the Slade. I went along late and I remember seeing Benny smoking outside in a grey tweed suit. He was leaning against a red-brick wall which, in the light of the setting sun, glowed the colour of a blood orange. This was before he was famous, when Benny's eyes sometimes softened and he could look like a beautiful loyal Labrador. He was waiting for Elaine, he said.

Two ponytailed men enthused about Magritte at the entrance to the exhibition. It was held in a large, whitewashed room and, apart from those two, it was empty and about to close. There were no purple sheep or horses with big testicles this time. There were some disturbing self-portraits. There was a football wrapped in the nippled skin of a sow. A dishwasher stood alone, filled neatly with dildos. There was an alarm clock surrounded by lots of little mackerel hearts. All I could hear was the sound of Elaine crying.

She lay completely naked on a broad white plinth, her legs positioned as though they had been forcefully spread. Around one of her ankles was a pair of childish yellow knickers. The insides of her thighs and her vagina were smeared with blood. Her nipples had matured, I saw, and their mottled texture reminded me of Daniel Parker's port wine stain. Scattered around her were business cards with corporate logos on them and the names of politicians – Ronald Reagan, Pol Pot, Margaret Thatcher. I knelt beside her and placed my hand on her plinth, near to the card of Rupert Murdoch.

'Lainey,' I whispered. 'It's me.'

In the years that followed, Elaine tried to convince me that her tears were fake. 'They were part of the art, Jim. I think that was pretty fucking obvious.' Earlier, representatives of Saatchi and other art buyers had circulated, discussing the various paintings and sculptures exhibited around my sister. They grew accustomed to her presence, Mum told me, later. They stood with their heels pressed against Elaine's plinth, standing back to value the art of her peers.

Jess arrived in our private room along with Jayne and Elizabeth Albright. Jess wore a black dress and excessive blusher. She deflected Mum's praise for Ladylike by insisting that we order lots of garlic bread. She wasn't yet a star, not quite, but Jess's face moved in small ways that would seem profound if filmed in close-up, and her voice was soft and completely calm and wouldn't sound eager if amplified. I avoided much of the hugs and loud hellos by going to the toilet, where, strangely for a pizzeria, a black man sat by a dish of coins, some Chupa Chups lollipops and a bottle of CK1.

'This is the real beginning of the twenty-first century,' Mum said, raising her glass of sparkling water. 'I mean, I know it's '05, but just look at these children of ours. *Look* at them.'

'Wait, Milly,' Elizabeth said, struggling to her feet. 'I wonder if anyone can help me. I'm at an absolute loss. Seriously. Why the bleedin' 'ell are we called the Albrights?'

Jess delivered the punchline loudly and in concert with the sisters.

'Because we wear bras,' Benny said.

I placed my hand in my pocket, gripped my phone and recalled the two photographs that were saved to its memory: Benny's self-portrait and the sexual shot. I fantasised about forwarding the latter to Irene Albright who, as we ate, was warming up in her dressing room somewhere in the Royal Opera House. Benny went to pour himself more champagne but found the bottle empty. He held it like a dead pet, mimed devastation and beckoned a waiter with one finger.

'Jesus, Ben. Why don't you rape a dwarf while you're in the mood?'

'The votes are in, Elaine. They've all been counted and the sad news is you're definitely not funny. Nice try.'

Elaine lit a cigarette. A grey seashell of smoke obscured her lips then dispersed. Mum explained to her sisters how Benny's irony was a sophisticated form of honesty. She said it was more authentic than, say, the bumbling faux Englishness of the actor Hugh Grant. 'And, of course, Hugh Grant was a man of the nineties.'

'And dreadful,' Jayne said.

'And he screwed a hooker,' Elizabeth added.

'Have that!' Mum stood and gestured with a slice of garlic bread. '*There's* the truth. The perfect English gentleman had sex with an American *pro*stitute.'

'A big fat one.' Elizabeth frowned.

'This face is a big black beautiful fucking prostitute who no one can resist.' Benny pinched his chin. 'Ha! Someone try to. Someone look at me and try to resist.'

Such jokes belonged to a no-man's-land between Poor Taste and Liberation. Mum blew a little whirlpool in her spoonful of soup. 'And so what about doing some actual acting, Benny? Or are you exclusively a phone salesman?'

Benny took one of Elaine's cigarettes. 'Ha!' He held it in his teeth and lit it, smiling as the smoke made his eyelids flicker. 'Oh, dearest Millicent. Fuck you from the bottom of my heart. Fuck you till the cows come home.'

In December 2000, Leanne Childe woke me early to peel parsnips, potatoes and to chop carrots. We sat at the table in the social area. We wore tinsel bandannas and played a Christmas CD. Mohammed came in and smiled at all our activities. He hand-brushed his hair into a side parting and went to the fridge in the large kitchenette. He removed a long sausage of herby lamb from his shelf.

'Pass me the milk, would you, Mo, while you're there?'

Mohammed took the five-litre carton from the fridge door and passed it to Leanne. She added some to her leek sauce and stirred it with a transparent thirty-centimetre ruler. She wore a novelty apron that gave the impression she had the torso of a French maid. Mohammed placed his frying pan on the one remaining hob ring. Leanne stepped to one side, giving him space to pour vegetable oil into his pan and add his long sausage. A calypso version of 'O Little Town of Bethlehem' was playing.

Mohammed peered into the cutlery drawer like it was a letter box.

'I've lost my knife,' he said.

'Oh, shit, Mo, sorry, I think I've got it.' I held the knife aloft by its blade so he could see its distinctive handle. 'I couldn't remember whose was whose.'

The scent of lamb joined with the scent of leek and Stilton. Mohammed diced an onion and added it to his pan. The aroma drifted over to the social area, where I sat at the table, cutting carrots into circles with a slightly blunter knife.

'It's not very Christmassy,' Leanne said, indicating the contents of Mohammed's pan. She crouched to check the turkey. She opened the oven and let the smell and the steam escape. Mohammed retreated from the hob to chop chilli. 'This needs basting,' Leanne said, pulling on two Homer Simpson mitts and reaching into the oven. She carried the turkey to the sideboard and having located a large silver spoon, she scooped oil from the base of the bird and drizzled it over its back. Mohammed crushed cloves of garlic with the heel of his hand then chopped them up with the chilli. Leanne removed a maroon rasher of bacon from the turkey's back and bit it. She went to the fridge, to her shelf, and took three fresh rashers and draped them over the bird. 'Once in Royal David's City' played.

'This is perfect,' she said.

Mohammed added the chilli and the garlic. Leanne returned the turkey to the oven. She removed the ruler from the leek sauce, banged it on the rim of the pan and wiped it on the suspendered legs of her apron. Mulled wine had been warming on the hob since first thing that morning. She stirred it.

'It looks like a lot of work,' Mohammed said.

Leanne observed him through the cinnamon steam.

'Crackers. In my house we pull crackers around now, after the Buck's Fizz.'

Leanne retrieved a red-and-silver cracker from a box in the seating area. Returning to the kitchenette, she bonked Mohammed on the head with it and, as he ground salt onto his meat, she challenged him to pull the cracker.

'Don't grab the middle because it's cheating. On three. One – two – *three.*'

Nothing.

'One – two – *three.*'

Again, the cracker didn't snap and so there was no bang, but this time they both kept pulling. They adjusted their stances and leant back. The contents of their pans sizzled and started to smoke. 'There must be something wrong with it,' Leanne spluttered. Mo glanced anxiously at his long sausage. He put his spare hand onto the cracker, bit his bottom lip and pulled hard.

'*There.*' Leanne was flushed and panting. 'But you shouldn't use two hands really. You cheated.' Mohammed dropped the winning portion of the cracker on the sideboard and liberated his lamb with a fish slice. Leanne unfolded a green tissue-paper crown. 'You have to wear this, Mo.'

'You can have it.' Mohammed took his pan off the hob and set it down on the sideboard.

'It's only a joke, but it's tradition. Stand still.'

The crown tore slightly above Mohammed's ear as Leanne pulled it onto his head. She bent her knees and stepped away.

'King Mo!'

Mohammed took a plate from his cupboard.

'Don't forget your other prize. The *toy.*'

'I'm eating now.'

'You have to play with the toy, Mo. It's usually shit but look, let me . . .'

Leanne took the cracker and shook its contents into her palm.

'Oh my God. A puzzle. Look, Mo.'

Mohammed stood in front of her holding his dinner plate in both hands.

'You have it, Leanne,' he said.

'No. Come on. It's a joke, really, but you've got to play with it for a second, just a second.'

The puzzle had a green base, not much bigger than a two-pound coin. On top of that was a transparent dome. Inside the dome there were three white balls. You had to guide the balls into three little grooves, which were only just big enough for them. On the hob, the lid of the potato pan rattled and wafted steam. Mohammed turned to leave, but Leanne held his wrist. She took his plate and set it down beside the cracker carcass.

'Leanne,' I said.

'What?'

A cloud must have drifted because sunshine suddenly streamed through the social area windows and caught on the bases of beer cans that brimmed the bin. Leanne turned to attend to the pan of potatoes. Mohammed held the plastic puzzle at its base with his thumb and index finger. He moved it from side to side, trying to steer all three balls into the grooves. He found it easy to secure two out of three. It was in trying to get the third ball to fit that he would dislodge one or both of the others. The only movement in the room was the small adjustments of his hand.

'Hey, Mo,' Leanne said, turning from the hob, holding a knife and a small piece of paper. 'Why do ghosts live in the fridge?'

Mohammed was still staring at the puzzle.

'Why do they?' I asked.

'Because it's *cool*.'

I swept the dead ends of carrots off the table and into my palm.

'I don't even get it,' Leanne said, laughing. 'Do you get it, Mo?'

Mohammed said nothing. He placed the puzzle on the sideboard, the three white balls in the three grooves. 'That's the point, in a way,' Leanne cried.

From 2003 onwards, viewers of *Big Brother* often complain that the programme isn't entertaining because the contestants are unrealistic and abnormal in terms of their hunger for fame. A common fear among contestants is what the editing process might do to them. They worry about whether their real selves will come across.

'That's the point, in a way.' The revelation was in Leanne's words. How frail they were. It was in the puzzle that lay completed on the sideboard. It was in the calm manner in which Mohammed picked up his plate and left the social area. It was in the handful of carrot ends that I placed among the beer cans on the bin's summit. It was in the punchline to the joke that hung in the air before settling somewhere, uncherished. It was in the way Leanne's shoulders hunched slightly as she stirred the leek sauce and wiped the ruler on the heaving breasts of her apron. The revelation was simple.

Benny stacked the pizza crusts on his plate, making a sort of elephant's graveyard of bitten bread. He slouched in his seat, still peeved with Mum. Waiters arrived with sorbets, cakes and coffee.

'It was a blow job,' Elizabeth said. 'Hugh Grant didn't *screw* the hooker. She gave him a blow job.'

'Holy smoke,' Benny said, shuffling upwards in his seat. 'Holy smoke, did Elizabeth Allshite really just say the word blow job? Hey, by the way, it's always baffled me, why are we called the Allshites? Seriously, I can't remember.'

Elaine dropped her cigarette into her sparkling water and followed the waiters out of the private room. Benny sat, vacant and pissed, his shoulders hunched. 'I'm serious. It's such a weird name. Why are we called the Allshites?'

It was only a silly, spiteful joke, but it seemed to wound the sisters. Jayne made a big deal out of pouring each of them some wine. Of the four, only Jayne had the capacity to soothe tense situations. It was a skill I attributed to her having worked behind the scenes of the entertainment industry.

'Have you written any good lyrics recently, Jim?' she asked.

'This is delicious,' Mum whispered, before sipping her coffee.

'I've been trying,' I said.

'Ha!' Benny said, as Elaine returned. 'Ha! I was joking. Why are we called the Al*brights*? Come on. I honestly can't remember. Why are we called the Albrights?'

'Let's see if you're still working in twenty years, Benny,' Jayne said. Her bleached hairline was fearlessly high. Her words, coming as they did from a former Hollywood producer, seemed to matter to Benny. He stood, bent himself over the table and smacked his own bottom, saying, 'I'm an idiot. I'm an idiot,' his fringe bouncing off his forehead and his face flooding with red.

Towards the end of my first year in Manchester, I went to the kitchen and found Mohammed struggling with the George Foreman Grill. He draped bacon onto its hotplate and broke an egg into a glass bowl. Another boy was sprawled, topless, on the sofa in the social area. 'When you think about it,' the boy said, 'we're all *literally* full of shit. Politicians, priests, porn stars. And blood. What exactly does the Koran say about threesomes?'

I didn't recognise the boy's voice at first. I went to the fridge, where a row of one-pint milk cartons, four in total, stood side by side in the door. Each was about half full. They had inflated slightly as their contents had soured.

'How are you, Mo?' I said.

Mohammed stirred a pan of beans with the thirty-centimetre ruler. The boy on the sofa stood up. His voice had lost the Mancunian tone it acquired in 1996. It sounded posh by 2001; it sounded brash. He said my full name several times, including my middle name, which as it happens is Louis. His hair was blond, but these days it was shaved to the skin on one side, but not the other.

'Harry,' I said.

It was like sniffing clean clothes, saying his name. Leanne came in to see how her breakfast was coming along. Mohammed lifted the grill's lid to show her the bacon.

'You can leave if you're not helping, Harold,' Leanne said.

The revelation that he and I had been friends at school was lost on her. She repeated that he (Harold) could either help Mohammed or leave. As I remember, Harry and Mohammed were the last guys to make Leanne breakfast that year. As that final term progressed, she'd sung less and less as she showered. She belted out 'Total Eclipse of the Heart' for most of January, but by April she was pretty much silent. According to the Internet, Leanne Childe moved to London after graduating in 2003. It says she worked in television for a while, as a runner for Endemol. There are photos of her on a night out in west London. She's posing with friends, all of them holding their drinks level with extreme, tilted smiles. Leanne does the same exaggerated pout in each one.

Leanne posts links to her blog on Facebook in early 2008. It is called 'Wild Childe'. In the first entry, she describes a trip to an art gallery and a sexual encounter with a married man. 'So there we are,' it concludes. 'Episode one. I'm not doing this in the hope of getting a book deal, by the way. I'm doing this to tell you the truth about my life. See you tomorrow, everyone!'

In 1974, Norman Mailer travels to Kinshasa with Muhammad Ali to report on the Rumble in the Jungle. Ali thrives in Zaire. He is followed by crowds and camera-crews. Ali has the ability to look into a camera like it's human. 'I've got a message for the children of the world . . .' Ali tells Africans that black people 'have been spoilt in America'. He says they have lost knowledge of themselves, have been turned into white people. For Ali, the camera represents an opportunity, a valuable resource, a mirror, a co-conspirator, the ear of the people, the eye of power. David Beckham rarely looks at the cameras that follow him. He does when he wears the sarong in 1998. In fact, he seems on the verge of coy laughter in that photograph. But mostly, his eyes deaden in the flash of white lights. It's as though the cameras don't exist.

George Foreman is tipped to slaughter Ali in the Rumble in the Jungle. He is younger, stronger and bigger. But the thing is, Ali learns to suffer. Mailer describes how he leans back on the ropes during training and allows his sparring partners to batter him. So when Foreman batters him, Ali suffers and survives and eventually counter-attacks and puts George Foreman down. Before the fight, Ali says he won't think about himself once it begins. He says he'll think about God and people becoming free.

Mohammed used metal tongs to remove Leanne's bacon from the George Foreman Grill. Harry stood on the sofa wearing a pink headband, smelling of smoke, his haircut perched on his head like a weathervane. I was lonely that first year in Manchester. Looking back, I guess Harry was, too. Having come to the city to study like me, he had also struggled to make friends. Back in Ridley, when we were kids, Harry's mum used to set the breakfast table last thing at night, before she went to bed. She'd set out the whole lot – jams, honey, butter dish, plates, place mats, bowls, all the cereal boxes lined up neatly. I think it helped her sleep, the thought of it all waiting there in the dark. Harry, her only child, was still cool in 2001. It wasn't that he affected uninterest in conditions of oppression. It is a hope, not a belief, cool. Harry and I moved into a house in Withington. There was a stranger's turd in the toilet when we were shown round. Our landlord, a Guyanese man with a long thick beard, shook the shower curtain to distract us and, when we moved in, the turd was gone.

I never saw Mohammed again after I left halls. I don't know his surname so I can't find him online. I never saw Leanne again either. That first post of 'Wild Childe' receives twenty comments. The second receives one. She stops posting new blogs after six weeks. She stops using Facebook in late 2008, which is pretty bold. Her last status update is a brief attack on the website. Her early tweets concern public transport in London and the success or failure of her cookery. After three months, she focuses more explicitly on the problem of happiness. Her third attempt to 'change my approach to the Net' is the most short-lived. She becomes desperate almost instantly.

We left the pizzeria in small groups and made the short walk to the Royal Opera House. Benny walked alone. So did Elaine. Jayne and Mum looped arms. Jess and I had to prop up Elizabeth Albright, who, over dinner, had drunk three times more than anyone else and so now swayed along the pavements of Covent Garden, steadied by her nephew and niece. 'You think I'm the crazy sister, don't you? Do you think I'm the happy one? Maybe I am the happy one. Jess, you like me, don't you?' Having spent the last years of the twentieth century starring first in *Starlight Express* and then in *Chicago*, Elizabeth Albright profited from a boom in musical theatre that began under Thatcher, prompted by Andrew Lloyd Webber's 1981 production *Cats*. In 1999, she declined the lead role in *Mamma Mia!* on the advice of her agent. ('It's just pop songs. It won't last.') In 2003, while playing Fantine in *Les Miserables*, Elizabeth suffered a fit, collapsed and had to be carried from the stage on a stretcher. She was diagnosed with exhaustion. By 2005, having rested for two years, she was considering several job offers from major West End musicals.

'I'm not happy,' she said, as we took seats in the small bar that served the boxes of the Royal Opera House. 'Everyone thinks I am. It's OK for Benny. He's young. I'm old. I used to be a man-eater. I did.' She feigned sobriety with a series of strange blinks. 'Five times,' she said, before suppressing a burp and releasing a breeze of brandy and garlic breath. 'I've been pregnant. Jess, I'm jealous of you. It's a good name for a band, Ladylike. In fact, it's perfect. You'll make it.'

As she had all evening, Jess dismissed the accusation of fame as only those who are on the rise can. 'I'm still me, Lizzie,' she said. It wasn't the first time I'd heard Jess say she was 'still me'. She'd been saying it since we both signed our record deals.

She told Elizabeth and me the story of Girl Thing, an English girl band signed in 2000 by A&R man Simon Cowell, who predicted they would be bigger than the Spice Girls. 'So you see you just never know,' Jess said. 'Girl Thing looked certain to happen, but then they just . . .'

'Failed,' Elizabeth burped, audibly, dismissing Jess and turning to me. 'I haven't read Milly's poems, Jim. I haven't read a single word. Is that awful?' Elizabeth smiled and sipped her brandy. 'I caught her at it once, your mum, Jim. We were on holiday in Wales. I was walking round a farmyard that was attached to our cottage, jiggling Elaine. She was only a baby. Your parents had been arguing about the moon landing at breakfast, whether it was real or whether the Americans staged it. I walked into a barn and there they were, one behind the other, Milly gripping the bale of hay, looking straight at me, and your dad, he was going at it hammer and tongs, eyes closed, oblivious until he actually *climaxed*.' Here Elizabeth laughed herself pale. 'Milly was so ashamed.' Elizabeth rose and staggered towards the toilet. 'She still is!'

Jess and I sat alone at the small circular table. On her cheeks, her blusher had lost the argument with paleness and fatigue. The blankness in her eyes looked deliberate. At the bar, men and women in tuxedos and gowns competed to be served and to order their interval drinks.

'Doggy-style's normal, Jim,' Jess said. 'That's all they were doing.'

'I feel sick.'

'I'm assuming you've deleted the photograph.'

'You do realise they were conceiving me in that barn, don't you?'

'Of course they weren't.'

'Of course they *were*.'

'Not in that position.'

'What do mean *not in that position*?'

'Jim, did you delete the photograph?'

'That's where I started, Jess. Doggy.'

'It could damage me. Delete it.'

Elaine entered the bar and gave Jess and me a joyless salute. I do not know which position my parents conceived my sister in. There are days when my hunch is missionary, but, generally, my suspicion is that Mum rode Dad like Dad was Santa Carlo Mist. It's only a hunch. By 2005, Elaine was a shift manager at a Revolution bar in Soho. She looked like an oldish boy in that red checked shirt. She looked thin. She'd read about fad diets in magazines found abandoned on bendy buses, or overheard strangers discussing weight loss while she sipped mint tea in the windows of Caffè Neros. She looked gaunt and asexual and her artistic ambitions were remembered with recourse to the same theatrical cringe that helped to articulate her memories of Nathan Lustard. She said she felt 'spanked'. She said since Uni she'd stood in loud bars holding a glass of white wine and not saying much at all really, but feeling years pass by like dead leaves in a weak wind, or some similar image. 'The world has pulled down my knickers and it has spanked me,' she said once. She removed any references to her Fine Art degree from her CV. She refused to accept money from Benny, though he offered many times to support her. The marriage became two-tier and Benny spent his money on solitary pursuits, which led naturally to melancholy and sarcasm. Surprisingly few people from Elaine's year at the Slade went on to be professional artists. I think one had a piece in a temporary exhibition at Tate Modern.

In our box, Mum had positioned her chair as near to the stage as possible. She was hunched over the balcony, looking down into the orchestra pit. The hum of the audience dimmed just after the house lights and lone tuning notes broke the silence of the auditorium.

It opened in 2000, Tate Modern, in a former power station on the south bank of the Thames. The power station closed in 1981, the year Elizabeth Albright wandered into a barn in Wales, jiggling Elaine.

10

In *La Traviata*, a courtesan named Violetta meets Alfredo, a Provençal aristocrat. They meet at a Parisian party and they talk about love, which, for Violetta, is nothing except the enemy of freedom, whereas for Alfredo love is everything.

In 1998, Harry was among the first at Queen's to get a mobile. When I asked him who he planned to call he answered, 'Home. And whoever else gets one, I suppose.' It was a burden, I think, being one of the first. His phone was large and never rang. It sat on his desk beside his pencil case and he'd occasionally tilt it to check he had a signal. Queen's banned mobile phones in January 1999, after several more pupils got them.

In Manchester, early in the twenty-first century, our friendship was reborn. Harry and I spent nights in the gay village. When doormen asked if we were gay, we'd say we were. We were middle class. We'd turned fourteen the year Beckham scored his wonder-goal. We lived above a shop called Videoscene in Withington and when we weren't in the gay village, we were in small clubs that played new music, normally a form of provocative electro, and these places were almost always slightly empty, kind of like deluxe nightmares, too cool to be truly popular, but three quarters full, I guess, with individuals sucking blood from stones, lobbying the DJ and expressing deep hope through clothes and semi-robotic, slightly insolent dance moves. The nights were held in old cabaret bars or bars in the basements of crap hotels. I'd sit on round, maroon-cushioned stools as Harry danced alone, having found that palatial loneliness that lies at the heart of fashion.

'I want the Internet, Jim.' He'd wake and enter the living room looking like he'd been horse-kicked in both eyes. 'How are we supposed to get it? We need a good laptop. Buy me one.' He made coffee in a stained pint pot and smoked two cigarettes as he drank it. 'I had the Internet in the 1990s. Do you realise that?'

In the early years of the century, Harry lined up his sentences along the border between Bullshit and Revelation. It was like conversing with a wooden mallet, talking to him. He'd find form around two and walk to Fallowfield to check his emails in a grocer's that had three PCs chained to a table in the back. He'd return, hours later, rain-soaked and invigorated, often with a baguette and a tub of hummus.

In this period, I believed I could lead a social revolution if I wore a Gucci suit instead of the traditional military uniform or, indeed, instead of a tie-dyed smock and dreadlocks. The thought gave my days considerable momentum, until Harry pointed out that it equated, when you thought it through, simply to becoming a politician. The tightening was permanent during this period. Jess was frequently in Manchester, seeking refuge from her stage school in Croydon. In general, girls weren't interested in me. The subtext of the things I said to them seemed to be an amazing sexual cowardice, and although I tried to eradicate this, most memorably by talking openly about sex as a form of aerobic exercise, it could not be done. That's the nature of subtext, I suppose. It's the troll beneath the bridge.

'Youth *is* an activism.' This was Harry. He spoke during this period, as I recall, using only two notes, both of which were out of tune (flat, I think) with the hoots, susurrations and engine noises of the actual world. We sat in the lower saloon, riding the 42 bus towards Withington at 2 a.m. one Monday in late summer. Jess was with us, which gave me a tightening so loose I felt sure it would ruin my life, just as needing the toilet can rid a restaurant meal of any genuine joy. In Rusholme, through the misted, key-scratched bus windows, Asian lads blew smoke from the chinked doors of modified Subarus. 'We've backed reality up against a wall,' Harry said. 'We've got the tit-head on the run. The world is obsessed with the end of things. The end of history. The end of hope. The end of belief. I could write a song about the end of my dick. Speaking's lying, right? Strip away all the lies and there's one lie left, and that's that we're capable of sincerity. We're not. Everyone *knows* we're not. You think you're Rimbaud, Jim. But you're more like Michael Barrymore. I'm actually *pro-capitalism*. I've got the balls to admit that. I mean money's an asylum, a wild fire, but I can actually conceive of hanging around all day writing pop songs. *That's* what we should do, Jim. Culture's another word for rubble, right? Or else it's a phase in human history that'll end in fifty years and be replaced by what I'm calling "techno-barbarianism".' Harry mimed the inverted commas but, in fairness, it was the only time I ever saw him do so. 'Fuck guitars,' he said. 'We'll make music on a laptop. We need a laptop. This is a transition period. Pressing the space bar is a definition of punk. I've seen adults on trains reading *Harry Potter* books, Jim. It's all rubble now. *The Simpsons* is going shit and, as the show's crappest character, Lisa is a martyr to her misguided belief in . . . well, her belief in belief. We'll never be as clever as clever people want us to be. I'm a dumbass. Good taste is how we defend our decision to give up and do nothing. Having a good time is the opposite of wasting your life. Youth *is* an activism. Let's start a band to avoid having to listen to someone else's. Do you see how that works?'

'No,' I said.

'Jim, don't spoil it.'

'I can't even play the guitar, Harry.'

'You're not listening. You sing, I'll play laptop. Life's good. If you ask me, she should never have done this.' Jess sat sideways on the seat in front of us. Harry reached over and fed his finger into one of several rips in her Minnie Mouse T-shirt. 'I mean, fashion's fashion but irony's guilt, right? You've ruined a good T-shirt, Jess. There's nothing wrong with Disney. I respect language. I think language is a wild animal. But these people *trying* to be clever. That's sad. That really makes me sad. These dickheads who grow moustaches and get into Soviet architecture but can't lick their girlfriends out because they own too many unread Kafka novels.'

'That sounds like you, Harry,' Jess said, inspecting her T-shirt. She'd made the rips before we went out using a Stanley knife. We were driving through the dead lands between Rusholme and Fallowfield.

'Is that fuck me, Jessica,' Harry said. 'I'll tell you what I think of Soviet architecture. I think it's fucking depressing. I don't read, bloody, hardback books full of photos of grim stadiums in Riga. Do you know what I like? I like thatched Tudor cottages with roses round the door. What's wrong with that? And then these dickheads who are *pretending* to be stupid. That's sad, too, but funny, I suppose. Look, we're here. Jess, ring the bell. I intend to rent a porno.'

We were still damp from the foam party we'd attended that evening. A night of chart music at the Ritz on Whitworth Street, the allure of which was mostly sexual, whereas the discos in the gymnasium at Queen's felt more connected to love. They made us long for love in the rural north. At the Ritz, we formed alliances with strangers on dance floors. We embraced each other and brought our heads together; we laid the foundations for white-morninged sex in red-brick terraces by singing 'Living on a Prayer'.

On 27 July 1996, having detonated a nail bomb in Centennial Park during the Atlanta Olympic Games, Eric Robert Rudolph flees to the Appalachian Mountains to hide. It isn't until Rudolph is implicated in two other 1997 explosions that the FBI feels certain that he planted the Atlanta bomb. The other bombs are detonated at a lesbian bar, also in Atlanta, and an abortion clinic in Birmingham, Alabama. Rudolph is on the run for years. He is eventually arrested in May 2003 in North Carolina. He is found freshly shaven and wearing brand-new trainers.

A few weeks after the Atlanta bomb, on 23 August 1996, 'The Declaration of Jihad on the Americans Occupying the Country of the Two Sacred Places' is published in the London Arab-language newspaper *Al-Quds Al-Arabi*. It is the first fatwa written by Osama bin Laden. He warns that US military presence in

Saudi Arabia will be met with guerilla warfare and jihad. Bin Laden describes the faith, determination and energy that young Muslims have for this conflict. He calls them 'youths'.

On 7 March 1998, Eric Robert Rudolph's older brother, Daniel, videotapes himself sawing off one of his own hands in order to, in his words, 'send a message to the FBI and the media'. The hand is successfully reattached.

Harry walked ahead of Jess and me. It was late. Withington High Street was cold and quiet. Harry still walked like a boy who thought, at night, about walking. But there was something touching about that, something touching about his love/hate relationship with style magazines and about how he rehearsed frowns after cleaning his teeth.

'Why do you let him dominate you?'

'Harry's Harry,' I said. 'I've known him all my life.'

'Jim. You *worship* him.'

The lads who ran Videoscene were always *all* there, four of them, standing behind the counter, key rings attached to their phones, saying, 'Right, mate?' in accents that were half Mancunian and half Pakistani. They sold porn on VHS from an old Sainsbury's shopping trolley by the crisps.

Fantasia was on television when we got home. It was the hallucinogenic passage in the film and I don't know if you've seen that bit, but it features the most beautiful-looking goldfish. It has wide, beautiful eyes. It's extremely sexy and alluring, but it's also very sure of itself. It reminded me of Dilly.

Harry sank into his armchair, holding his rented copy of *Big Busty Whoppers* and blowing smoke at the various women posing on its cover.

'These youths love death as you love life.'

'Such a beautiful goldfish. *Look* at her. Jess, you're missing it. *Look* at her.'

★

'Our youths believe in paradise after death. They believe that taking part in fighting will not bring their day nearer; and staying behind will not postpone their day either.'

We used to buy drugs from a guy called Kam who drove round south Manchester in a red Saab with a couple of white girls listening to techno very quietly. You'd climb into the back of his car and steal looks at the cold thigh of the girl beside you. Kam would twizzle in his seat and shake your hand, pushing a bag of weed or coke or pills into your palm.

'Safe.'

'Safe.'

He did a year in Strangeways early in the twenty-first century.

'The best of the martyrs are those who do not turn their faces away from the battle till they are killed . . . A martyr will not feel the pain of death except like how you feel when you are pinched.'

The name Veronica Rio appeared on the television screen. I remembered how Daniel Parker did keepy-ups with a tennis ball in the teachers' car park, and how I believed that the ability to do so would solve the problems of youth, like the problem of Kate Reynolds, or the problem of unleashing love. And I thought about how, in the end, he and I simply sat on a bench by Lancaster fountain and sold porn for money to buy tracksuits. I can easily make complaints about pornography, particularly if I've recently orgasmed or if I recall the level of intimacy I experienced with Dilly.

Veronica Rio belonged to an older generation of porn actresses, who acted in films that were influenced by conventional cinema, although they normally involved a cultural regression to a world of one-dimensional, archetypal characters, like maybe a milkman shags a listless housewife. There's a humour and a tackiness that the directors and actors are incapable of avoiding. The films can't help but tell you that it's all good-humoured.

Feelings ran deeper with Dilly. We were earnest. He wasn't a milkman and neither was I. And although Dilly's smile expressed happiness first, such was the intensity of his glee, the longer you looked into his eyes, the more convinced of his melancholy you became.

Contemporary porn – Amateur, Gonzo, Point of View, for example, these all acknowledge the camera in some way. They're mostly comprised of close-ups and often a slow-voiced Californian, a dude with a grain to his voice, he's saying something like, 'Look at the camera, baby' or 'Why don't you show the camera those titties? Are they real?' Often, one of the participants is holding the camera or someone who's having sex is looking into it. Time can vaporise. But contemporary porn is no less conservative than the early-nineties films of Veronica Rio, really. To watch porn is to watch porn. Masturbating to porn is like pretending to be dead; it's very relaxing. An open attitude towards porn becomes evidence of personal liberation. Over coffee, someone might say, 'I'm watching too much porn at the moment.' I say this. I say this to myself. It's possible I'm the only one who says this. I don't so much say it as think it to myself during runaway moments when bleakness and elation merge and I drink water straight from the tap and reflect candidly on matters of the soul, concluding, normally, 'I am too free, but I can cope.'

'I remember Veronica Rio,' I said.

'These women are fucking gone in the head, you know.' Jess sat beside me on our old, foul sofa. Our living room was littered with Harry's debris. His CDs, his newspapers, his cigarette packets, his style magazines. 'That's why they get their tits so big,' Jess said. 'They don't know what they look like. Their brains are damaged.'

'She was in *More Than a Handful 4*,' I said. 'And *Frankenpenis*.'

'I'm going to bed,' Jess said. She went to the door and Xed her body in its frame. 'Are you coming, Jim?'

'Those youths are different from your soldiers. Your problem will be how to convince your troops to fight, while our problem will be how to restrain our youths to wait for their turn in fighting.'

'*Video Virgins 7, Anal Nymphettes, Ass Busters Inc., Busty Porno Queens, Truck Stop Angel, Girls Who Take It Up the Ass 21.*'

'*Cousin-fucker 1*,' Harry shouted. He'd taken off his shirt and was standing on the glass coffee table. It was about to crack. He was beating his chest with alternate fists. 'What about *Cousin-fucker 1*, Jim?'

'Death is truth and ultimate destiny, and life will end anyway. If I do not fight you, then my mother must be insane.'

There was static on the screen when I woke the next day. Jess picked her way across the living room and unplugged the video so that BBC1 came on. Harry stirred in his armchair, coming round like a child, with a rubbery face and bewildered eyes.

'Where is this?' Jess asked.

I recognised the towers from the establishing shots on *Friends*.

'Manhattan,' Harry said.

We watched a replay of the second plane hitting maybe a hundred times, maybe more. Harry opened the Limoncello his mum brought him back from Naples. It was a big moment for him. He couldn't decide if what we were watching was hilarious or serious. He rolled a cigarette on the *Big Busty Whoppers* case. When the first tower fell, we lay down in front of the television. Next door's tomcat visited and sat on the windowsill for a while, scratching its ear with a rear paw as the second tower fell. I was nineteen. Lately, when I'm lost online, I sometimes rewatch the Twin Towers falling. The towers that fall on YouTube are different, less hypnotic than those that crumbled on the day. People ask where I was when 9/11 happened. I say I'd been to a foam party and woken hoping to watch *Neighbours*. In the evening, I hurried between a Cumberland stew I was cooking and the lounge. Harry said it was getting boring. He was posing. It's likely he struck poses in the womb. And saying things were boring was how we made them stop. He'd done it once to our friendship, down in the garden back in Ridley, the week before 'Wannabe' went to number one.

We went to bed early after eating the stew. Jess instructed me to look away as she undressed. On my bedside table, a piece of dark chocolate melted under my reading light and spread across the cover of a children's novel that was there. Jess was drunk on very cheap red wine and Limoncello, which is a sickly feeling. She hopped as she removed her socks. 'OK, you can look now,' she said, performing a strange curtsy, lifting the hem of her torn T-shirt to reveal her yellow knickers. 'Why are we called the Albrights? Why are we tall and flat chested? No offence to your mum, Jim.' Her sigh smelt of lemons as she sat on the bed beside me.

'Jess?'

'This sounds serious.'

'Do you think I'm talented?'

She took a circular tin of lip balm from the bedside table and removed the lid. She turned her fingertip on its slick surface for a moment and then applied some, closing her eyes and stretching her lips against her teeth in a way that reminded me that, behind her face, there was a skull. She gripped a cigarette with glossed lips and lit it, allowing a pure, uninhaled cloud to float from a gap at the side of her mouth. She looked at me. Her answer was in the smoke. In the way it drifted.

We climbed into bed and we spooned. Jess shuffled backwards against me and pressed her bottom into my groin. The effect of this, the sad tightening, made me want to go somewhere private and shatter my erection with a mallet as though it were made of green glass. But, instead, I pressed myself against her, rubbing slightly. I moved my hand under her T-shirt and stroked her.

'Love,' I said.

She brushed me off like my hand was no danger at all, like

it was a neutered, bald tarantula. A moment later, she reached over her shoulder and begrudgingly pulled my arm across her chest like a seat belt. She made a sort of huge rucksack out of me. The slightest thrust or rub from me and she'd have shrugged me off once again. She'd have gone to sleep on the sofa or with Harry. So I lay there with a rigid penis, clinging to her back, and I thought about the towers for a while, then about the future and then I thought about Archie and the boys of Kendal Under 11s. I pictured Berky in a sunlit kitchen, enjoying the feeling of his feet on lukewarm linoleum, cutting a sandwich in two for his lunch box, watching his wife through the window as she walked backwards up the drive pulling a wheelie bin.

In 2001, three months before the planes crash into the towers in New York, the glamour model Jordan stands as an independent candidate in the UK general election. She runs under her real name, Katie Price, as the candidate for Stretford and Urmston in Manchester. Her slogan is 'For a Bigga and Betta Future'. She promises free breast implants, more nudist beaches and a ban on parking tickets. She receives 713 votes.

During Act One of *La Traviata*, Elizabeth Albright's head lolled forwards and hung like it was half severed from her neck. A strand of saliva linked her lower lip with her lap. Benny slept, too, though high notes woke him and he adopted an air of intense concentration, before immediately falling asleep again. I got a slight tightening while watching the opera. The horniness seemed connected to reckless melancholy. At the end of Act One, Violetta stands alone on the stage and sings about her love of freedom. It is clear she is posing. It is clear she has fallen in love with Alfredo.

I can't bring myself to write down the name of my and Harry's band. Our name was the word we hoped to hear as we were pulled from the darkness and introduced to the world. It was a new name for the two of us and, as such, not so much a rebirth as much as proof that we yearned for one. The band began in Harry's bedroom, with him knelt down in front of his new laptop, trying to program a beat. After half an hour's work, he pressed the space bar to unleash it. Its tempo was faster than disco, but slower than techno, and had an exciting rigidity we related to. 'Now, you sing something over it, Jim. Anything. Sing anything.' Harry passed me a lightweight microphone that was plugged into his stereo. I sat, listening to the beat and I thought about the boy who had drummed in Harry's old band, Monkey Eats Man. I didn't remember his name, just that he was a small, pale nerd with sad eyes and thin brown hair. And that he had no rhythm at all and, the truth was, he only drummed for Harry because he owned an expensive kit that was completely immune to his playing.

I brought the microphone to my lips and sang.

On 15 June 1996, the day Gascoigne scored his wondergoal at Wembley, a van with Irish number plates parked on Corporation Street, Manchester. At 10 a.m., still several hours before Nathan Lustard carried Elaine down the hall and into the Music Room, the van exploded. It was the biggest bomb to detonate in England since the Second World War.

On a wintry day in 2003, Harry and I sat on a bench in Whitworth Park, Manchester. The bench and paths were dulled by night rain and the sky was dark white. A photographer crouched in front of us, rocking slightly on her frog's legs.

'We deserve this, Jim,' Harry whispered, without moving his lips or looking at me. 'We so do. We're a good band.'

The song we wrote was called 'Inside the Explosion'. There were others, of course, but that was the good one. It was manufactured on heavy Czech vinyl and released as a limited-edition single by two Mancunian music journalists. It did well in the indie clubs and on night-time radio. We opened an email account that incorporated the name of our band and that felt professional, felt almost like seeing our name up in lights.

'I know that you call sex lines, Jim,' Harry muttered. I glanced at him. He frowned in the direction of the camera. 'I hear you through the walls,' he whispered. His frown raised the temperature of his eyes, but brought no creases to his face. 'And I know you buy loaves of economy bread.' His lips barely moved. He was still looking straight ahead. 'To have sex with,' he said.

'Moodier,' the photographer said loudly. 'Even moodier, if you can, and stop whispering.'

'You think you deserve to be blown to smithereens, Jim. You don't. It's fine that you make love to those loaves. And we deserve this. We're a good band.'

I followed Harry's gaze to the camera lens. The camera clicked several times and a flock of pigeons landed beneath a nearby statue to eat the breadcrumbs a little boy was throwing.

'That's the one,' the photographer said, standing to inspect her view screen.

We signed our record deal at Madame Tussauds. We posed for a photograph with Britney Spears. The rumour was they melted Gary Barlow down to make her. We had a five-album deal and twenty thousand pounds each. We asked for free iPods but they said no. As soon as we'd signed, the label told us they considered 'Inside the Explosion' to be what they called 'a tastemaker release' rather than a hit. They set us the challenge of writing an album that contained songs that could be played on national radio during the daytime. We rented a room in an old mill in east Manchester to write it in. I was the lyricist; Harry did the backing tracks on his laptop. Our A&R man was Nigel Grove-White. 'Love or Sex,' he said. 'Write about Love or Dancing or Sex or, at a push, Death.' He was thirty-five, wore clean red Converse with a grey suit and had a Union Jack pin-badge on his lapel. 'Write about Sex *and* Dancing. Or Sex *and* Death, or Love and Death, or Love and Dancing, or Dancing and Love and Sex *and* Death, or Death and Sex *and* Dancing!' His iPod was as white as the teeth he laughed through. His laugh was the sound Dilly made when, having unplugged his little valve, I squeezed the air from him.

Robbie Williams doesn't rejoin Take That when the band re-form in 2005. His feud with Gary Barlow and the others is too deep. Robbie Williams's favourite footballer is Francesco Totti.

In February 2006, Iraqi insurgents kidnap an Italian journalist, Giuliana Sgrena. On being released, Sgrena describes an event that reduced one of her captors to tears. It was watching Francesco Totti walk out onto the pitch wearing a T-shirt with 'Free Giuliana' written on it. The insurgent idolised Totti and couldn't bear to be disapproved of by him. He wept.

On 14 June 2004 Francesco Totti plays for Italy against Denmark in the European Championship. He's running back towards the halfway line when he turns and spits three times in the face of Christian Poulsen, the Danish midfielder. After the game, having been red-carded, Totti tries to deny the offence. Even when confronted with the footage, he says, 'A trick film. That's not the real Francesco.'

In the 2006 World Cup final, during extra time, Totti watches from the substitutes bench as Zinedine Zidane headbutts an Italian defender hard in the chest and then turns and walks away from the pitch, past the gold trophy and into the dark.

There's a roadside shrine in the hills above Rome. There are photographs of mangled cars, which suffered terrible crashes but, miraculously, no fatalities. Totti takes his shirt to the shrine, the one he wore against Denmark. It's white and dirty and is accompanied by a handwritten note which reads, 'I beg forgiveness, Most Holy Virgin of Divine Love. Never forsake me. Your Francesco.'

11

During the interval, the auditorium emptied. The audience re-located to the gallery bars to discuss the opera and play parts in a roar of voices, the remnants of which I could hear, as I sat in our box, looking down at the rows of burgundy seats and at a skinny tuba player, who sat alone in the orchestra pit. I fantasised about murdering Benny Giles and fleeing to a prostitute with milk skin, a double chin and big boobs, a rented mummy, I suppose, a woman to confess to. Jess sat beside me. She hung an arm off the balcony and performed pendulum swings, watching me as a safety curtain descended from the rafters to shield the stage.

'Did I ever tell you, Jess, about the glass pizzas?'

'All our lives we've been watching opera. *Why?*'

'Did I, Jess?'

She shook her head.

'A few months ago,' I said. 'Harry and I were rehearsing and we both got hungry. We went and got pizzas from a takeaway in Miles Platting. We took them back to the practice room to eat, OK, but we quickly realised that both pizzas had a thin pane of glass inside them, underneath the cheese and the toppings. We weren't angry or surprised, at least not as much as you might imagine. We walked back to the takeaway with the glass pizzas and we complained, not aggressively, but, you know, we said it was unacceptable. They made us two new pizzas but this time they didn't put any glass inside them. We went back to our practice room and ate.'

In 2003, Benny Giles paid cash for a vast, open-plan apartment in Bethnal Green, east London. Its centrepiece was a beautiful, mint-green chaise longue. The front windows looked down into

Brick Lane and out to the skyline of the City, where cranes spent the days turning slowly, lifting girders and pallets of bricks, before bowing to the sky around five. 'Am I a celebrity?' Benny lay on the chaise longue wearing silk pyjamas and a trucker's cap. 'Am I though?'

'You're a dick,' Jess said, from a corduroy beanbag. We'd spent the day marching against the invasion of Iraq.

'I can't believe Kate Moss was there today,' Jess said, stubbing out her cigarette in the soil of a cactus. 'She was actually *there*. With us.'

'The war's one of the few things Kate Moss won't endorse,' Benny said. 'I endorse it. I hate the Arabs. Pass me a Haribo.'

Elaine came in from the rain, spat the word 'fuck' at the floor and dropped shopping bags on it. Benny ate a fried-egg sweet and brought a fresh fag to his lips. Its first glow announced a silence during which Elaine splashed a set of keys down on the sideboard, unpacked the bags and wiped the coffee table with a blue cloth, drawing a horribly dry, artificial cough from Benny, but no words. He stayed silent until Elaine was in their bedroom and had closed the door.

'She's worse than your fucking dad.'

'Don't speak ill of my husband.'

Mum emerged from the bathroom pursued by a cloud of fluorescent-lit steam. She wore a white robe and had her hair turbaned in an orange towel. She picked a rosebud from a vase on the windowsill, de-thorned its stem and slid it behind her ear. 'A peace movement began today,' she said, sitting beside Benny on the chaise longue. The wings of her dressing gown fell to reveal the inside of a reddish, mighty thigh. Benny sniffed the way coke users do, conspicuous in his attempt to seem innocuous.

FHM makes its first attempt to catalogue the hundred sexiest women in the world in 1995. The 1995 list is the only list to be topped by a supermodel − Claudia Schiffer. It's also the only *FHM* list of sexy women to contain dead women − Marilyn Monroe and Audrey Hepburn. Kate Moss comes twenty-second.

'I'd like to try some of that, Benny, if you wouldn't mind.'

Benny smiled angelically but said nothing.

'Auntie Mill,' Jess said, 'you're not saying –'

'Why shouldn't I try some?'

Benny gathered his legs to his body and looked at me.

'I'm entitled to try some, since you're doing it, Benny. Do you need a razor blade because I've got one in my washbag?'

Benny broke blocks with his cash card and swept the cocaine into lines on a small pane of glass, which he kept on the coffee table for precisely that purpose. Mum flexed her fingers and kept looking at me. When I was very young, we went to Margate and I saw a skeleton dancing on the seafront. It was dancing beside an old man and I didn't notice the strings that linked the skeleton's limbs to the man's fingertips. I thought it was an actual dancing skeleton. For a pound, the old man sold me a see-through bag of cardboard bones and I walked along the seafront with Dad and after five minutes or so I burst into tears. I was still crying pretty badly when Dad sat me down on a bench, where a woman was gutting mackerel, and he assembled the bones into a skeleton and tied the little strings to the fingers of my hand. Maybe it was the heat, or maybe it was the smell of fish guts; I couldn't stop crying. My hand hung by my side and the skeleton dragged behind me as we searched Margate for Elaine and Mum.

Mum pushed a rolled-up tenner into her nostril. She crouched over the pane of glass and her voice turned nasal. 'It's almost yoga, this, isn't it? Look at my posture. I'm halfway through a Sun Salutation.' She was surprised by the ease with which the powder vanished.

'Sniff,' Benny said. 'Sniff, Millicent. Breathe through your mouth.'

After Mum, I did a line and then Jess. Mum insisted that I sit on the chaise longue with her; we talked about the different slogans we'd chanted that day. Everyone thought George W. Bush was a real cunt, though, to me, he had one of those faces that doesn't age as such, but kind of imprisons its own youth and preserves it somehow, so even when he's talking about bombing countries you can't help thinking a little boy's saying it all. I went on the march to be with Jess. I was drawn to her. I had been since the nineties, when she'd performed 'Wannabe' while making love to a column of air.

Benny smoked a fag like he was licking chocolate from a gold teaspoon. Mum stroked the knuckles of my hands and gradually delighted in the small movements of her mouth – a subtle orgy between lips, teeth, tongue.

'Should we wake Elaine? Elaine. Such a beautiful name. Could I have one of those, Benny?'

'Seriously?'

'Yes seriously! I smoked when Julian and I got together.'

A moment later, Mum lay on her back, allowing smoke to drift, unblown, from her mouth and bathing in the light of her eyes. When the cigarette ended, she went to the bathroom for a long time and returned with a schoolboy's quiff gelled into her hair. 'Coke's very me. Get more. I'm your mother-in-law. I'll pay.' After the second gram, Mum removed her arms from the sleeves of her dressing gown so its top half hung like a samurai skirt. I think maybe her special bras only came in white. When we kissed her goodnight, she was lying on the chaise longue, writing in her notepad. 'I've got to finish this. Yes, you guys go to bed. This is the breakthrough for the new collection.'

Jess and I slept in the spare room, which when Benny purchased the flat was intended to be Elaine's studio. Jess climbed into the single bed and I lay down on a pink lilo on the floor. The bedside lamp clicked off and somewhere a dog sounded desperately lonely. I put my hands in my underpants and cradled my testicles. A bus's brakes winced on Bethnal Green Road and the dog continued to bark. Jess twisted abruptly in her bed. My testicles felt ludicrous. In the darkness, my cousin was looking at me. I could tell by the mood of the room.

In the morning, the red tissues on the coffee table spoke of a long nosebleed. Mum lay asleep on the chaise longue. Little bits of twisted tissue plugged her nostrils. Elaine was furious with Benny. 'She survived cancer. What have you survived?' She lifted the duvet and unveiled his big clothed foetus. '*Nothing*, Ben. You've survived *nothing*.'

'I haven't.' Benny half sat up and groped for the covers. 'I promise I haven't.'

My approach to lyrics was simple. On page one of a notepad, I wrote a list of all the people I'd ever loved. Beside it, I wrote down all the people I'd ever had sex with. In 2004, I spent days walking around Manchester's Millennium Quarter, the area they built following the 1996 explosion, reading the two lists and thinking. In the eighteenth century, the area been a warren of narrow streets known for witchcraft and prostitution. In the late nineteenth century, those narrow streets were cleared and grand buildings were erected to house the centres of global trade in cotton and corn. I used to pee in the Corn Exchange, which is a shopping centre now; I once stroked a fleece in Fat Face for a while before deciding not to get it. In Selfridges, women in lab coats sprayed the air in front of me with a Britney Spears perfume called Curious.

When no lyrics came to me, I left Harry in Manchester, in our rehearsal room, where he was trying to create a sound that would enable our music to stand out on daytime radio. I went to London, where time behaved differently, where the afternoons dissolved like aspirins and the days died in clubs, late, with Benny putting his arm round strangers, hanging off them, holding their phones in the air. (Look who I bumped into!) 'I need a shag,' he'd say, as we walked back to Bethnal Green. 'Did you see those beautiful whores? I'm famous. You're going to be. We should *have* them.'

My friendship with Benny developed in the months after I signed a record deal. There's a magnetism that occurs when you stand on the edge of fame. You're attracted to other famous people, even if they're repulsive; they emit warmth. You want to combine yourselves and witness your effect on the anonymous; share the public gaze in order to intensify it. It's basic chemistry. It's the reason low-level celebrities look for love together. It was the reason I saw so much of Benny. His drug dealer was a haggard gingernut who lived in a former factory in Shoreditch. Outside her living-room window was a metal winch, which she – her name was Dinky – described as 'this beautiful decoration'. She camouflaged her drug-dealing and her drug-taking by affecting love for life. 'I love the sky today, don't you? My grandad used to work here, did I say? I don't know if it's this exact building, but it *was* Shoreditch. He made furniture. What are you two here for, crack?' We'd leave her staring at a word search and go for lunch. The afternoon would drift by in pubs and parks or sitting on the chaise longue playing Grand Theft Auto.

In 2004, our band came fourth in a respected cool list and it was like when the plane accelerates on the runway; Harry and I felt the powerlessness of lift off. We played a gig in a club in Liverpool the day the list was published. I remember bar staff at the venue wanted photographs and autographs. The promoter was nervous around us, repeatedly asking us if everything was to our satisfaction.

'Go and demand the Internet,' Harry said. 'Say we won't play unless we get it.'

There were cartoon sex organs inked on the dressing-room walls. On the ceiling, a swear word was written in huge letters, the last of which was faint where the marker pen had run dry. Harry ate a Conference pear and, having got nowhere near its core, he dropped it onto the floor and sucked a biro, which splintered instantly in his mouth. He pondered a piece of paper that was blank except for a wandering fly. 'Tell them we won't perform until we've checked our emails, Jim.' There was a knock on the door and a boy entered clutching a 7" copy of 'Inside the Explosion'. A Liverpool fanzine had run a competition to meet us and the boy had won. I don't remember his name, but it was one of those whimsical surname-names, like Thorney.

'I can't tell you when precisely Picasso painted this,' Harry told the boy, pointing to a piece of graffiti with a drumstick, 'but the veins on the shaft and the pubic detailing suggest it was during the real glory days.' Beside the penis was a woman with an exaggerated quantity of pubic hair, a sword through her head and swastikas instead of nipples. Even in this period, it got me down that I'd never seen Kate Reynolds in the nude. I regularly fantasised about the two of us standing naked in the old coal shed at Queen's, me with a safe penis and a bunch of flowers, her smoking a joint and stroking her beautiful hairy beaver. Hers was a kind of mystic vagina. I used to imagine it a great deal. I used to imagine I could press my entire face against it and allow her hot juices to dry on me like a mask. The boy wore blue undistressed jeans and a red T-shirt (the Strokes) that was many sizes too big. His quiff, having been sculpted in a world of post-shower promise, had wilted and become crusty. He had a slight lisp and was cross-eyed. Neither problem was severe, but they combined, along with the big T-shirt and the collapsed hair, to give his presence a lack of clarity.

'Who are you here with?' I asked.

'I'm on me own,' he said, in his soft Scouse accent.

'Have you seen this thing?'

I handed him the magazine containing the cool list. He looked at the photo of Harry and me sitting on that bench together, staring sternly from the page. We'd pulled similarly serious faces when we created the band's email account, or when we first tried on our table-tennis strips and posed back to back, arms folded, for my wardrobe's mirror.

'I've met these guys,' the boy said, turning the page and pointing to the band that came first in the list. 'They're banned from playing here because they trashed the stage,' he said.

Harry spat a bit of biro onto the floor. He took the magazine from the boy's lap and folded it in half. 'I'm sorry, Tooley,' he said, 'but you look like the kind of guy who's got access to the Internet. I don't mean that as an insult.' The boy admitted that he could access the Internet in his father's study. 'I had the Internet in the late 1990s,' Harry said. 'You're part of a spike in global population caused by the Industrial Revolution, Tooley. I don't mean that as an insult. You're part of a boom in youth culture that in a hundred years' time will be considered incredibly embarrassing. So are we. The celebrity and the suicide bomber are spiritually linked. They've got very similar convictions about freedom, explosives and morality. What websites do you go on in your father's study? Is there a lock on that door?' Harry was twenty-two and happiness was a mystery. His was a religion based not on faith but on higher education and blind rage. 'The afterlife and the after-party are very similar places. There are virgins in this venue right now, Tooley, standing at the front of the stage, waiting for us, leaning against the barrier.' Harry's relationship with words had become strained by 2004. Each one was umbilicalled to a cosy controversy. The boy looked at the floor.

'Do you think you'll start a band?' I said.

The boy shook his head.

'Come on,' I said, patting his shoulder. 'You should go for it.'

'I wonder if yous'll make it,' he said.

In the next room, our support band took to the stage, greeted by light applause and some solitary female screams.

'We already have,' I said.

On 30 April 2007, Kate Moss launches her first range of clothing for high-street retailer Topshop. She appears briefly in the window of the branch on Oxford Street, London. Out on the pavement, many members of the public wait to buy her clothes. Her appearance causes a frenzy among them, separated, as they briefly are, by a pane of glass.

The longer I sat with Jess during the interval of the opera, the more miserable I became. I tried to wake Elizabeth Albright, who was asleep on a chair at the back of the box. She looked at me like I wasn't there and then rubbed some dribble into her lap. Her head lolled and strands of permed blonde hair fell over her face and quivered in the breeze of her snores.

'Let's go get ice cream,' Jess said.

In Act Three of *La Traviata*, Alfredo's father tells Violetta she must end her affair with his son. His relationship with a courtesan has brought shame on the family. Violetta eventually agrees and travels to Paris to resume her life as a prostitute. When Alfredo discovers she's gone, he assumes she's betrayed him and travels to confront her, unaware that his father's influence lies behind everything.

'Let it melt,' Jess said, as I tried to eat the ice cream with a tiny plastic scoop. The interval bell rang and we climbed a wide staircase and passed through the gallery bars. Waiters rushed about us with trays, gathering empty glasses and bottles. We paused by the entrance to our box. An usher urged us to take our seats. Jess waited till he'd walked away and came very close to me.

'I need your advice,' she said.

'Voicemails make me nervous.'

'Will you listen to me?'

'Harry keeps leaving them.'

'The label have suggested I have surgery, Jim. They say it's best to do it before I'm famous. Get it out of the way.'

'What kind of surgery?'

'My breasts . . . Jim.'

From time to time, I find myself wondering why, in 1997, I tried to eat the front cover of the *Sun*. If you'd asked me then, I think I'd have said that I longed to make love to a Spice Girl. But actually, I think I did it because I wanted that front cover as deep inside me as possible. It was like eating skin.

The usher reappeared and insisted that Jess and I return to our box. The auditorium was dark as we took our seats. The curtain had risen and Irene Albright lay centre stage in a large bed carved from a dark wood. She wore a white foundation and a disheveled blonde wig. This was Violetta's sickbed. I cupped my hand over my cousin's ear.

'Have the surgery,' I whispered, and Jess nodded. 'It's the logical choice.'

Pedestrians in Grand Theft Auto III are made out of separate polygon parts (limbs, a head and a torso). This makes it possible to detach these things using firearms or explosives.

The night before the opera, Benny and I walked to the launch of Ladylike together. The plane trees were in bloom on Portland Place. We'd spent the day on London Fields, where we'd eaten Subways and I'd tried to convey to him the stir Elaine caused when she nailed all those condoms to a piece of chipboard.

Ladylike were launched at the Royal Institute of British Architects. Male models guarded the entrance. They wore Ladylike T-shirts and had their hands tied behind their backs and leather masks over their mouths. We gave our names and felt the dumb pride of the guest-listed. In the foyer, a beautiful girl recognised Benny from his adverts and, for a moment, as she lost her cool, became flushed and requested his autograph, he looked poisoned by joy. We drank beer beneath chandeliers, surrounded by journalists and elegant people, who spoke in the notes that lies and birdsong share. Later, when the free drink ran dry and faces were rouged and puffy, those present would speak in slack code about what they'd witnessed and, amid talk of taxis and going on somewhere, would decide whether Ladylike were bad or good.

I've heard some footballers weep in the moments that follow their orgies. Call girls mention it when interviewed. I felt similar after being with Benny. He drank several beers quickly and became cruel. 'I hate the Chinese, Jim. I detest them. I've started following them into Topshop and laughing at them. Hey, give me that.' He raised my phone above his head, pulled the face that had made him famous and photographed it. Returning the phone to me, he stooped to kiss the skin beneath my earlobe.

'Whatever,' he said, violently, trying to shoo some dread from his mind.

The four Ladylike girls bounded through lights and dry-ice wearing miniskirts and vests. They danced around the stage at random, pointing and smiling at people on the front row, occasionally colliding with each other, unleashing pouts, bringing their index fingers to their cheeks and rolling their eyes. Jess didn't mime standing-up sex with a column of air. The whole thing looked intensely professional. They performed their first single, 'Silly Boy'. They followed it with a song called 'Sorry, But You Stink'. Beside me, Benny was in stitches. He buried his face in my chest and his forehead left a peach-coloured make-up stain on my shirt. '*Wow*, they're shit. *Wow*, they're the shittest thing I've ever seen.' Ladylike's third song was a ballad called 'Not So Strong'. Its conclusion was a cappella, which Jess performed as a solo. Her final note ended just after she closed her mouth and smiled. Four young men strode across the front of the stage with bare chests and sarongs. Jess's man knelt in front of her, bringing his head level with her crotch. An uptempo beat played and Jess and the other girls feigned comical orgasms as the men mimed licking them out. It was quite a dubious novelty song called 'Roxette Boxset'.

I went outside to get some air. It was dark and Portland Place was quiet. I watched the small waves of slow cars that the traffic lights released and breathed in the calmness in between. I took out my lyrics notepad and scanned the list of the people I had loved and the list of people I'd had sex with. Returning to the venue, I descended some stairs and found a peaceful, unisex toilet. I entered in time to see Mum disappear into a cubicle. I lowered both seats in the one adjacent to hers and for a while there was silence. Just when I felt sure it was the silence of the night, or the silence of London, or the silence of the whole planet, Mum sighed, farted softly and urinated. I heard the bleep of her phone and then her voice, which sounded calmer than it ever had.

'Hello, Sheila. Millicent Albright here. I'm in London. I was wondering if we might meet. Carol's been awfully vague as to why you won't take the manuscript. What have you got against *Cucumber Sandwiches*, eh? I'm at my niece's launch tonight, then I'm watching my sister sing tomorrow, so it's all go. We can sort this out, Sheila. Call me.'

I heard the toilet roll rattle and rip. Mum left the cubicle and rinsed her hands, singing quietly, '*I'm sorry, sorry, sorry, but you stink. I don't care what anyone thinks.*' I could hear her over the hand-dryer's drone. '*I'm sorry, sorry, sorry . . .*'

In 1999, at the launch of *Lady Beast*, Mum stood at a lectern beside a display of her books. It was evening and we were gathered in a bookshop in Notting Hill. 'Those of you who know me,' she said, 'know that this is the real me.' Elizabeth Albright tried several times to perform the poems on Mum's behalf. ('I will, Milly. Make everyone be quiet. Everyone. *Shhh!* Milly wants me to . . .') I had to take her outside to sober her up. We walked to a road near Notting Hill Gate, where the facades of the houses were painted in pinks, pale yellows and blues. 'My agent used to live round here,' Elizabeth said, as she perched on a low wall outside a pea-green home. 'Francis Hems. Has your mum ever mentioned Francis Hems, Jim?'

I was seventeen. My aunt was framed by the bay window of the house. She felt she was 'put on this earth for musical theatre' and no one really argued with that. She looked drunk and quite old, sitting on that wall. She shook her large perm with both hands and took some slow, sobering breaths.

'Your parents came to Stratford for an opening night of mine once. We all went out for a late supper – your parents, Francis Hems, me. It was the first time I'd seen your dad drunk. He devoured some butter thinking it was cheese. It was so embarrassing, the way he tried to keep it together. I went back to my digs but your mum and Francis went for a stroll by the Avon while your dad slept in the car. They found a bench and Milly opened up to Francis about all sorts – things to do with *our* dad. The next thing he knew she was touching him!'

My aunt looked up and seemed sad not to find me laughing.

'If you knew Francis, James, you'd see how hilarious that is. Milly groped him! They call him the Queen of Soho. But that's not the funniest thing. The funniest thing was that once he rebuffed her, Milly stood on the riverbank and started singing a song. I can't remember what, but some show tune. *Your sister*, Francis always says, when I bump into him, *your bloody sister, standing there singing in the middle of the night, no training, a horrible voice, trying to persuade me to represent her. Me*, he says. He's got such a camp voice. *Me!* That's exactly how he sounds!'

By the time I returned to the main room Ladylike had finished their set and the stage was empty. Benny approached with a slack jaw, looking coked-up and distressed.

'Where's Jess?' I asked.

'Probably fingering herself in her dressing room. Ha!'

Benny's sentences were like pork loin; with a sharp enough knife you could cut off the prime irony and make crackling from the sincerity. He started adding 'Ha!' to the ends of his sentences in the final weeks of our friendship.

'Seriously, Benny, where is she?'

'Probably being made to gape by that nigger who writes for *The Times*. Ha!'

His mouth hung open. He tried not to smile. It seemed possible that Benny's mouth would never close fully ever again. That it might hang, half closed, half open, for ever more, not smiling or grimacing, but simply there, an unhappy gap, an entrance and exit for air.

'Benny.'

'Beh–neee,' he said, deriding my tone. 'Oh, I hate you, too, Jim. You've failed me. Why aren't you famous yet? Jess is *there*, look.'

Benny pointed across the bar to where Elizabeth Albright was trying to push through the crowd of people that surrounded her niece. I went over and attempted to do the same, but couldn't get close to Jess either. 'The *cute* one.' A pink-haired man pinched Jess's shoulder. 'Your *voice*, my *God*.' He handed her a glass of champagne and predicted that Ladylike, and Jess in particular, were going to be huge. 'I'm going to be drunk!' Jess said, and at that moment, as people laughed, looked at each other and nodded in appreciation of her, I went to the bar, and did my best to mingle. It was less than a day before Benny would call me a clothed piece of shit, but that was how I felt really. A woman in ethnic jewellery held court beside a yucca plant. She looked like a plump Karen Carpenter and maybe that was the reason I lingered on the outskirts of her circle, trying to find a way in to the discussion of the band.

'They're manufactured,' I snapped. 'They don't write their songs and Jess was miming.'

Several faces tilted towards me, each voided by tiredness, alcohol or make-up, each looking bored or a bit disgusted. I wasn't quite sure what to say. I made myself beam with a strange pride and claimed I was only saying what everyone else was thinking.

'No, you're not. No one cares.' Karen Carpenter wasn't Karen Carpenter. She was Irene Albright. 'It was a mixture of recorded and real singing and that's fine,' she said, standing close to me, trying to prevent the others from seeing me. 'You're jealous, James. And you're drunk. Go home.'

In Grand Theft Auto IV, the cross hairs are easy to aim at specific parts of a person's body. It's orthodox to murder a prostitute after sleeping with them. In videos posted on YouTube, players frequently immobilise her with a knife and then, as she lies on the floor, screaming, the cross hairs, more often than not, scan to her crotch.

I drifted around Bloomsbury, where I got the hiccups and hailed a taxi. In Bethnal Green, Elaine was asleep on the mint-green chaise longue. I lay down on the floor beside her and used my coat as a pillow. I searched for 'magnificent bust' using my phone's limited search engine and when I drew a blank, my mind stalled and I fell into a kind of shallow coma.

Crazy Frog goes to number one all over Europe in May 2005. He is a computer-animated frog who impersonates the sound of a motorcycle engine and rides around a city on an imaginary motorbike. It is the first hit record to be known predominantly as a ringtone. The media discusses how something so bad can become so popular.

I woke in the middle of the night to the sound of Benny's voice. Moonlight pooled on the windowsill, where a fat cactus stood alongside a bronze statuette, an award from Benny's Young Vic days. Elaine was still sleeping and I was still holding my phone as I stood and staggered towards Benny's bedroom and gently pushed at the door. His bedside light was angled so it shone onto his face. His hair was sweaty and swept away from his forehead; a line was visible, just below his hairline, where his make-up ended and his skin began. Jess was looking at me.

They were doing it in the position that I was conceived in. Both naked. Both pale. Jess's eyes were grey and I thought about how those slow, see-through creatures must seem to one another, when they pass on the beds of the deepest seas.

An online biography of Girl Thing begins, 'They're fun, they're fresh, they're kitsch and they're cool. They're Girl Thing.' It continues, 'Be yourself, have a good time, and you can't go wrong.' In her autobiography, *Being Jordan*, Katie Price describes how, in 1998, a Dr Prakesh showed her how durable the silicone implants were by insisting she give them 'a good old punch'.

After considering it for a month, Jess decided against breast enlargement, though two fellow Ladylike members decided to go through with it. Their debut single, 'Silly Boy', was added to daytime radio playlists, but received poor feedback from listener groups and was widely ridiculed in the press and online. A last-minute tour of nearly one hundred regional radio stations couldn't prevent it narrowly missing the top 40 and entering the UK chart at 51. The band was dropped a week after 'Sorry, But You Stink' failed to receive any notable airplay. Their debut album, *Show Up, Show Off*, was never released.

But all Jess knew, as she gripped the bed sheet in Bethnal Green, was that their launch had gone well, and that tomorrow the Albrights were going to the opera. I held up my phone and I photographed them, capturing the moment when Jess made a bid to wriggle free of Benny's grip. 'Get out, Jim,' Benny shouted. He was thrusting like a wild animal, holding her in the position. 'Get out!'

12

At the end of *La Traviata*, Alfredo comes to Violetta and says that it doesn't matter to him that she's a courtesan. They plan to leave Paris and be together for ever. However, Violetta is suffering from tuberculosis. She climbs from her sickbed, staggers towards her love and dies at his feet.

By the time Irene stepped through the curtain to take her third bow, the entire auditorium was standing to applaud her. Mum leant over the balcony and cheered her sister at a volume she'd never quite reached before. She'd spent a long time wanting to make those sounds. 'Brava! *Bra-va!*' Roses, thrown from the stalls, landed around Irene. She looked up and acknowledged her family with an intimate smile and wave.

The rims of Benny's nostrils were lightly frosted with cocaine. He sniffed, but nothing changed. This was after, as Mum and I stood with Benny and Elaine, waiting for Irene in a corridor backstage. Jayne had taken Elizabeth for a sobering march up and down Bow Street. Benny had stolen a pistol from a table of props and was waving it about. 'OK, look, guys,' he said, pointing the pistol at the side of his head. 'Jim'll only tell you this if I don't. Jess and I made love last night, after her concert. How could I? That's what you're thinking, isn't it, Elaine? How could I?'

'Don't even say that as a joke, Benny.'

'I'm not joking, Milly.'

'There are *limits*, OK? There's a line, Benny. Don't cross it.'

Benny pulled the trigger, the pistol clicked but that was all.

'I fucked Jessica Albright,' he said. 'I promise. From behind. I'm sorry, Elaine, but —'

'*Benny* —' Mum glanced nervously down the corridor — 'there's a line. It's not funny.'

'He isn't joking,' Elaine said.

'He is. He *always* is.'

'He isn't, Mum.'

'No, I'm not,' Benny said, recocking the pistol and shooting himself again. 'I did it. No one's using the R-word here, but I have to say she was pretty out of it.'

The Age of Irony was ending for Benny. It bequeathed him a slim soul, a discordant voice and a wooden heart. Mum tore flakes of white paint from the wall as she steadied herself. 'You didn't,' she whispered, covering her entire forehead with a hand.

'Yes, I did.' Benny was loose-limbed and titillated. 'Yes, indeed I did.'

There wasn't a line. And even if there was, Benny had crossed it ages ago. He'd crossed it in search of a promised land, where strangers knew his name and knew he was destined to be the white Morgan Freeman. 'My excuse is I was drunk.' He smiled at Elaine and shot himself in the head again. 'Doo doo doo, doo doo doo . . . Monkey is funky tiddley tunky, monkey is hunky biddley bunky . . . Will you forgive the little monkey?'

'Ben, I'm pregnant.'

Benny's limbs lingered in the crouch position he'd adopted in order to perform the monkey dance. I pictured the small thing in Elaine's womb and wondered which of the positions had given rise to that cashew nut of genes and heart. I was in no doubt as to which one it was. 'Oh, wow.' Benny's mouth was threatening a smile. 'Oh, boy.' He put the pistol to his head and pulled the trigger. There was a loud bang and a puff of smoke. He fell at our feet, holding his face and screaming. One of his horrified eyes looked up at us through splayed fingers. His loud apologies were muffled by his palms.

No one went with him to the hospital. Elaine called an ambulance and she and I watched from the pavement, as Benny was carried past, sitting on a stretcher, nursing his face with an ice pack. The burn he sustained, along with a semi-sordid kiss and tell that appeared in the *Sun* the following month, put an end to the phone adverts. He was replaced by an animated question mark called Seymour. He split from his agent after a furious and hypothetical argument over which television programme he was most suited to, *Big Brother* or *Celebrity Big Brother*. Benny waved to us as the ambulance doors closed.

There were celebration drinks in Irene's dressing room but Elaine and I didn't go. We rode the Tube back to Bethnal Green and sat on the chaise longue watching television. She didn't say much. She gathered her thin limbs and said she'd taken the pregnancy test during the interval. We considered ordering a curry, but in the end we didn't. It was difficult, just sitting there with her. Each time Benny's advert came on, we changed channel.

The missed calls from Harry that evening culminated in a voice-mail, the gist of which was that a boy from our year called Bamber had died in Iraq, and that Harry finally felt he had created a sound that would allow our band to stand out on daytime radio. I travelled to Manchester, to where we rehearsed, in the east of the city, in Ancoats, in a half-derelict cotton mill on Bradford Road. Not far away was the City of Manchester Stadium, for which Tony Blair laid the keystone in 1999. In 1998, the Trafford Centre – the gigantic mock-rococo shopping centre built on the ring road – opened. All new Mancunian buildings were a response to the '96 bomb. The facades of many were comprised almost entirely of glass. In Ancoats, the blood-brown 1970s tower blocks of Rochdale Road still thumped the sky, but were derelict now and looked like CD racks; empty balconies like empty slots. A process of regeneration was happening across England. But progress was a psycho. It put steel in the windows of some buildings and built new ones full of small flats. People could live inside these flats, just as I floated in Mum for a while. Progress commandeered nineteenth-century buildings and then, as the economy weakened, left them to crumble behind fences that showed conceptual drawings of new ways of living, where blurred illustrations of humans lingered in paved squares that looked neither public nor private. '1842' was carved into an archway that led to a courtyard full of oil puddles, scrap metal and at least forty neatly stacked cabinet freezers. I climbed a rusting fire escape and phoned Harry from outside a locked door. For eighteen months, we'd rented the room and tried to create new pop music. Harry would loop beats on his laptop. I'd plug a microphone into a guitar amp and stand with my notepad, reading the two lists, occasionally singing spontaneously, other times just watching Harry as he fingered the mouse pad, oblivious to the sadness his looped beats caused and how their incessancy ground me down. Some days we studied Prince songs like scientists, trying to isolate and emulate magic elements. Other days we mapped out Britney's song structures on big sheets of sugar paper, or bought four-packs of lager and forty cigarettes and tried to engender a pre-sonic vibe. Four men came up from London, one by one, to assist us with our songwriting. They drove into the mill's courtyard in mid-range sports cars and dragged Pro Tools rigs from the back seats in the rain. Months started to pass by. Grove-White, our A&R man, called occasionally and said we had a future. But something made it difficult to see. It was like looking at a white sky through a window speckled with raindrops, trying to determine whether rain was still falling. We'd trek right across the city most days to check the band's email in an Easy Internet Café in St Ann's Square. All the computer screens had had crosses scratched into them with keys or knives. It was an hour and a half round trip to read spam about drugs that might enlarge our penises or new ways of making money online. We'd get back to Ancoats, tired, Harry would tap the space bar and trigger the looped beat. The space bar broke eventually, but worked if pressed in a certain way; there was a knack to it, but it often took several attempts. In the room adjacent to ours was a boxing club for boys. Trainers shouted instructions as the boys worked the bags. Harry was oblivious. He sneezed twice and knelt on the dusty floor. I sat on the old red sofa, beside an area of pigeon shit and a poster of Kurt Cobain. Harry switched on his Casio keyboard, checked all the dials were in the right places and adjusted the volume slightly.

'I tried to get the Internet,' he said, indicating a switched-off wireless router on a pile of pizza boxes. 'My dad had a mobile phone in 1995.'

The secret to a radio pop song was to write about love or sex or death or dancing. The other secret was to have a signature sound, something listeners could identify you by. As Harry played me ours, a volley of punches were thrown next door and plaster fell from the ceiling, where rusting pipes led nowhere now and nothing hung from two gigantic hooks. Cotton is manufactured in that room for less than a century. The Mill closes down in 1960, in the period when, according to Norman Mailer, white people are becoming cool. Harry's sound was a blend of metallic textures and lunar vibrations. I listened to it very carefully. It arrived with force and then echoed away.

'There,' Harry said, looking up. 'Do you think it's cool?'

Harry never apologised for cheating on me with Fiona Hohner in 1995. I hadn't been waiting for an apology as such, but, in that moment, it crossed my mind that one would've been nice. He looked small, crouched over his retro keyboard. He might at least have consulted me before going to the coal shed with her.

The two of us walked to a greasy spoon in Miles Platting. We chose a table in the corner that was chained to the floor. A grey woman watched us from behind an old yellow till. Soon after Harry and I entered, the place filled with a lunchtime crowd of men in high-visibility bibs and rigger boots. Some removed hard hats to reveal baseball caps, or flapped newspapers to life, or lit fags.

We started a MySpace page a month before we were dropped by our label. As I remember it, no love was unleashed. Harry picked up a menu and flicked its corner where the laminate and the paper separated and curled. The grey woman swept then mopped the floor beneath the electric-blue insect killer. 'One day,' Harry told me, 'I'm going to make an acoustic album. I'll write songs about what it's like to be young nowadays, as everything's changing.' He laid his hands flat on the tabletop and splayed his fingers. 'I'm tired,' he said. 'I want control . . . I'll go somewhere like southern India or Chile, Jim. Just me and a guitar.'

Four workmen left the cafe. They fastened their coats against the cold and crossed the street, singing in unison, '*We are not, we're not really here. We are not, we're not really here.*'

People I've Loved	Had Sex With
Kate Reynolds	Dilly
Evie from *The House of Elliot*	Pillows
Harry	Leanne Childe
Elaine	
Jessie Spano from *Saved by the Bell*	
Jess	
Aunt Jayne	
Francesco Totti	

In 2003, Manchester City Football Club begins to play its home games at the City of Manchester Stadium, near Ancoats. The last Manchester City goal to be scored at their old stadium, Maine Road, is scored by Marc-Vivien Foe, a Cameroon international. It comes in the 3-0 defeat of Sunderland on 21 April 2003.

Many photographs are taken on the day the team play their last game at Maine Road, in the city's notorious Moss Side. After being demolished, Maine Road is replaced by a development called the Maine Place; a complex comprising shops, leisure facilities and apartments. The photographer Kevin Cummins, famous for his portraits of Manchester musicians such as Ian Curtis and Morrissey, documents the final match at Maine Road. His photos capture the architectural intimacy the stadium shared with the surrounding terraced houses. He publishes them in a book in 2006. The book's title takes its name from a popular Manchester City chant: 'We are not really here.' Once, in our practice room, after four cans each, Harry looped a beat and started dancing. 'It's recording, Jim,' he shouted, clapping along to the kick drum, his eyes squinting, biting his entire lower lip in appreciation of the groove. I let my notepad fall from my hands and patted my thigh to the rhythm, standing in front of the microphone. Harry picked up a sheet of flesh-coloured sugar paper, which contained a detailed structural breakdown of 'Toxic' by Britney Spears. 'From your heart!' he said, tearing the paper to pieces, looking at me with eyes so intense it was as though they were reaching out like hands. *'Give me your love,'* I sang, to a melody that rose. I closed my eyes. *'Give me your love!'*

We sat on the old red sofa and listened back to what we'd recorded. Harry blamed digital technology for the lack of vibe. 'It's zeros and ones, Jim. It can't capture the unheard.' As I listened to myself sing, the image of a huge hotel came to mind. It was bigger than any building could ever be. Its front wall was missing and this afforded me a clear view into the millions of small rooms, in which people lived, seemingly, one in each, some sitting or lying quietly on the bed, some making hot drinks using single-portion kettles, but most beating their fists against the dividing walls, saying their names.

In 2003, two months after Maine Road was demolished, Marc-Vivien Foe is playing for Cameroon against Colombia in the Confederations Cup in Lyon. He is running alone through the centre circle when he suddenly collapses. Though efforts are made to restart his heart, they fail and he is pronounced dead on the pitch. The cameras capture the whites of his eyes, looking up in what is a death stare. He is twenty-eight. Fans of Manchester City lay flowers against the largely demolished Kippax stand at Maine Road.

In the France '98 sticker annual that Daniel Parker and I completed, I recently noticed something strange. Normally, in their portraits, the footballers are smiling or else they're looking stern. The one exception is the portrait of Marc-Vivien Foe. In his, he has closed his eyes.

In October 2005, Mum confirmed that her poetry collection, *Cucumber Sandwiches*, would not be published and that she would, as a result, return to teaching. We were sitting at the kitchen table, back in Ridley. Mum slowly turned the pages of a catalogue of breasts.

'The publisher said it was too tame. They didn't understand that it's your father's diced penis in those cucumber sandwiches. It's diced England. *When they cut off my breasts you brought me cucumber sandwiches.* He did that, you know? He came in with a plate of them. Me, half-dead. This is a C cup. What do you think?' Mum turned the catalogue so it was facing me and pointed to a photograph of a nude female torso.

Mum had her breasts reconstructed at a private clinic in Cheshire. I sat in a waiting room, sedated by subliminal pan pipes, watching an Eastern European receptionist covertly dissolve crisps on her tongue. Windows held the day at bay with long organza curtains and standing between those was a lush fern and a portrait of a woman with a cleavage the colour of strong tea and a look in her eye that suggested an impossible ease with the universe.

Irene Albright came for moral support. She and I sat on a pink settee together. She read *Closer* for a while, then rolled it up, gripped it like it was someone's wrist and gave it a Chinese burn. Her phone kept ringing; I guess it was her agent. *La Traviata* brought Irene great success, a new recording contract and numerous job offers. She'd been able to finance Jess's stay in Ibiza, where Ladylike had relocated to try and get a buzz going in the hope of securing a new record deal. Their management were attempting to move them into edgier territory, encouraging the girls to make a dance-pop album called *Mistakes and Pisstakes.*

I went in to see Mum on my own. Two bags hung above her bed, one of blood, one of water. I stroked her forearm for ages because I wasn't sure what else to do. Mostly, I tried to ignore her bandages.

Mum sang at the Midland Hotel, Morecambe, on New Year's Eve 1989, our first year in the north. She wore a beige ball gown and sang jazz standards for what was mostly an elderly audience.

In between songs, people called out requests for wartime numbers and in response the pianist invariably played the opening bars, only to be waved to a stop by Mum, who apologised, explaining that she didn't know the words.

There was a plastic flower on the piano that night that moved mechanically to sound. It had a smiley face and wore sunglasses. I stood beside it at the midnight countdown. '*Three . . . two . . . one . . .*' The flower struck a pose for each number the audience shouted and then it moved vigorously at 'Happy New Year', as people cheered, embraced and pulled party poppers. Shortly after midnight, Mum's set was cut short by a group of men. They gathered at the piano, placed pint glasses round the plastic flower and took over.

On the way home, driving along the coast road, Mum's gown was trapped in the taxi door and it flapped in the dark outside my window. She made us all promise not to tell her sisters that she'd sung. 'There's no need to report this,' she said. It was 1990.

I sat by her bed for an hour before she woke. She kept closing her eyes and opening them again, as if she expected to see something different. All she'd have seen was the room and the bandages around her chest. She reached for my hand.

Irene stayed with Mum and I caught the train into Manchester, where I had begun renting my small bedsit on the outskirts of the city centre, towards Cheetham Hill. I watched the suburbs come and go. The supermarkets, the rows of red-brick terraces, smokeless chimneys, artificial sports fields, the old tower blocks, the curry houses and parades of run-down shops. As the train approached Piccadilly, sunlight caught the glass towers of the centre and they became pillars of reflected light. When I imagined what was beneath Mum's bandages, I found myself thinking about a time capsule we buried at Ridley Primary in 1991. It was a big deal at the time. They were relaying the infants' playground and so it was an opportunity, so they told us, to hide things that would 'speak to the future about today'.

I left the train at Piccadilly and walked to the Northern Quarter. I stood on Spear Street. Above me, I could hear people toasting some kind of success on a roof terrace. Black sacks of rubbish were piled on the corner of Stevenson Square, spilling their contents through rat-bitten slits. They say if a man wanders alone around a strange city, he'll instinctively find his way to the red-light district. I think Freud said that. Manchester wasn't strange to me, I suppose. I walked down Shudehill, following the tram tracks down Balloon Street towards Victoria. I stood on Corporation Street, right where the bomb exploded.

Dad and I once played Combat Bombastic on the beach in Cornwall. He pursued me with zombie-arms with his tongue hanging from his mouth. My legs were weak with wanting to escape and with wanting to go on the run for a while but, most of all, they were weak with wanting to be caught. Mum watched us from a bamboo mat, the wings of her book draped over her pale thigh, its cover curling in the heat. Her sun hat's limp rim shaded her collarbone, her mouth and concealed her eyes completely. Elaine lay on a pink towel, scanning the beach for anyone else trying to untie the trick-knot of being fourteen and a girl. She wore circular sunglasses that refused to stay on her face. She patted her crown to check that an orange braid was still there. Dilly lay at her feet with sand stuck to his damp underbelly. 'Target apprehended!' Dad wrapped his arms around me and we fell together. 'Combat Bombastic. Prepare for detonation! *Three . . . two . . . one . . .*' When he exploded, he pressed his mouth to my ear and made a raspy, apple-scented sound. His spittle tickled and I rubbed my ear with my shoulder. To be inside the explosion, to be the bubble that bursts, was intimate.

From Corporation Street, I walked along Cross Street and up into Chinatown. I stood on a dark backstreet at the rear of a kebab shop. Through its door, a young man shaved strips of doner meat from a vertical spit while two others took orders at the counter. Mayonnaise mesmerised a big-faced boy as it oozed from a teat and swirled on his chicken burger. The guy at the doner spit stopped carving. He picked up a yellow container and brought it to the back doorway to empty it into a drain. He saw me and paused. In the years since we'd last seen each other, Daniel's stain had changed. It had turned a darker purple and the eyebrow it enveloped had been pierced. He banged the base of the container till he was sure it was empty. He turned and went inside.

The England manager, Fabio Capello, ends the international career of David Beckham. When justifying Beckham's exclusion from the squad, Capello says, 'He's a little bit too old.'

I slipped through a doorway further down the street and climbed some stairs. They were lined with fairy-lit mirrors. At the top, I rang the doorbell. The lock buzzed and I pushed through to a reception area, where a warm-eyed woman with a brittle bouffant sat at a desk, speaking on a mobile. 'I like Center Parcs,' she said, catching my eye and indicating an empty waiting area. I took a seat. 'Ah, but they do it out like a winter wonderland,' the woman continued. 'The staff dress as elves.' On a flat-screen television, the scrolling news concerned bombs that had exploded on a bus and on tube trains in London that morning. We'd followed the story on the radio, as we'd driven across Cheshire to the clinic. We were horrified, but not mystified, and on some level we were at ease with the idea of people making themselves explode. 'Imagine being one of them,' Mum said, leaning forwards in the passenger seat to adjust the volume. 'Imagine buying your ticket.'

I was shown into a room that looked down onto Portland Street. The bed was oddly high and there was a mirror fastened to the ceiling above it. After a few minutes, a girl arrived dressed in nothing but her underwear. She was Chinese and smelt of soap. She called herself Jordan, though it was clear she felt little affinity with the name. In fact, quite the opposite. She removed her bra, pushed her knickers to the floor and stepped out of them. The air was thickened by talcum powder, perfume and body creams. Jordan patted the bed then stood on her tip toes and held her legs slightly apart. As she applied lubricant to her vagina, she frowned and looked up into the mirror.

'Listen,' I said. 'Tomorrow, telephone a newspaper about this. *Kiss*,' I said, indicating the bed. 'And then, tomorrow, Jordan . . . *tell*.' I made the phone sign with my hand, brought it to my ear and twiddled it. Jordan looked at me through slim, blinking eyes. Her teeth were terribly crooked. She patted the bed again. 'Do you understand?' I said.

I brought an invisible microphone to my lips, pulled an anguished face and sang the chorus from 'Inside the Explosion'. Two years previously, it had done well on night-time radio and earned us a record deal and fourth place on an internationally respected cool list. Jordan didn't recognise it. I was about to get my phone out to show her some pictures of Harry and me, when her own phone started ringing. She rushed to her handbag and answered it. It was clear from her impatient tone who it was she was speaking to. The way she rolled her eyes and shifted her weight from foot to foot while tutting and sighing, it reminded me of Elaine, how she threw a party once in Ridley while our parents were away.

When Harry and I moved out of Withington in July 2005, he threw a large glass sweet jar full of copper coins into a skip at the end of our road. He moved to London and got work as a songwriter. He wrote a song called 'Heaven' using the sound he had created for us. He played a role in an eighties pop revival that was gathering pace in the music industry, writing songs for some major pop acts.

Jordan lost her temper and whined loudly into her phone. It was at this moment that a seagull clambered into the room through the open window and flapped wildly against the walls and the furniture. It landed on the bed and then flew forcefully at its reflection in the mirror above. Its scream was so loud. The bird was deranged. It knocked a portrait of a naked woman from the wall and caused Jordan to drop her phone. 'It's cool,' I said, lunging and trying to snatch the bird from the air. 'I'll get rid of it,' I said. Jordan ran into the corner, where classic porn played on a muted television. I kicked her knickers towards her and took a horsewhip from a table beside the bed. I used it to try and drive the seagull back towards the window. It kept swooping out of the way and flying at full speed into the door, as though it wanted to make its way deeper inside the brothel. I abandoned the whip and used a big pink beach towel to get a grip of one of the bird's sharp feet. I carried it with difficulty across the room, having to shield my face from its huge wings. I pushed it back out into the night and pulled the window shut. Even so, Jordan continued to panic as she attempted to thread her feet into her knickers. I held her shoulders and shushed her, telling her several times that the sea bird was gone, to be quiet and to calm down. 'I'm a table-tennis player,' I said, attempting to soothe her. 'See?' I adopted the 'ready stance', knees bent, shoulders hunched, and I mimed a backhand chop with the horsewhip. 'Your national sport,' I said, but she only whined even louder than before. Without ever deciding to do so, I demonstrated an attacking forehand and whipped Jordan hard across her chest. She covered her breasts with her hand and her forearm and I tried to gather her in an embrace and to muffle her howls.

They were other customers, I think, the wild, righteous men who burst into the room in various states of undress. They wrestled me to the floor and dragged me through the warm, powdery air, past the irate woman with her swaying bouffant, to the summit of the fairy-lit staircase.

Crazy Frog is vilified for possessing a human scrotum. Complaints from parents lead to the scrotum being blurred out in his adverts. The Japanese do the same to erections in porn. It's connected to shame. His second album, *Crazy Frog Presents More Crazy Hits*, peaks in the UK album chart at number 64. Someone called animekitten1 recently commented on Crazy Frog's video. 'i love how at the end he just stares into your soul nonstop for 10 seconds.'

The men made few additions to the damage done to me by the staircase. I was dragged into the backstreet and punched by a bold man in Bart Marley boxer shorts and polished loafers but no socks. Lying in the road, I watched the muscles flex inside his lightly hairy calves that appeared jaundiced in the street light. The idea of shouting for Daniel crossed my mind, but then I was kicked again, and then I was walking home, slowly, as if I was up to my waist and wading against a river's flow.

On a bridge near Charles Street I took out my phone. It was my fifth. The flip phone. I got blood on the keypad as I flicked through my photographs. The self-portrait of Benny and, from the same night, the photo of him with Jess. I deleted both and let the phone fall into the river. The following day, drops of blood mapped a route between Chinatown and my bed. I called my mobile from a payphone in the Arndale Centre. A recorded voice said it was switched off.

LOVE LIFE

13

You fall in love with Grand Theft Auto III very early in the game. It happens when you first drive into Liberty City. It happens because nothing happens. It's morning, the sun's shining and you're driving alone along lively North American streets. A destination has been suggested, but that's all – nothing is mandatory. It happens when you realise you are playing outside the structure of narrative. No one is going to make you do anything. Time is not going to run out. You are free. It happens when you realise you can leave your car and stand still on a pavement as fellow pedestrians wander past and speak. It happens, you fall in love, on your first day in Liberty City, when you see how dusk brings golden twilight, how the nights bring darkness, how each day dawns and it rains.

I received news this week that I wasn't expecting. I can't find a way to write it down. I've taken to doing online creative-writing tutorials. They stress the importance of 'likeability', which feels a bit vague. The tutorials are united in agreement with regards to the importance of appealing to the senses. Today, I wrapped a Manchester United scarf around my face so that I could smell my own breath. It smells of lung. Does that work, 'of lung'?

You can undertake the missions in Grand Theft Auto, but it's better to wander aimlessly. It's better to stand on the Ocean Boulevard and let pedestrians stagger past, repeating their set phrases. Living outside narrative is a definition of happiness, I think, and actual cities fill me with lust. I could replace every word I've written with that one. I get the tightening in British cities. Lust leads to weak orgasms and a feeling like I'm lost in a desert that used to be a seabed and I'm nailing planks of driftwood together.

In Grand Theft Auto III, you play a convicted bank robber who wears green combat trousers and a black bomber jacket. There's a series of in-game perspectives to choose from. One gives the impression you're inside the skull of your avatar, looking out of his eyes. The most popular perspective views the avatar from behind and slightly above. It's the same perspective JFK is filmed from in 1960, as he is followed through a crowd of his supporters by those American film-makers and their innovative lightweight video camera. Those film-makers believed their camera had, effectively, turned their audience into JFK.

I love my memories of Liberty City. Hours passed, but I didn't notice. A year of my life went by like the Queen in a horse-drawn carriage. It waved and I waved back, like I waved at Elizabeth Albright when Stan King drove her down Main Street in his cream VW Beetle. I lived for Grand Theft Auto III. I don't regret playing it. It was like I could hold my brain like I can hold my breath. Years ago, when I was nineteen, I'd wander down Deansgate muttering 'Busty big bosoms' under my breath. Like a ship sailing with its anchor dropped, I passed shops, muttering those words and churning the seabed. In the letter I wrote to the prostitute, Jordan, I tried to describe this insufferable lust. I told her about the tightening and about those boys who walked down into the London Underground in 2005 with rucksacks on their backs, or the men who steered the passenger jets back towards New York; those guys could tell you about lust, about fame, about what the tightening is. I apologised to Jordan for striking her with a horsewhip. I blamed lust, but I said it was only a theory. I didn't want to seem overly confident, callous or full of neat excuses. For my lust I blamed culture. I'm a grown man, Jordan, I wrote. Then I imagined myself as a sea monster.

Of course I'm sorry I whipped you, but imperatives of reproduction being undeniable, what kind of world do we want to live in? I've thrown that net out to sea so many times! I've seen dolphins swim in and out of it like they don't know it's there! I grew up in the rural north of England. Am I right in thinking you are one of the rural Chinese poor? Please do not think this a rude presumption. I am simply trying to establish our connection to one another, aside from our meeting last year in Manchester. I did not mean to enter your place of work. I get so horny and a million bluebirds take flight in unison, each holding a good idea in its beak like a twig. They made us long for love in the rural north. I can't stress that enough. They really made us long for love. But then all you want is sex. And then you don't want either. What a shit-heap!

Do you know Katsouris, the Greek delicatessen on Deansgate? I get the feeling it's the kind of place in Manchester you won't have been introduced to. If this is the case, perhaps I could show it to you? They do a cheap but delicious English breakfast, but also a range of Mediterranean sandwiches. I'm leaving my phone number at the bottom of this letter and invite you to text me to make the necessary arrangements. If you prefer, I could simply guide you there, make a few suggestions as to what's especially nice, and then, as I say, I could leave you to it. We need beliefs, Jordan. Like a pumpkin skull needs a candle's flame! I'm so tired. I'm so horribly tired of it all. My mother was a Socialist in the early seventies. She dated men who planned, in their adult life, to take down the system 'from the inside'. This was before she married my father, who voted Conservative in 1997 and might well have voted for the planet to be folded up like a knitted sweater and put away in a drawer. I suppose your mum is a Communist. Is she? I suppose what I'm saying is when did you arrive here and are you lonely?

I went to Chinatown to deliver the letter. It ran to so many pages that I had to roll it into a scroll and secure it with a violet scrunchie. I waited for Jordan in that same small room above

Portland Street, the room that the seagull had flown into. The Jordan who came to me, however, was mixed race and from Merseyside. I handed her the letter and left in a manner that I fear, in retrospect, was unorthodox and hysterical. The truth is the tightenings get looser every year. These days, I keep my penis in my underpants like it's a red rose or a box of chocolates. I fell out of love with Jess when she entered the real world, or seemed to enter it. Perhaps I was jealous. Everyone who becomes famous goes insane. It should be a deterrent, but it isn't. People want to go insane. It's the only freedom I can imagine. The only real holiday from morality.

Last week, at the smoothie stand, I asked Peta out to the cinema. We stood side by side, removing the stalks from strawberries and slicing them and I couldn't think of anything to say that might put us at ease. In the end, I asked if she liked the actor Will Smith and it turns out Peta loves him. After the lunchtime rush, I put on my coat to leave and she came close to me. 'I want to date a few more guys from the website. After that, Jim, maybe we could go out.' She held a wet knife and a handful of gooseberries. It isn't the most romantic situation. I'm being pitted against the hundreds of thousands of men who use whichever dating website Peta's on. She doesn't trust me, I don't think. Or she has no faith in our life at the smoothie stand.

By noon each day I feel quietly outraged by the world. I get tightenings and enjoy a strong rapport with the religious. Sitting in the back of his Saab, waiting for the handshake of weed, I once told Kam how much I admired Islam. 'I love how serious it is.' I pulled myself forwards using the headrest of the passenger seat. 'The ridiculously sincere deference to Allah!' It was around the time when Viagra was becoming popular. I remember because Kam offered me some.

'I'm twenty-two,' I said.

'And?'

The luminous rubber skeleton that hung from his rear-view turned one way, then the other. His car smelt of Burger King. I was always pretty good at buying drugs because I'm polite and instinctively jittery around illegality. The scent of Burger King lacks the sweet, rictus bliss of McDonald's. That night at the drive-thru in Morecambe with Jayne Albright, after *Independence Day* in 1996, that was my very first McDonald's. I ordered a Hamburger Happy Meal. It was an honest mistake.

As an actor, Will Smith is good at waking up. He wakes up very well in *Independence Day*. He's good at shuffling round kitchens in boxer shorts and a vest, rubbing his eyes, slugging milk from the carton in the glow of a fridge. I've a feeling he wakes up well in *I Am Legend*. Maybe even *I, Robot*.

Any description of my heart would begin with the image of me standing in a phone box on Tottenham Court Road. It would describe the cards that prostitutes leave in those places, the ones with the sexy picture and the contact number. It would explain that I'm standing in the phone box on Tottenham Court Road because my phone's out of battery and I need to call Mum. In the image, all except one of the cards has been torn down, shredded and left on the floor. Over the phone, I ask Mum what it was that attracted her to Dad that day, on the corner of Stryd Fawr and Friars Road. As she tells me, I take down and fold the one remaining card. Later, I dial its number on my recharging phone. I cancel the call after one ring. In the letter of apology I wrote to Jordan, I asked how *her* heart might be described. I said maybe hers was one of the cards that was taken down and shredded. I said it wasn't for me to speculate. I asked what other men are like.

By 2007, having spent eighteen months playing but not mastering Grand Theft Auto III, I was broke. When I interviewed for the smoothie stand Peta said I was the palest person she'd ever seen. And you must remember, Peta's Polish, so that's really saying something. She took a rasberry from a Tupperware box and fed it to me.

'Are you a druggy?'

'No.'

'Dying?'

'I'm prepared to work hard.'

'Have you ever eaten fruit?'

Peta brought in a family photo album to work yesterday. All her male relatives look like He-Man figures so I can understand her lack of interest in the idea of my cinema trip. I'm writing this in the Arndale Food Court. I'm eating a Big Mac in the seating area allocated to Kentucky Fried Chicken. It's quite a tormenting situation. I think the best way to write about my news is to write about Kate. Tomorrow is Harry's stag night and, after that, I intend to travel to Morecambe, which might make things clearer. The problem is that the more recent the things I write about are, the worse I seem to feel. Last year, when I Skyped Mum, she showed me my dusty copy of Eminem's first single and asked me, quite sincerely, 'Is this worth anything?' She subsequently lay each of my CDs on a green velvet cushion and photographed them three times before uploading the most flattering image. She emailed me each time one sold.

'3p, James! "Gangsta's Paradise" sold for 3p!'

In the paperback edition of *Being Jordan*, Katie Price disassociates herself from Lolo Ferrari on page 90. She cites the rumour that Ferrari wasn't allowed on planes in case her breasts exploded. 'Now *that's* what I call weird,' Price says.

Lolo Ferrari has breast-enlargement surgery twenty-two times. She is said to suffer from a form of dysmorphia – a strong conviction that her body is repulsive. Her husband, a Frenchman named Eric Vigne, lines up her replacement in the months preceding Lolo's death. He finds two sisters whom he dubs the Silicone Girls and pays for a series of operations to inflate their breasts and launch them on a tour of clubs in Eastern Europe. On trial for Ferrari's murder, Vigne describes his wife as 'the goose that laid my golden eggs'.

'I love the feeling of general anaesthetic,' Ferrari said. She dies in the year 2000, aged thirty-seven. In the late nineties, hoping to launch a pop music career, she releases two singles, 'Airbag Generation' and 'Set Me Free'. She also records a cover of Thelma Houston's hit, 'Don't Leave Me This Way'. The song is never released.

In 1994, when our table-tennis strips faded to pink and the letters on my back read 'horn' not 'Thorne', Harry and I asked the butcher's in Ridley to sponsor Ridley C. Two hunters sat on stools outside, plucking pheasants that they dangled over silver buckets. The hunters were in charge of the beating jobs, which Harry and I had applied for the previous summer without success. Beaters were boys who beat the bushes with sticks and scared pheasants into the sky to be shot. Inside the butcher's, the air was cool and hygienic. The butcher was a red man. I handed him our letter, which outlined the sponsorship deal and I told him we'd wait at the War Memorial for his response. It was a lush afternoon and the square was dazed. Harry was certain the butcher would agree. He was mentally spending the money, talking about getting new kits, new bats, a new table, a team minibus, even suggesting we buy a wooden bench for what he called 'the inevitable crowd'. Across the road, beyond the old lamp post, my dad watched us from the window of the spare room. It was six months or so since I'd found him lying drunk on the bedroom floor at Irene Albright's, since he'd warned, 'Don't let people get to you.' The butcher emerged from his shop and spoke a word to the hunters. He displayed himself for them, squinting in the sunlight, pressing his hands against the small of his back, hoisting his stained apron with his gut. Harry whispered the word 'please' and squeezed my wrist. The butcher collected the bald pheasants from the hunters, glanced over to us and shook his head.

'We asked for too much,' I said.

We had asked for ten thousand pounds. Within the week, we'd been rejected by all the businesses in Ridley, including the cattery on the outskirts and every one of the dairy farms. Harry blamed me. I'd argued against typing our proposal on a computer because I feared it would seem impersonal. I looked up at Dad in the spare-room window. I hoped he was thinking, Son.

Date: 09/12/2009
Subject: stuff

Hey Jim,

Long time no nothing. How are you? You will be shocked to hear I'm getting married! She's called Sandra and she's a psychotherapist. My stag night's in Manchester next week and it occurred to me you might still live there. Do you? What are you up to? Sandra is forty and says there's stuff you and I need to talk about. Stuff about the band but also stuff about when we were young. You know you look very hacked off in your Facebook photo and you never write anything on there. Are you OK? Join Twitter. What do you do? Send me your mobile number.

Hope you can make the stag weekend.

Harry

I've finished my Big Mac. It tasted like a holidaying alien's first attempt at a double-burger. It was delicious. I'm going to write about Kate now. It's lunchtime and the Food Court's heaving.

14

In November 2008, less than an hour after she joined Facebook, I sent Kate Reynolds a message saying 'Hey'. A month later, in fact just before Christmas last year, I sheltered in the doorway of a Caffè Nero near Westminster Tube Station, listening as cars tore through gutter-puddles and watching a necklace of ruby brake lights drag through the darkness over Westminster Bridge, above which the palace was gold in the heavy rain. I wore preppy, nautical style clothes, a pink polo shirt and a navy-blue tank top, items I purchased from M&S using my fruit-crushing funds. The clothes implied maturity, but also that I wasn't hostile to affluence. I changed into them that morning, having worked the dawn shift at the smoothie stand. I caught the Megabus to London and the journey took close to seven hours. As I sat on a dusty seat, bus-sick and brittle, looking down at the cars jammed on both sides of the M6, I rehearsed a smile to greet Kate with. But by the time I arrived at Victoria, the smile was so far-fetched that I decided against it, in favour of a subtle frown that was suggestive of reading novels, a high caffeine diet and, I suspected, indifference to television. Around seven that evening I leant against the coffee-shop window and watched the rain fall from the sky and thin clouds obscure a crescent moon.

'James Thorne. Hey.'

'Hey.'

From the way she flinched when I embraced her, it was clear I was supposed to have simply kissed the air beside her cheeks.

'Ooh, hug,' she said. 'OK.'

In 1996, at the Queen's Summer Fair, I'd asked Kate Reynolds if she'd go out with me. I had told her, 'You could be my Beaver.' The reason she gave for not being able to was, 'We've got exams.'

We were in the school corridor and two versions of 'Wonderwall' were playing. 'Sorry, Jim,' she'd said. 'I have to study.'

November rain eased to drizzle and we walked along Whitehall to Trafalgar Square. A decade wandered with us like a lost tourist. Kate told a story about a senior colleague who seemed stranded between pervert and buffoon.

'He sounds awful,' I said.

'Oh God, Jim, he is. That *thing* that men become. That horrible ridiculous thing.'

Kate chose a pub that was popular with young civil servants like herself. Waiting at the bar, jiggling pocket change, were boys who had bounced from university with dry armpits and almost-long hair, as well as good girls who lacked boom and posh cackles, but who had neat ponytails and genuine senses of humour. I stood among them and waited to be served. When I went to pay, I produced a gooseberry from my pocket. I dropped it at my feet.

'How did you get down?' Kate said, once we were seated.

'The train into Euston,' I said.

'You look no different.'

'You don't.'

Kate's small laugh concluded with a sigh and a headshake, mine with a glance at my hands. The mood of her eyes shifted between guarded and inquisitive. She wore a brown work suit with a sky-blue shirt. She still had a magnificent bust. 'I brought this,' she said, placing a small object on the table. And for a little while, we stared at it, as if the object might speak, as if it might say 'Hello', in a way that would have made us happy, but also made us burst into tears. It was a badge. It read: 'Women Are Manufactured'.

'I googled you,' she said, sipping her beer. 'You're the first thing that comes up, you know? If you type in my name you get some Australian woman.'

I had googled 'Kate Reynolds' the previous evening, but I didn't admit to having done so. Her trails, when I found them, were short and fairly typical. There was a 2003 article on Elfriede Jelinek, written during Kate's time, so read her biog, at Oxford University, and published on a website that was now inactive. She'd joined Friends Reunited in 2004 and listed her interests as This. Is. Weird. And, of course, there was her recent Facebook profile, where her photo wasn't of her, but one of the witches from *The Wizard of Oz*. I was surprised that she'd googled me and I took it as a compliment. Somehow, if you shone a torch down into that cellar, I looked up. Only it wasn't me, really. It was me, aged twenty-two, sitting on a park bench with Harry. Me signing a record deal beside a waxwork of Britney Spears. Me onstage.

Kate made a shelf by entwining her fingers. She rested her chin there. 'I was at St Hilda's College,' she said. 'I did stuff for the anti-war alliance and I think that counted against me in the end. Were you on the march in '03?'

'I was, yes,' I said. And I saw it instantly, from above, that huge crowd of people that weaved through London that day and among it, somewhere, separate, Kate and me. The thought was nice and appalling and ultimately pretty maddening. I realised how much I wanted to make contact with her. Those were the exact words. Make contact. And now, five years after that crowd dispersed in the darkness and rain around Marble Arch, we were sitting at a little wooden table.

'I already feel drunk,' Kate said, stroking a sliver of foam from her top lip and glancing towards the bar. 'We're being watched, by the way. We probably look like an Internet date. Whitehall is lonely. Everyone is lonely. I once passed Tony Blair in Portcullis House, maybe three years ago. It was just the two of us in a long corridor. I could feel it, Jim. The loneliness. There was something really fucking abject about the two of us, walking towards each other, both wearing suits. Blair nodded, but didn't smile. He looked lonely.'

Kate played with the badge on the tabletop, batting it from side to side with her index fingers and I pictured her standing on our doorstep in Ridley, wearing her 'New Labour' sash, encouraging my parents to vote.

'Did you say hello?'

'I gave him *the look*.'

'He reminds me of my mum.'

'I gave him the look, Jim. I let him know that I was available, that I was . . . *there*. How depressing is that?'

A group of young men assembled round a *Lord of the Rings* fruit machine nearby. They lamented their losses with backwards steps and by saying 'For fuck's sake' in loud, big-tongued voices.

'Anyway, I'm at the Home Office for the foreseeable future. The long-term goal is to be an MP. I can't believe I just said foreseeable future. It's been a weird day at work. He's older, my boss, he's fifty, he's fat, he's married and he farts in his sleep after he comes. I'm fed up, Jim. I'm so fed up. I'm so fed up it's actually quite funny.'

'You always were.'

'I'm lonely. What do you do? What do you do exactly? What are you doing tomorrow, for example?'

Part of me wanted to run back to Manchester, pull on my cap and apron and wash and crush a fresh batch of gooseberries. 'The band got signed,' I said. 'But I lost interest. Lately, it's been . . .' One of the young men slapped a button on the fruit machine and it urinated pound coins. The others celebrated with whoops and by half climbing on each other. As the coins were scooped from the tray, some of them posed for a photograph, pulling faces I associated with elation, contorting their eyes and mouths quite drastically. I guess they were dicks, but they were probably likeable if I'd got to know them. A phone flashed and their tableau dismantled. They formed a circle and shared out the coins. '. . . I live off the royalties of pop songs I've written,' I said.

'Seriously?'

'It's called a passive income.'

Kate took our empty glasses to the bar and spoke to people there whom she clearly knew. She returned with salted peanuts.

She ate them alone, leaning back in her chair, wearing a curious smile. She poured the last of the nuts into her mouth, splayed the packet and licked salt from the reflective lining.

'I'm writing an album on acoustic guitar,' I said. I leant forwards, my arms triangled on the table and my hands clasped. 'I'm going to travel round Chile or southern India, just me and my guitar. Although I've got a home studio up in Manchester.' Kate folded the nut packet neatly. Once it was possible, she tied a knot in it and pulled it tight. 'That's great,' she said. 'I'm fed up, Jim.' She gathered a swathe of her long brown hair, making a brief hand-ponytail, then she brought it over one shoulder so it fell down her front and she could fiddle with the tips of individual strands. 'I finish work every night, go to the gym then eat Rice Krispies.'

'I want to write mature pop songs.'

'I dream I'm on a cross-trainer.'

'You've done well.'

'I work, work out, wank, cry, then fall asleep!'

'I thought you were a feminist.'

'Oh, Jim,' Kate said, reaching across the table to pinch the back of my hand. 'I am. Let's eat. If we stay here I'm going to start crying.'

'Simone de Beauvoir never married.' This was later, on the escalator down into Charing Cross Tube. 'But she did share a long and stimulating relationship with fellow philosopher Jean-Paul Sartre. Sartre's nickname for Simone was "Beaver" . . .' We kissed till we got to the bottom, where we held hands and stepped off. The Tube wind blew and a train came clattering into the station. 'You're amazing,' I said. The doors bleeped. 'Believe me.' They hissed and burst open. We sat alone in the carriage and Kate described her expulsion from Queen's, how she'd been caught in the coal shed smoking a joint and reading *The Handmaid's Tale*.

'My sister lost her virginity in that coal shed.'

'God, Jim. *Elaine Thorne*.'

'I hardly see her any more.'

'That thing she did with the condoms. I had a massive crush.' Our train slowed into Finchley Road. 'Puberty was fucking shit,' Kate said. 'I could cope with it now, I think. But it happens at the shittest possible time.'

The staircase to her flat smelt of junk mail and rotten carpet. 'We call it West Hampstead,' she whispered as we climbed. 'But it isn't quite. You'll have to shush.' We crept down a hallway and into her small bedroom. She had flatmates, she told me, but didn't know what they were like, except what she'd learnt from monitoring their food cupboards. 'They make no noise,' she said. 'I miss the north, Jim.' Kate removed her jacket. 'We've lost our accents.'

'I haven't.'

'You sound like you're from nowhere.'

'Eee-are,' I said, to prove her wrong. I planted kisses on her throat and her collarbone, unbuttoning her shirt. 'Eee-are.' Kate lay on the bed and shuffled out of her work trousers. I pulled my pants to my knees and touched her, saying 'Eee-are', the way we did at Queen's to get attention. ('Eee-are, Berky.') That sound, 'Eee-are', was cleansed of meaning now. I sounded like a lovelorn donkey, calling across dusk fields. I'd been licking her vagina for a minute when I opened my eyes and saw that Kate had no pubic hair whatsoever, just a vaguely stubbled pubis. She pushed me onto my back and took the tip of my penis in her mouth. What I remember about Pamela Anderson's 1998 sex tape is how happy and carefree she and her lover are. I remember they're on holiday somewhere, telling jokes and being good to each other. He's a rock star, I remember, her lover. He climbs into the driver's seat of a 4x4 and lets his tall penis stick out of his shorts. I remember how attracted they are to each other. How they can't keep their hands to themselves.

'What's the problem?' Kate said. The dim lights of eyes were visible in the darkness of the bedroom. 'Am I doing it wrong?'

Later in the video, there's a close-up of their sex organs, mostly

Pamela's. I don't enjoy that bit, even in my memory. But early on, when they're bantering and there's a sense of fun and love; that bit breaks my heart.

'Touch yourself,' Kate whispered.

'It's because it's you,' I said.

'Just relax. Make yourself hard.'

I lay beside Kate, rubbing my soft penis and recalling an encyclopedia I'd had as a child. On the central pages was a drawing of a pubescent boy and girl standing naked beside a man and woman. Harry and I used to study them. We used to point at the man and say, 'Look, they've got it wrong!' I lay between Kate's legs and she positioned my penis. 'OK, Jim. Come on.' I established a momentum I was sure I could sustain. It was extremely slow. 'Oh, Kate, darling,' I said. 'I love you. I *love* you.' I buried my face in the pillow and continued with my thrusts.

'Jim?'

'Oh, Kate —'

'You're soft again.'

'I think it's because it's you.'

'Your willy's like a Flump.'

'Yes.' I laughed. 'Yes it is.'

Kate reached into her bedside drawer and produced a tube of lubricant. She applied some to our hands and we lay side by side, kissing and rubbing our privates with lubricated fingers. Kate whispered my name; her tone stranded between piss-take and praise. Her moans were somehow off kilter and recalled the sympathetic sounds the dinner ladies made when we grazed our knees on the playground of Ridley Primary, when they used to put their arms around us and, inspecting the wound, lovingly vocalise our pain with soft, low moans. Long before Kate climaxed, I came silently onto my stomach.

In the morning, I woke to rain and the sound of tree branches tapping on the window. Kate entered with wet hair, wearing only a white blouse. She pulled a high-backed chair in front of a full-length mirror and watched her reflection blow-dry its hair. She skipped across the room to turn on the radio. Returning to the mirror, she applied moisturiser to her forehead and cheeks. Having done so, she looked deep into each eye and drew round them with eyeliner. She dressed; first putting on a pair of stockings and a black skirt, then apparently changing her mind and putting on a pair of grey trousers. She thickened her eyelashes and added blusher to her cheeks. She glossed her lips. She took a silver ring from an enamel bowl. She removed a chain from a hook beside the mirror and fastened it round her neck. The Josef Fritzl case was mentioned on the radio. Kate lay beside me on her bed. I turned her hand in mine and drew a circle on its palm with my fingertip.

'I still think about Walter,' I said.

'I haven't been north in three years.'

The item focused on logistics, on the practical problems Fritzl encountered when imprisoning so many women for so long. There was an interview with his psychologist in which the Austrian's childhood was discussed, as well as his claim that he knew his second life was wrong but that it simply, over the years, became normal.

'The modern world disappoints Walter. And I'm part of it.' Kate brought her face level with mine. Her teeth were beige and her kiss was lukewarm and tasted of liquorice. 'They don't know to escape, these girls. They assume it's normal to be living down a cellar. But you do, don't you, when you're young, you always assume everything's basically normal . . . Look at you. Look at Jim Thorne, lying in bed with nothing to do! Do you really earn a living just from royalties?'

I nodded.

'What are you doing today?'

'I was thinking maybe my acoustic album,' I said.

'But you don't have your guitar.'

'I'll just buy one.'

We kissed until Kate pulled away, closed her eyes and

impersonated me: 'Oh, darling, I love you, I *love* you . . . Do you know you kept calling me Dilly? Who's Dilly? One of your groupies?'

'It was nerves.'

'It was cute . . . Eee-are.' Kate massaged her breasts through her blouse. 'Eee-are, eee-are. What does "Eee-are" even mean?' She smiled for her mirror and pulled a dead face for it. She re-glossed her lips and said she was hung-over.

'I think it comes from "Here you are",' I said.

The radio bleeped for 9 a.m.

'Here you are,' she said.

'Yes.'

15

Harry stepped onto the platform at Manchester Piccadilly, raised the handle of his suitcase and wheeled it towards me, trying not to smile. He was luminous, laundered, had lovely stubble and was far from pea-headed. His blond hair was short and combed neatly to the side. His walk was hurried, almost lolloping and I knew immediately that he'd somehow found happiness. He stopped beside me and yawned melodiously. 'How are you, Jim?' We crossed the station concourse, out of pace with one another, talking about Harry's journey and then about train travel in general. We walked down into town beneath a grey, rainless sky. Pre-Christmas Manchester was in a whirl and featherbrained and the Market Street shops looked violated and scandalised. People smoked or else they exhaled visibly. We opted for a Japanese restaurant near Castlefield because Harry had read a positive review. As we waited for our food, he accessed the restaurant's Wi-Fi on his smartphone, operating the touch screen using a cotton bud.

'The Internet,' he said.

'My phones always break.'

'It's so convenient.'

'I trust Nokias, weirdly.'

'I've got BBC weather on here, the music sites I like, my Twitter . . .' Harry angled his phone towards me. He animated his Twitter with one tap of the cotton bud. On his feed, below two or three Tweets directed at specific followers, he had written, 'Meeting an old school friend . . . #awkwardsilences'.

He placed his phone on the table. He broke his chopsticks out of their wrapper and turned one with his fingers like a drumstick, looking at me. He told me about his DJing. He used his phone for that, too. He picked it up and showed me an application that simulated a vinyl-scratching effect. He showed me a game in which, by stroking the screen with the cotton bud, he threw screwed-up pieces of paper into a waste-paper basket. 'It's like a barbarian wringing a rabbit's neck,' he said, and something about his delivery, his lack of enthusiasm, I suppose, told me that such remarks were rare these days. His accent had a hint of cockney and the majority of his sentences related to technology or to the raw practicalities of his life. He handed me his phone; I narrowly missed on my first attempt but, on my second, I landed the paper in the waste-paper basket. Our meals arrived and, on reflection, I think I praised mine too much. My sudden enthusiasm for the sushi seemed to elevate Harry somehow and trigger an interrogation of my life.

'So, you make smoothies?'

'I co-run the stand.'

'Oh, Jim. Does your mum know?'

'I don't see her.'

'Isn't it hell?'

Nearby, an elderly couple ate noodle soup silently in a sunbeam. A stem spoon had found its way onto our table. Harry picked it up and fondled it for a while. He had the energetic air of a man who believes in sparkling water. He was skilful with chop-sticks. At one point, he sprayed his Adam's apple semi-covertly with Paco Rabanne and by doing so affected the flavour of my fish. His words, these days, made ornaments out of living things. ('Sandra probably won't conceive. We'll adopt.') I'd once played high notes onto his penis.

'The band failed,' he said, 'because you sabotaged it. You self-sabotaged. You were scared of getting what you've always wanted.'

'It was a weird time.'

'Fame, Jim.' Harry held my eye. 'All your life you've been desperate for fame.'

He finished his Coke. Ice cubes slid down the glass to his lips. He allowed one into his mouth and I anticipated the grotesque crunching of it. But, instead, he let it melt on his tongue, until he could drink the water down with one neat swallow.

'I've never wanted to be famous,' I said.

Harry smiled softly at the stem spoon. He placed it on the table without making a sound. 'I'm here, Jim,' he said. 'I've made it. You were an Albright, but *I've* succeeded . . . You've still got really bad BO, do you realise?' I nodded. 'I think part of you wishes we still played for Ridley C, Jim. Part of you wishes the butcher's had given us the ten grand and we'd built the ping-pong stadium. You know which part of you I think wishes that? Your heart.'

In June 1997, my sweat problem began. A maths class was disrupted when girls sprayed me with Dewberry body spray and Impulse to try and mask my smell. The armpits of all my school shirts yellowed. I wore Elaine's blouses sometimes, for respite. There was a three-week craze of calling me BO Baracus and holding your nose and singing *The A-Team* theme when I arrived anywhere.

Harry adjusted the lush fleece collar of his leather jacket. What a mature collar it was – expensive without seeming so and neither young nor old. I was on the verge of tears. My Adam's apple swelled and Harry sipped from his empty glass. He picked up the stem spoon and contemplated it solemnly. Harry's security was founded on his mother's decision to lay the breakfast table last thing at night. That, and the fact he had a television in his bedroom. It all must have made reality very persuasive and I think that accounts for his success. I concentrated extremely hard and so no tears fell. I tried to prepare a defence of myself, but there was insufficient time. 'Hey, Julian!' Harry stood up abruptly and called across the restaurant. '*Julian*, we're over here!'

The haircut of Julian Straw was yet to be slept on. It was shaved on both sides, left long at the back and gelled at the crown into a Sonic the Hedgehog spike and then, right at the front, styled into a short, sideways sweep. His haircut spoke of solutions to the universe I suspected to be entirely workable. He was an ox-like brunette, slightly overweight, and his brilliant hair turned his pimpled face into a sad side show. He took the stem spoon from the table and bonked Harry on the head with it. Having done so, Julian Straw's confidence drained and he blushed. 'How are we? Big night for the Fat Bayonet, eh?' His voice was an attempt at blasé but contained a nervous quiver. 'When did Manchester become Milton Keynes, eh?' he said, with a cautious chuckle. He said he needed a shit, a shower and a shave. Later, he would preface weak revelations with the words, 'I shit you not . . .' As a schoolboy, I suspected he would have spent his lunch hours with popular boys but been made to suffer for the privilege and excluded from all memorable moments of solidarity. At thirty-one, he had the grey-blue and blurting eyes of a man who would almost certainly marry the next woman to hold his penis, the Fat Bayonet, and feel it wince then stiffen.

'Julian, this is Jim,' Harry said. 'A friend of mine from school. Julian's my best man, Jim.'

We went to a karaoke bar in the Printworks. Julian had booked a private pod for the nine stags and, on arrival, I drank an entire silver bucket of sweet cocktail through a pink roller-coaster straw. When it was my turn to sing, I sang 'Money for Nothing'. I sang well, though everyone was already too drunk to notice. Harry was presented with a spiked drink and, though he protested, Julian led the stags in a chant for him to down it. We were in Manchester's Millennium Quarter, right where the bomb went off. When I went outside for air, a pink limousine pulled up and four girls climbed from it, tottering on very high heels, holding beer cans, looking at their exposed toes as they walked with their shoulders hunched. Their clothes were cryptic and suggested nudity, but also its exact opposite. A transvestite on stilts stooped to give me a leaflet. A person dressed as a giant Corona bottle tripped descending the kerb and ran to find their balance. Girls dressed as schoolgirls swarmed the smoking area, distributing promotional condoms and sachets of lube. A boy filmed himself smoking a Cuban cigar. A hammered man peed against the window of the Co-op and stood in the wet pattern as it trickled towards a drain and entered it audibly. Julian Straw smoked beside me.

'My dad was called Julian,' I said.

'Remind me how you know Harry.'

'School.'

Julian put the entire orange section of his cigarette into his mouth. He was sweating round the eyes. He spoke in the low, slow voice favoured by the extremely pissed. He opened his mouth to let the wind steal smoke from it. 'I shit you not, matey.' He put a heavy arm over my shoulders. 'You're going to wake one day and see something on the news like . . . something like . . . all Virgin Atlantic planes are grounded. No oil is entering Liverpool . . . America's bust, dude . . . You'll walk to a . . . to a fucking . . . ATM machine . . . Dude, I'm not trying to scare you. I'm scared. I want to start a family.'

We returned to our karaoke pod and found Harry on the stage with his arms behind his back. A familiar progression of chords was playing. Harry's unlit cigarette looked like a thermometer. As a young man, he had played very attacking table-tennis. A good player will combine attacking play with defensive strokes and I'm thinking specifically here about the backhand chop. Thirteen years on from his performance in assembly, he sang 'Wonderwall' like a preacher lambasting a sublime new sin. He sang in an exaggerated nasal voice, trying, I think, to lampoon the original version of the song. He failed to begin the second verse. He brought his fist to his mouth and filled it till sick seeped then squirted from between his fingers. In a hollow hour, we gathered in Julian Straw's suite at the Hilton, where he unpacked the contents of his suitcase onto the bed. 'What even are these?' He held up two identical fancy-dress costumes – plastic packs containing star-spangled fabric, red-starred tiaras, thick bracelets and red and gold bustiers. He began lining up chairs in the corner by the minibar. Two girls were let in. Someone tried to make a docked iPod louder, hitting the + button many times to no real effect. The girls removed their overcoats and draped them over an armchair. Both had thick, curled, dyed hair. They sat on the bed, close to each other, not nervous, but not at ease. They observed the drunk stags that were strewn around the suite, all lost in thought, slow conversation, or, in Julian's case, in the task of arranging chairs. A stag approached the girls holding a beer can level with his heart. He rolled his eyes quite secretly, trying, it seemed to me, to apologise in advance, to absolve himself of guilt. He asked them what they did normally. 'Nothing,' said the girl with blonde hair. 'This,' said the girl with black. The girls then spoke about their respective rotas, leaving the stag to stand alone, sipping from his can, nodding, and then walking backwards in small steps to take a seat with the others. It was as though time had never passed. Drunk, the stags looked teenage, flushed and smiley. Julian agreed to pay extra if the girls wore the costumes. It was during the negotiation, as one girl read the back of the packet, that we learnt they were Wonder Woman costumes. This news amused both girls but they still insisted on the additional money. The blonde girl received a stack of notes from Julian, which she counted by the window before sending a text. The other opened one of the packets. 'I'd wear these out,' she said, holding aloft a pair of star-spangled hot pants. Both girls had large implants. Harry grabbed me by my wrist, dragged me into the bathroom and locked the door.

The door handle twisted violently, but Harry was oblivious; he climbed into the bathtub and lay down, looking lost on the border between Drunk and Upset. He let his head fall back onto the fleece of his collar and he gazed at the silver showerhead as it dripped slowly onto his pointy brogues. 'They're elite, Harry,' Julian shouted, knocking on the door as he spoke, still twisting the handle. 'Your last night of freedom . . . Dude.' Harry lay in the bathtub with his eyes closed. I perched on the sink. In the other room, Julian Straw clapped twice to disperse the stags. 'Everyone meet in the lobby tomorrow morning at seven . . .

It's over.' Uncherished boys like Julian became focused, cold-blooded adults who nick-named their penises, were religious about banter, energised by ease, at peace with the Premiership and psychologically reliant on work and the Internet. 'You stay where you are, ladies,' he said.

In my Grand Theft Auto years, I watched porn on the Internet and I remember the lists that accompanied the clips. The lists of the sex acts the clip contained. There was a formula to them – an orthodoxy. In his 1941 essay, 'On Popular Music', Theodore Adorno argues that, for market purposes, all pop songs are inherently similar. He calls this 'standardisation'. In Microsoft Word 2001, Manet is considered a spelling mistake, but Monet isn't. In an interview for the *Sunday Times*, Katie Price's second husband, *Celebrity Big Brother* winner Alex Reid, gives the percentage of his life that he would like to keep private. It is 10 per cent. 'We have to be somewhere,' Walter told me, years ago. 'It's an immense pity.' These days, I take my phone to the toilet with me. It's a small slice of nowhere that takes the edge off here.

For Adorno, the lack of formal innovation in popular music means that, essentially, when you come across a new song, you needn't bother listening to it because you have, in effect, already done so. The song has, in Adorno's term, been 'pre-digested'. To disguise this fact, the song is 'pseudo-individualised' by a guitar solo or a rap, a riff, a different singer, a new band, a fresh haircut, a strange sound.

Harry and I listened from the bathroom as the remaining stags vacated the suite. We heard Julian ask the girls what services they offered. His tone was intimate. Their answer was a string of deadpanned acronyms, full-stopped by the scrape of a cigarette lighter. We heard it all, Harry and I; him lying in the bath, me perched on the sink.

Wonder Woman first appears in 1941, the year 'On Popular Music' is published. Adorno is worried that, under capitalism, culture will become something that requires 'no effort', something that is simply 'relaxing'. I found porn addictive. I try to imagine it without the sex. I try to imagine the editors editing it. I try to imagine the participants wailing having recently been born.

'Meet The Fat Bayonet.'

Julian Straw directed the girls, instructing them into positions or demanding specific services. His voice was youthful. He worked as a financial adviser for Santander. Harry had gone to him for advice after receiving his first significant royalty cheque for his song, 'Heaven'. As Julian devised Harry's investment portfolio, the banter had escalated. I imagine it was terrifying. They agreed, so Harry told me, to meet for a pint and then a curry that very night.

As I listened to Julian and the Wonder Women, I tried to think about cave paintings, but I couldn't imagine who had painted them. I capitulated and pictured Julian and the girls. I compiled a mental list of all the positions they adopted and the acts they committed. Although I couldn't see them, it didn't matter; Julian's demands were blunt and vivid and the love they made was orthodox. I ran the taps so the sound of water drowned the sounds of the sex, but we still heard Julian orgasm with a loud, quivering scream, like a ghost on its debut haunt. It was as his howl subsided that I knelt beside the bathtub, drunkenly ruffled Harry's hair and reminded him that he was a TT Prince of Ridley. Harry said nothing. In fact, both rooms fell silent until Julian Straw spoke in a low voice, drained of energy. ('I shit you not, girls. A revolution's coming. I'm not saying this to scare you . . .') Half an hour later, when Harry unlocked the bathroom door, Julian lay on his front, naked and asleep. The two costumes had been left neatly folded at the foot of the bed.

At seven the following morning, we gathered in the lobby to travel north in a minibus to the Lake District. We carried rucksacks and climbed into a fine mist, sweating the alcohol, looking down at our boots, hearing the scratch of Velcro as we unfastened colourful cagoules and began to pant. We barely spoke. It was overcast and the mountains were slate grey. All the trees had suffered somehow, or looked that way – stricken. We peered down at the lower, greener peaks and at the floor of the valley, where long, uneven drystone walls enclosed dark meadows and flocks of sheep. It was a four-hour climb to the summit of Scafell Pike. We stood, the nine stags, looking across the peaks to where a white helicopter hovered. We were higher than it. We ate pies. Julian skidded down a scree to shit in the privacy of several huge boulders. The spike of his hair remained visible, hovering among the rocks, which, according to a plaque, were one and a half million years old. When he lifted it above his head, Julian's phone was the highest thing in England.

'I can't get the Web. Harry, you got signal, matey?'

'Mine's dying,' Harry said. His phone lay on his palm and lit with a low bleep. It displayed a farewell routine, full of twisting colours, and then it went dark. In the Lake District, tarns gather like tears in the dips and hollows of the hills. On the descent, we stopped by Burnmoor and snoozed in the heather. The sun shone. Out on the tarn, small birds fished. Some of us removed our boots and socks and soothed our blisters in the water. I felt strangely happy, but also that a gentle wind or a bird taking flight would send ripples right through that sensation.

16

I phoned Kate on New Year's Eve last year and we each confessed to having spent Christmas alone. She said she'd cooked a nut cutlet and eaten it in tears in the shared kitchen of the empty house. We confessed to being slumped on sofas watching muted televisions and to being quite drunk. I booked a Megabus to London.

Sex was a problem Kate and I solved by lying side by side and kissing each other and by using lubricant on ourselves. Rather than get angry or vindictive, she accepted my problem and enjoyed the solution, which can't be called mutual masturbation, I don't think, as we didn't interfere with each other, but could be called, perhaps, Shared Self-Love. Masturbation, performed in tandem like that, had a no-nonsense charm. It gave moments in bed a magical pragmatism. Kate's index finger moved around her underwear like a child playing beneath a blanket. It was riveting. Afterwards, our embraces were warm, silent and lasted five minutes. Then, more often than not, we'd dress, go out for dinner and I'd update Kate on my acoustic album and we would, generally, proceed with our relationship with the generous diplomacy and emotional swiftness of people approaching thirty. I bought more and more cardigans, tank tops and V-necked jumpers and it was a period of strange joy.

'I'm writing pop songs for an adult audience,' I said. This was in a Pizza Express on The Strand. 'When it's finished and I sign the record deal, I'm going to buy a place in London. You and me together, I was thinking.'

'Are you kidding?'

'We've known each other a long time. When you think about it.'

Kate drained her bottle of beer and said her life choices were seeds she'd planted without thinking. They'd been watered by rain, had sprouted stalks, developed leaves, grown trunks and become tall trees with branches you could tie a rope to. She looked out into the evening at the people on the pavement. 'We could build a tree house,' she said, skewering an olive with a cocktail stick. She chewed it slowly, looking up and to one side at nothing in particular. 'You can run down dead ends in your twenties,' she said, 'because there's time to run back. I'm sick of trying to achieve something.'

Those London Pizza Expresses were made largely of glass. We learnt our order off by heart. A ramekin of olives, two bruschettas, beers, an American Hot for me and a Fiorentina for Kate. It felt like maturity, the ease with which we ordered.

'I think I can love you,' Kate said.

I took an olive from the bowl using my fingers. I put the fruit into my mouth, grimaced then gradually became tolerant of its bitterness. 'You know it's actually pronounced bru-*ske*tta. Not bru-*she*tta,' I said. 'I've been saying it wrong.'

Kate nodded and her mood lightened. She picked up the menu and sat sideways in her seat. 'I might have cannelloni,' she said. She didn't. She ordered a Fiorentina and said it was a bad time to invest in property. 'Let's be sensible,' she said, muting the tail of her sentence as a waiter came to check on us. 'I've got zero savings,' she said, quietly, as he left. 'The truth is, I'm in debt, Jim. Could you ask your mum to help us with the deposit?'

I cut my pizza into slices. I held one by its crust and it flopped like a tongue and all the topping slowly slid down onto my plate.

'I'll use the advance from the acoustic album,' I said.

'How much will it be?'

'Plenty.'

'Let's be ordinary, Jim.'

'And I love you,' I said.

Kate spiked an olive, leant forwards and, still chewing it, smiled.

I'm writing this at the Midland Hotel in Morecambe, in the restaurant, sitting at a table beside a white Christmas tree. Elderly ladies are taking tea and eating scones in the conservatory. Beyond them, through the windows, Morecambe Bay is a beautiful lead colour. The tide's high and I've been watching waves crash against the limestone sea break and streak upwards, drawing my eye to the mountains in the distant north, before spraying the jetty, where there's a line of fishermen, all in gloomy cagoules.

My room here is small and doesn't have a sea view. It looks out onto the old railway station, the Apollo Cinema, the Superbowl and a KFC. Further down the promenade, they've demolished Frontierland, the funfair modelled on the Wild West. Elaine and I went once with Dad in 1993. The log flume broke with us at its summit and we teetered there, looking across Morecambe Bay, at the fishing boats the tide had marooned in the harbour, at the grey horizon and the Irish Sea. An awkward mood developed, and I think it did so, not because our log was stuck, but because the Midland Hotel was so conspicuous. Dad dangled his arm out of our log and dipped his fingers in the water.

'It's quite nice up here, isn't it?' I said.

'Why does everyone have to stare?' Elaine waved to the crowd of spectators that had gathered at the foot of the steep slope. 'Hello, yes, we're stuck, isn't it amazing?' A seagull landed on the prow of our log. It lingered there, looking at me, all but its beak, its eyes and its grey wings blending with the sky. It squawked. Elaine shooed it away and it flew along the coast towards Blackpool. Further back along the log flume was a log of restless boys. One peed into the flume and begged Elaine to watch. Another made a pretty specific accusation about my sister's recent past. Elaine flicked a sly V and her face cycled between smiles and frowns. Fifteen minutes later, as our log jerked into life, the heckling was over and Elaine was communicating covertly with the boys. They were writing a love letter that they intended to float to her in a crisp packet. Dad's eyes didn't soften and he didn't blink as we descended at speed into the deepest section of the flume. People cheered as we cowered in our splash. There was a rumour someone was raped on the ghost train and that's why Frontierland closed in 2000. I don't believe that. I think it closed because, when you finally got round to going, it wasn't as good as you had hoped it to be. It was open for almost the entire twentieth century.

Kate and I went public with our relationship in June of this year. We went to a dinner party, thrown in a white, Regency end-terrace in Holland Park. We were the youngest couple there, though not by much. The hosts were hip, had invested in good cutlery and attached baby monitors to their belts, through which a child sometimes called out to them from his sleep. Most guests worked in political PR. We ate pumpkin soup and talked about the death of newspapers and how lonely-making certain websites were. ('But hang on, I met Jim on Facebook. It can't be so bad.') Between praise for the scallops, predictions were made about the future. A discussion began and eventually raged during which guests raised their voices and half stood, pointing at each other, forecasting a planet of empty ocean, dead soil and dwindling numbers of nomadic humans. The debate concluded with a slurred prayer concerning a Hackney allotment and moved to a discussion of *Sabrina, the Teenage Witch*. It was twice confused with *Clarissa Explains It All*. 'Clarissa explained *nothing*,' Kate said. Everyone was drunk. We ate home-made ice cream. It was argued that the central paradoxes of feminism, masculinity and love could all be found in the on/off relationship between A.C. Slater and Jessie Spano in *Saved by the Bell*. Coffee was served with a very dry panettone and we retired to the lounge, where a joint was lit and an acoustic guitar leant in the corner by the flat-screen television. We tried to remember the names of the specific ThunderCats. One guy, a prematurely bold Liberal Democrat spin doctor, recited the entire opening monologue from *The Raccoons*. A copywriter from Reuters impersonated the rodent sensei from *Teenage Mutant Hero Turtles*. As I did my He-Man impression, a little boy in blue pyjamas side-stepped through the gap in the door. He stood with his hands clasped, looking at us, explaining that he was frightened. He put one little foot on top of the other until his father picked him up and took him away, stroking his hair and saying his name, Ralph, tenderly.

'Play us one of your songs, Jim.' I looked up to see Kate, holding the acoustic guitar by its neck. She was hoping, I think, to redeem me in the eyes of her new friends following the failure of my He-Man. 'Entertain us before the world ends.'

The guests gathered in front of me on the rug and began fidgeting, giggling and prodding each other. 'I haven't even heard these myself,' Kate said. The male host appeared in the doorway clutching yet more bottles of wine. 'A *gig*. Fantastic.' He killed all the lights except a steel anglepoise, which he twisted so it shone in my eyes. I strummed the open strings and adjusted the tuning. 'There's no need for that.' The male host sat on the rug with the others. 'I tune it electronically.'

I remembered how, years ago, staring out over Irene Albright's garden, Dad had said, 'Don't let people get to you.' I wondered who he'd meant by that. Whether he'd meant the Albright sisters, or whether he'd meant people like those who sat cross-legged and smiling on the rug. People who talked about their lives in the same matter-of-fact ways footballers talk about football. Or whether he hadn't meant them at all. Whether he'd meant himself. I rested my thumb on the tight nylon strings.

'Come on, Jim.' Kate nodded. 'Play.'

Mum's 1989 performance isn't mentioned in the history of the Midland Hotel I read at the bar last night. 'The Midland Hotel was built in 1933 – the year Hitler came to power!' It had a funny style, the leaflet. It described the beauty contests that were held at the Midland until the mid-seventies and how they were stopped 'when feminism was invented!' 'Though in some ways, this was a contradiction,' the leaflet continued, 'since the Miss World contests had high audience figures throughout the seventies! So go figure, as they say!'

The barman stank of smoke and broke a glass as he tried to dry it. As he collected the shards with his hands, he described the raves that took place at the hotel between 1993 and 1995. 'I've been in this very room when it's been practically falling fucking down with people dancing.' His conker-coloured hair, though not receding, covered a relatively small area of his head and he'd grown a goatee to tackle the vagueness of his chin. 'We used to go out onto the beach and watch the sun rise over the bay,' he said. 'You never came?'

'I was too young,' I said. 'My sister did.'

'Who was your sister?'

'Elaine Thorne.'

He swept away the last splinters of glass and sold me another beer. 'This place has been derelict for most of the noughties,' he said, setting down the drink on a paper napkin. 'It's now a what's-it-called, a remake.'

'A renovation.'

'A reconstruction,' the barman said. 'Do you know why the raves stopped?' I sipped the beer and shook my head. 'Someone got shot,' he said, leaning across the bar till his goatee hovered above my drink. 'A guy came here dressed as a Nazi officer and someone shot him in the heart.' It was as the barman described the death of the Nazi that a young man, who I'd noticed earlier eating lunch with his parents, approached me and asked if I was Jim Thorne. Before I could reply (I intended to lie) he said he remembered 'Inside the Explosion' and asked me for my autograph. The barman went in search of a pen and paper but, in fact, I always carry a biro and so I suggested that I sign the historical leaflet. The young man asked if I still made pop music and I told him I was visiting my mother. The young man, like Julian Straw, had fresh, intricate hair. His fringe had clearly been straightened with hot tongs and then gelled so it covered his eye like a patch, before falling to a mousy-brown point near his nostril.

'It's a shame you didn't make it,' the young man said.

He took the signed leaflet and walked away. I turned to face the bar and felt dizzy. My brain felt sugary. I had to look at the barman to check he wasn't concerned for me. The light of a deco chandelier blurred. The barman, in a distant voice, asked me if I was famous. His tone contained a note of betrayal. I nodded vigorously, gripping the marble bar with both hands, breathing deeply, suffering from a horrible kind of asthma of the mind. I crossed the foyer, keeping my head bowed. I held the banister tightly as I climbed the spiral staircase.

'At least play *one song*. I'm a yummy mummy. I'm like your target market.'

I lifted the guitar off my lap and told everyone that I was sorry. I twisted the anglepoise so it shone onto a framed portrait of Banksy's Kate Moss. The silence lasted till a match was struck and the second joint glowed in the lips of the male host. 'I'll play something,' he said, coughing on the smoke and taking the guitar. A fruit bowl circulated and I chose a peach. Kate climbed onto the sofa and held my hand. Our host played a version of 'Independent Women' by Destiny's Child, and although people saw this was funny, they also saw what a proficient guitarist he was, and how his voice broke and sounded lovely when he sang falsetto. The truth is, I wanted to say, the truth is most people can sing pretty well. That's the point of singing. But before I could say this, he launched into 'Give Peace a Chance' and encouraged us all to join in on the chorus, which we did, with much laughter and swaying. We must have woken his son again because his wails played on the baby monitor. I pictured the boy in his bed; saw the look in his eye as our singing woke him.

'Listen! Ralph's crying in tune. Keep going!'

Later that night, I pushed Kate against her bedroom wall, kissed her, scooped her breasts from her bra and bit her nipples. 'You fucking stink,' she said. She tore my shirt open. 'I could smell your BO at dinner.' I grabbed a chunk of her hair and pulled it till she said 'stop'. She lay on the bed and I undressed. I crawled over her and bit her nipples again, throttling her neck till she pinched me. 'From behind, Jim.' She climbed onto her hands and knees. 'As hard as you can.' I lowered her knickers slowly. She gripped the bed sheet. Firmly and rhythmically, I spanked her. I spanked my childhood sweetheart at a tempo fractionally faster than 'Give Peace a Chance'. She winced after each spank and ordered me to strike her harder. 'Ask me who I am, Jim.' She turned her head to look at me. '*Ask me!*'

'Who are you?'

'I'm the Wicked Witch of the West!'

'Who *are* you?'

'*I'm the Wicked Witch of the West!*'

I never read Mum's unpublished poetry collection *Cucumber Sandwiches*. But I know, because she told me, that it wasn't just poems about breast cancer; it was also, she said, poems *about* poetry.

'*Yes,*' Kate said. '*Harder.*' I struck her pale bottom with a flat palm. The report of each spank reverberated round the small room. 'Now, Jim. Fuck me as *hard* as you can.'

In the 1992 film, *Saved by the Bell: Hawaiian Style*, a chain of hotels called Royal Pacific is trying to buy out the Hideaway, which is a small, independent hotel owned by Kelly Kapowski's grandad. To make matters worse, the sacred ground of a Polynesian tribe is also under threat. When Jessie Spano hears about the underhand tactics being employed by the owner of Royal Pacific, she says, 'That's typical behaviour of the large, money-grabbing corporations of the nineties!'

I held Kate by her waist and thrusted as forcefully as I could. I pictured us as we would seem if viewed from the high-backed chair where Kate applied her make-up each morning. It struck me, as I did so, that I was no longer having sex. I was, I realised, *about* having sex. I felt myself soften inside her.

'Don't stop, Jim. *Harder.*'

In her sex tape, Katie Price holds a vibrator to her clitoris while a *Celebrity Big Brother* contestant penetrates and films her. She closes her eyes. She steadies one of her huge fake breasts. The video ends with the *Celebrity Big Brother* contestant pushing his toe inside her. She has shaved a heart into her pubic hair.

'*Harder*, Jim.'

I returned to my thrusts and found I was approaching orgasm. Kate was, too. She said so in a breathy, slightly pained voice. I thought about how, in 1996, we'd had exams and how I'd got Bs and Cs and she'd got As. I spanked her as hard as I possibly could. I came inside her as I spanked her like she was a glamour model. Like she was a child. The following evening, we ate at Pizza Express near Waterloo Bridge. Afterwards, I knelt on the damp grass near the London Eye and asked her to marry me. Nearby, on the riverbank, people had painted themselves silver and gold and were pretending to be statues.

Following our engagement, Kate became keen to see Manchester. She wanted to visit Walter, too, and build bridges. I tried to dissuade her with warnings about the reality of life in northern England. I told her Mancunians stand still on escalators. I told her they talk about hope to their hairdressers and their haircuts begin to embody this hope. She drove north in a hired Citroen Picasso. She didn't ask where my home studio was or why it was I lived in a bedsit. 'Oh dear.' She flopped onto the bed, laughing at how steep its slope was. 'Jim, it's fucking *filthy* in here.' Kate slapped the mattress and dust particles exploded from it. We lay together and it was suddenly clear that we'd fallen in love. From time to time we kissed, but the kisses led nowhere. We must have opened the laptop, because I remember watching Saddam Hussein get executed. Underneath the clip, someone had written :(

We searched for properties for sale in north London. While Kate scrolled through pictures of immaculate living rooms, I speculated on how much my advance for the acoustic album would be.

'It's adult-orientated. Adults still buy music.'

'I'd like somewhere that's ready to live in. Somewhere we can move into quickly.'

'They're songs *about* youth, but *for* adults.'

'We need a place near primary schools.'

Later, Kate somehow made a meal out of the contents of my kitchen. I'd never have thought it was possible. She found a dusty tin of Economy Chopped Tomatoes, some pasta twirls, a tin of sardines, a tiny bit of red wine and some herbs I didn't know about. She said it would've been vastly improved by an onion and some garlic, but I thought it was delicious. I told her it was one of the nicest meals I'd ever had, which was true. On my bookshelf, she found a book on fruit smoothies and I told her I didn't know where it had come from. We lay in our clothes on my sloped bed. We hadn't tried to have sex again since the night of the Holland Park dinner party. We weren't doing Shared Self-Love as regularly either. Before we went to sleep she set an alarm on her phone.

'My parents moved to northern Spain and I was left with Walter.' The following day, we drove the Picasso north to Sea View. The people in passing cars looked on the brink of tears and the wind-screen wipers winced when they crossed the glass. It rained heavily all the way. 'It was only meant to be for like six months.' I was soothed by Kate's ability to drive. She glanced at me between sentences to see my responses. 'Walter had all these plans to make me a radical. He dressed me in red dungarees. Gregory had a heart attack at a Goya exhibition in Bilbao.'

'Who's Gregory?'

'Mum joined some group. Like nudists bored with the twentieth century. What I remember about her is this sense that she was absolutely gagging for it. That's why she didn't marry Walter. Gregory, my dad, was this big, dumb guy who reckoned to like yoga. He had a long dick. I know because he could store two full toilet rolls on his morning glory. He'd do it for Mum and me on Sunday mornings. In Spain, Mum did acid in a forest, living in tents, trying to get into techno while they waited for like sex computers or whatever. She sent letters. She was fucking mental.' And after that Kate talked about the condition of the road, then about a holiday in Norfolk she'd been on in the eighties, then about watching Green Day at V '98, then about how being young is such a con, then about how politics is the shell but the egg has been blown, then about the possibility of bombs at the Olympics, then about her strange sexual awakening while watching *The X-Files* and then about her stance on returning ill-fitting clothes and I just watched her, I didn't watch the road, and I listened.

At Sea View, Walter opened the front door, but only a little. The ruddy tip of his nose poked out from the shadows of the hallway. He beckoned us in and we stood in the gloom on a rink of unopened bills. Walter limped in the direction of the kitchen, where the Aga was stone cold and the Belfast sink contained soil, dead leaves and a shattered plant pot. He walked towards Kate. 'You're here,' he said. He wore an old scarlet dressing gown, leather slippers and a tartan scarf.

Our arrival shocked and tired him. Kate changed his bedclothes and he lay on them, smiling at her. Once he was asleep, she began to clean. I sat with Walter and read a football magazine I found beside his bed. He had clearly sold his books. I found an academic diary, but the entries were infrequent and concerned *MasterChef*, football and brief descriptions of how his energy levels fluctuated. Kate kept coming in to show me half-full packets of tablets she'd found. She sat on Walter's bed and googled their names on her laptop, researching the symptoms they treated. Walter woke around ten to find me sitting by his bed, eating a takeaway pizza. He patted his bedclothes, brushed his forehead with his fingertips and watched me.

'Football is men running around on the lawn,' he said, indicating the radio on his bedside table. His smile was slow and irresponsible. 'I support Manchester City,' he said. 'I've always hated the effect of money, but nothing came of it so bugger it, I thought, I support Manchester City.' He propped a large, boomerang-shaped pillow against the headboard. 'You're the boy who came to make badges.'

'I'd like you to listen to me, Walter.'

'When was that?'

I leant forwards, weaved my fingers and examined them.

'Kate's downstairs,' I said. 'She's seen your tablets. We're both very worried.'

'At death's door, son, here's what I'll do. I'll twist the volume knob and hear someone talking about a game of football that's yet to happen. OK?' Walter rubbed what remained of an eyebrow. His face had dark spots and looked almost sunburnt. 'They'll be talking about who might play in this game, who might score in it and who might win.' Raising himself on an elbow, he spoke like a man outlining a grand conspiracy theory. 'I'll listen with interest,' he said, lifting his hand and, with his fingers, miming the turning up and the turning down of the volume. 'I'll be dead when the game is played,' he said, as the smell of baking drifted into the bedroom.

'I'm writing an acoustic album,' I said. 'It's about youth, but it's for adults.'

'About me?'

'No, *youth*, Walter. Being young now.'

Walter looked at me, then at his clasped hands. 'If rooms could talk, they'd giggle,' he said. There were footsteps on the stairs. 'The older the room, the louder the giggling, don't you think?' Kate arrived carrying a rolling pin dusted in flour and wearing a red headscarf and a blue shirt of Walter's.

'Jim, I need you to go to Tesco.'

'I've just been saying how worried we are.'

'Here, I've made a list.'

'I'm not insured.'

Kate held out a car key and a folded piece of paper. 'The roads are dead,' she said. A rather fraught silence ended when Walter's head flopped back onto his special pillow.

'Go to Tesco, little boy.'

Kate watched from the landing window as I tried to start the Picasso. It took time even to bring the headlights on. She was still there, silhouetted, looking down, as I edged the vehicle slowly out of the driveway. I stalled between the gateposts, but quickly re-engaged the engine. I managed to progress in bursts of first gear out of the drive, along the narrow lane and out of her sight. I stalled again where the landscape lilted and, this time, I slumped against the steering wheel and took deep breaths. I looked through a gap in the trees to where a low moon shone a line of light onto the calm surface of the sea. The supermarket was situated on the outskirts of Carnforth, a small town, not far from Ridley, with a train station famed for having been the set for *Brief Encounter*. I found a loaf of bread that had been reduced to 1p and I held it in my arms like a stray cat. The aisles were bright and deserted. The cheese department was a morgue. Kate's shopping list requested the most mature Cheddar available and that took quite some time to find. The fruit section really depressed me. I pressed the plump end of a pear into my right eye socket, trying to soothe an ache that was growing there. Since the start of my relationship with Kate, I'd truanted from the smoothie stand and missed many shifts and missed many calls from Peta. I'd maxed two credit cards and negotiated two loans at the bank.

Only one checkout remained open, right at the back of the store. A line of closed checkouts shrunk gradually into the distance, as far as a huge rack of colourful magazines near to the main entrance. I read the till attendant's name badge as she scanned my products.

'Fiona Denning,' I said.

'That's me,' she said. She scanned the bar code of the Cheddar and her till gave a life-support bleep.

'Fiona Hohner,' I said.

Fifteen years previously, sitting beside me on a bus, Fiona had mimed male masturbation as we travelled back to Queen's from the Inter School Jazz Contest. Her hand had blurred and I'd wondered whether she knew the first thing about it. Some time later, she'd gone to the coal shed with my best friend. Nowadays, she wore a beige tabard, a name badge and greeted me with tired eyes. She was thin-lipped, but her name didn't rhyme any more.

'Is it true Harry King made it as like a music producer?' she asked. 'Is that true?'

Behind me, someone else was unloading their shopping onto the conveyor belt. Fiona greeted them in a morose voice and turned to me.

'It's saying "card refused". Have you got some cash or another card, Jim?'

I searched through the different compartments of my wallet. 'I've made it, too,' I said. I had two Nando's loyalty cards, a Subway loyalty card and a Costa Coffee loyalty card. 'I'm buying a house in London,' I said. I had a membership card to a casino I couldn't recollect visiting. Fiona smiled apologetically at the next customer, who was stroking the handle of his empty trolley. I turned to face him and began to wave my finger at Fiona. 'She once sat beside me on a bus,' I said. The emptiness of the super-market amplified my voice. 'I remember thinking, there's no way you rub it that fast. But you do, don't you? You do rub extremely fast. I mean, I suppose there are various techniques and it depends on the man. But it is fast, isn't it?' The man lifted a leek from the conveyor belt. He concentrated on it, looking rather forlorn. The light above Fiona's checkout was flashing. She folded her arms and communicated silently with some shelf stackers who had congregated nearby. Beyond them, jogging out from the cereal aisle, was a young security guard.

On 30 December 2006, men put their camera phones onto video mode at an army base in Kadhimiya, Baghdad. Masked men in bomber jackets couldn't get close enough, I remember. Only Saddam looks calm. I heard he was stabbed six times after he dropped. No one quite captured the fall, did they?

When I arrived back at Sea View, only the dining-room light was on. Kate sat at the table, looking at a seafood pizza, but not eating.

A pair of orange cigarette butts stood up straight in a terracotta ashtray. I took the seat I'd taken years ago, when I'd come to help design badges. On the walls, the pictures of bearded men with machine guns had gathered another layer of dust. It looked as though they were standing in mist. Kate took a silver Zippo lighter from the table. It lit first time and she smoked.

'Jim, why are you limping?'

She tapped ash into the dish and made sure to topple the two butts.

'I'll sign a contract for my acoustic album,' I said.

'I feel so stupid.'

'Acoustic music sells, Kate.'

'Can you play the guitar?'

'Yes.'

'Tell me the truth, Jim. Can you play the guitar?'

Kate stood and walked to the mantelpiece. There was an ornament there, a Mrs Tiggy-Winkle, a hedgehog wearing a bonnet, holding a broom made of dead branches. She stroked the ornament's bristles.

'I make smoothies,' I said.

Kate turned and tried to speak. She shielded her eyes with a hand and breathed so deeply I thought she might faint. 'You've been clinging to me,' she said. 'And I've been clinging to you.' Again, she stroked the bristles of the human hedgehog. 'I wanted to be with someone who knew me when I was young,' she said, as I limped towards her. 'You used to follow me round school, Jim.' I kissed the collar of her shirt twice and held her as tightly as I could.

Bright orange lights circled across the ceiling. A large vehicle bleeped as it reversed onto the gravel driveway. We went to the window in time to see a man in fluorescent overalls climb from the cab of a breakdown truck and deliver instructions to its driver. 'Bit more . . . Bit more.' The remains of the hired Picasso were lifted by a hydraulic mechanism and lowered slowly onto the driveway. Kate drew the curtain. She was suppressing tears.

'I never learned,' I said. 'After Dad.'

Kate went out into the night wearing Walter's leather slippers. I watched through a gap in the curtain. She signed some forms, leaning against the crumpled bonnet of the car. Later, we cleaned our teeth, side by side, beneath a little strip-light. We slept together in her old bedroom, where someone had painted over the sky in magnolia. I woke to an oblong of bright sunlight on the duvet. Kate was still sleeping. I went to the kitchen, made a cup of tea and peeled a tangerine. I crept barefoot onto the driveway to inspect the car. It was a beautiful sunny morning. The clouds were barely drifting at all, just hanging. The Picasso looked much worse than I'd imagined. It was hard to believe I'd done so much damage while driving so slowly.

Kate was pregnant that morning – there it is, my news. She texted me to tell me so last week, before I left Manchester and came here to Morecambe. I was at work when her text arrived and, for an hour or so, I crushed gooseberries silently and made 'Top of the Mornings!'. Peta and I went for a cigarette and there, standing outside Ladbrokes on the high street, I talked about Kate. I talked about how I met her in Textiles in 1996. I mentioned the rumours about her wild pubes, about how we made badges with Harry King, about how we only had sex once, after a dinner party, and how other times, sexually, it was Shared Self-Love.

I like imagining life before the fanfare of expectation. I like to think about the foetus in Kate's womb on our final morning together at Sea View. Neither of us knew it was there. She lent me a hundred pounds and kissed me goodbye at the cashpoint in Carnforth. She didn't look me in the eye and she barely spoke. I walked down the hill to the train station, looked back and she was gone.

17

This morning, I sat on the shingle beach at the back of the Midland Hotel. The sun rose, though I didn't see it do so on account of the clouds. No plaque commemorates the blow job Elaine gave Nathan Lustard there. I thought about scratching a remembrance into one of the limestones. I ate a bacon sandwich as I sat there on the shore. Small waves offered me a tatty seagull feather, before dragging it back, before offering it again.

In Ridley, where I arrived shortly after eleven, the butcher's does not exist. It has closed down. So, too, has the pub, the bakery and the post office. They're second homes now, with unnaturally large front windows that offer views into empty living rooms. Beige curtains hang where dead pheasants used to. A glass coffee table sits on the spot where Harry and I presented our letter to the butcher. There's an ornament on it; a white baby with wings.

Mum sat on the window seat in what used to be my bedroom. Outside, wind shook the tree above the Italian Courtyard and the fragments of sunlight that she was sprinkled in danced then dimmed. The mantelpiece was painted black. Above it, a brass birdcage hung from the ceiling on a golden chain. A green, grey and yellow budgerigar gripped a perch with its claws and sang. A little boy sat on the floor, playing with a long-necked, long-tailed dinosaur. This was Thomas Thorne, the only son of Elaine Thorne and Benny Giles, parents whom Mum once referred to as 'the hippest couple in England.' I sat on a suede pouffe and Mum came to sit beside me. We embraced and I remembered how, at Ridley Primary, in 1991, I wrote a poem for the time capsule that they buried beneath the infants' playground. The poem was about table-tennis. I imagined aliens reading it, years in the future, all of them gathered round and really engaging with each stanza. Below the poem, I drew a picture of Harry and me in our red strips. I really exaggerated how pea-headed Harry was. I couldn't remember what it was that he contributed to the capsule.

'This is your uncle James, Thomas,' Mum told the boy. 'He's come for Christmas. Isn't he funny?'

The boy blushed. He held the face of the dinosaur level with his own and giggled through his teeth, sending out sparks of spittle. 'I don't know,' he said, in his cluttered, salivary, three-year-old tongue. Shortly after this exchange, he abandoned the dinosaur and left the room, calling for Elaine.

'Pop died,' Mum said. 'She was run over. I found her on the War Memorial, completely flattened . . . Do you know about Elaine's tattoo? She says it's ironic but it covers her entire back, so I don't see how it can be.'

'What is it?'

'It's a human skeleton. He's wearing a top hat, smoking a cigarette, rolling a pair of dice with one hand, while in the other he's holding all four aces.' Mum returned to the window seat. I went to the mantelpiece and watched the budgerigar peck the skin beneath its green wing.

'I ran into Stan King the other day,' Mum said. 'Harry's doing well.'

'I was on his stag night.'

'He's getting married, he's a record producer, he's bought a home.'

'There's something I need to tell you, Mum.'

'He used to be square, do you remember? *You* were the talented one. How did Harry King become cool?'

The budgerigar improvised a fragment of melody. Mum continued to talk about her encounter with Stan King. All I could think about was him marching down the corridor at Harry's sleepovers, hissing, 'For Christ's sake, boys – *sleep*.' What a celebrated pube Harry's first was. We should have kept it. We should have preserved it in Sellotape and built a religion round it.

'Some of my pupils have tattoos,' Mum said. 'They're primitive. The result of ritzy spinelessness and self-importance. A *skeleton*, James. Elaine's a recruitment consultant, you know. She's already got a skeleton . . . When I was young I used to think, I wish birds didn't fly away, I wish they'd perch on my finger and get to know me.'

Mum's laptop was on her bureau. Her screensaver is a photograph of her and her sisters. They're standing in the entrance of a yellow marquee. It took chemotherapy to give Mum some perspective on her perm. She admits that herself. In the photo, she resembles Charles II.

'I've been thinking about Dad recently,' I said. I closed the laptop and looked at her. She crossed her legs and angled her body away from me. I tapped the cage but the budgerigar said nothing. Mum's mouth hung open; she looked at the ceiling and played a soft drum roll on her knees. 'Have you now?' she said. She folded herself in half by sliding her hands down her shins and feeding them into her fleece-lined boots. In this position, her voice became strained.

'You don't always do what you feel is right in life,' she said. 'Often you do the opposite.'

I've never visited Bangor in North Wales. But I found the corner of Stryd Fawr and Friars Road on Google Earth. I discovered Stryd Fawr just means High Street and that the area's pretty glum. On the corner of Stryd Fawr and Friars Road, there's a Bargain Booze and a tanning parlour. It was cloudy on the day the Google van drove through Bangor and photographed the corner where my parents met.

'I got a girl pregnant,' I said. 'But she hasn't kept it.'

Mum's hands were still buried in her Ugg boots. She arched her neck to see me. It accentuated the red rims of her eyes. 'Why?' she whispered. She sat up straight. '*Why?*' And this time, I heard the spectres of words she hadn't said. The wind shunted the window and the house prickled and ticked in the cold of winter. The word 'Why' stood like a fortress in the peace of the room. Mum watched me from its ramparts as I bit my lip and looked away.

'I don't know,' I said.

Those words were pleasant to say. I repeated them. Mum stood, walked to me, took me in her arms and held me to her breast. I let myself be held. I was crying and crying.

I stayed up late in the Music Room, watching *Cocktail* on television. Elaine sat in our antique chair. Only her cheek and the tiniest tip of her nose were visible to me. I asked about her job, but she didn't want to discuss it. I told her how lovely Thomas seemed and she turned to me.

'Jim, you know I'm not really a recruitment consultant, don't you?'

When Elaine was ten and I was seven, she used to sit as high as she could in the apple tree, watching as I dug a hole beside it. When the hole was deep enough, she'd crouch inside it and I'd lay planks of wood over her. I'd ask her how it was in there and she'd say it was nice and relaxing. She slid from the apple tree once and landed in the gooseberry bush. She tore some culottes that Mum had sewn using a pattern she'd owned since the seventies.

'I live with a footballer,' Elaine said.

'OK.'

'Partly for Thomas's sake. But also, I like him.'

'Is he professional?'

'He plays in London. He sees other women, but he likes us, Thomas and me. We might be opening an art gallery together. He funds his own football academy in West Africa. He loves tattoos.'

'Who is he?'

'If I told you his name, Jim, you wouldn't understand. The money he earns confuses him. He collects shields.'

Preparing cocktails is easier than preparing smoothies. During the section of the film that's set at the beach bar in Jamaica,

Elaine yawned, came and kissed my forehead and went to bed. Her teenage diaries are stored in a cupboard on the top landing, outside her bedroom. The racing-green exercise book labelled '1995' remains my favourite.

8 August

Things eaten:
1 bowl of cabbage
1 lemsip
1 carrot (a massive one)

Feeling shitty so slept all afternoon. Dad knocked on my door at some point. Creepy. I took two pills at the Midland last night. The music was fuckin' ace. I saw Nathan near the end and gave him a BJ on the fuckin' beach. I hate myself. He was pulling my hair, wearing his pissy pants. Elaine, what were you thinking?!?!?! People were fuckin' watching. Have a THROW UP day tomorrow. Don't talk to anyone. Sit on your own. FUCK EVERYONE. Go to the library at lunch.

On Christmas Day, the kitchen smelt of roasting meat and the floral tang of the Albright sisters. The surfaces were cluttered with vegetable offcuts, peelings, used mixing bowls and some old black-iron weighing scales that were dusted in flour. Mum directed us all from the head of the table, which was extended so far that it made crossing the room difficult. Her sisters sat down one side, Elaine and Jess down the other, where there was also a place set for me. Thomas Thorne was given his own little table by the window. Out in the Italian Courtyard, dead hanging baskets hung completely still and the tree was nude and damp. On the table, a turkey gave clouds of steam to the spotlit air above. There were white napkins, a scarlet tablecloth, silver place mats, a baking tray of apple and walnut stuffing, ornate white serving bowls of sprouts, potatoes, red cabbage, leek sauce, carrots; long silver spoons reclined in each. Mum carved the turkey with a bread knife and a special fork. Irene and Jayne Albright helped Elaine to serve and circulate plates piled high with food. Elizabeth Albright took two bottles of red wine from where they'd been breathing on the counter, having matured in the cellar. She toured around the table filling everybody's glass.

'You're sitting here, James.' Mum indicated the seat to her left using a forked slice of meat. The seat would have left me opposite Aunt Jayne, which was a nice idea in theory. Jayne had allowed her bleached hair to grow out. Her natural colour was a mixture of grey and mahogany. Irene, meanwhile, had also gone natural. She had a huge head of what was very nearly white hair. It shone, along with the turkey, under the kitchen spotlights.

Elizabeth Albright wore a green prosthetic nose. She was halfway through a month of pantomime, *Snow White*, in Stoke-on-Trent. She would have to leave early on Boxing Day to be in the Midlands in time for the matinee. It was a large green nose, the tip of which hung lower than her scarlet lips and on each of her cheeks were two large warts, which, like the nose, had been attached to her face using an adhesive so strong it would last until Epiphany. 'They call it *semi*-permanent,' Elizabeth had told us, on arrival that morning. 'What does that even mean?'

I lifted up the large earthenware bread bin from its home in the corner and carried it to the window. I set it down opposite Thomas Thorne at the children's table and sat on it. Thomas Thorne laughed hysterically and pointed at me while looking to his mother, smiling and open-mouthed, seeking an explanation. He shouted a word I didn't catch and made a Legoman bounce around on the floret of his broccoli.

'You can supervise Thomas's eating,' Elaine said, shushing her son and looking at me. 'Uncle Jim's going to help you eat, Tommy.'

'That can be the Men's Table,' Elizabeth Albright said, rising in her seat so she could see where I was. She had to arch both eyebrows to see over the brow of her nose.

'I can't dine at an asymmetrical table,' Mum said, sitting down in the place intended for me. 'We can imagine that Daddy's sitting there.' She indicated the empty place at the head of the table. '*Yes*,' Elizabeth said. 'To Daddy.' No one responded to the toast, not even Mum. Nonetheless, Elizabeth raised her glass to the empty place. From where I was sitting, on the bread bin, level with their tabletop, I could see a jungle of full wine glasses, cutlery and female forearms, but I couldn't see as far as my invisible grandfather, Charlie Albright. I did however have a good view of the six pairs of women's legs that were conducting a secret meeting in the gloom beneath the dining table.

'Everybody eat,' Mum said.

I picked up a stray Legoman, bounced him across to Thomas's plate and made him whisper, 'Howdy.' I bounced him back to my plate and sat him down in a cove between two roast potatoes. The scrape and ting of cutlery was quickly drowned out by pleasure-groans, delivered from mouths still full of food. There were moaned, one word reviews of different parts of the meal. 'Heavenly carrots,' Elizabeth Albright said, refilling her glass. 'Heavenly gravy.'

'Oh my God, Jess.' Irene Albright addressed her daughter with feigned urgency. 'Tell everyone about Carter.'

'Mum, no, it's not –'

'Oh, come on. He's amazing . . .'

'Who's Carter?' Elizabeth asked.

'He's Jess's *fiancé*!'

There was a choral guffaw on the adult table. I leant forward and looked into the eyes of my nephew. Reflected in them, I watched the Albright sisters climb from their seats to kiss and embrace Jess. They all looked small and warped.

'Let's eat, let's eat,' Jess said, as she received the sisters. 'We've not even set a date.'

The four members of Ladylike ended up working as holiday reps in Ibiza. They performed Ladylike songs on Saturday nights for the holidaymakers. A camera crew followed them for a fly-on-the-wall documentary called *Ibiza Uncut*. 'It was so staged,'

Jess had told us, earlier that day. 'They basically bought us vodka and filmed us drinking it. They didn't feature us in the end, thank God.' Jess moved to Bristol after Ibiza, where she trained as a youth worker. She started running in the evenings and volunteered for various charities. She was baptised through total immersion into the Church of the Seventh-Day Adventists, a process that involved a long letter to Elaine, apologising for her sexual betrayal with Benny in 2005, a letter Elaine described as 'mawkish and really depressing'.

'OK, so Carter's a graphic designer,' Jess said, once everyone was back in their seats and eating. 'We met at church fairly recently. Then again at the soup-kitchen. And then it turns out Carter *loves* going to art galleries, so he invited me to London on what turned out to be a date –'

'Tell them what he collects!'

'Right, OK, this might sound weird. Carter collects board games. Not to play with, but as collector's items. He knows how weird it looks, believe me, but he loves them. His aim is to curate a board game museum.'

'Tell them how he proposed!'

'OK, Mum. Does everyone remember Pooky, my toy mouse from when I was little?' Under the table, one of Jess's black ballet pumps hung from her big toe. She jiggled it as she spoke. 'Well, one day, Carter sent me a link to a YouTube video, while I was at work, and it turned out to be a stop-motion animation, something he'd made himself, God knows how. He'd animated Pooky! He'd made Pooky sneak out of my bed and down onto the carpet. Pooky kept scurrying in and out of the shot, bringing colourful letters with him, like fridge magnets, each time. Eventually, Pooky spelt out *Will you marry Carter?* Then he performed a funny little dance next to the words.'

'Jayne, isn't that amazing?' Irene gripped the wrist of the former Hollywood producer.

'It's fairly easy to do,' Jayne said. 'But very fiddly. He sounds sweet, Jess.'

'He sounds soppy,' Elizabeth said. 'I'll tell you all a story. Last week, I was beaten to a part by a woman who couldn't sing, couldn't dance, couldn't act and had *zero* experience. A camera crew followed her wherever she went, even into the audition. She was a celebrity.'

'Which one?' Elaine asked, abruptly.

'How should I know?'

'And so what's your point?' Elaine said. 'Because everyone's looking for a way out, Lizzie, right? Most celebs start out poor. You'd do anything for a part, wouldn't you?'

'I'm fifty-three, Elaine. I'm an actress. I want to act, to play great parts, to –'

'I miss Los Angeles,' Jayne interrupted, as if she hadn't been aware that her sister had been speaking. 'They can really *do* fake in California. They don't have our hang-ups about celebrity, money and whatever. Maybe it's because America had so little to lose. I miss the Indian jewellers on Pioneer Boulevard, the flea market on Melrose Avenue. I hate London. I miss working on my laptop in Starbucks, West Hollywood, sitting out on their patio. It's only superficial if you look at it superficially. And now it's ending, really, America. I'll miss it.'

'I'm with Elizabeth on this one.' Mum's chair scraped against the floor and produced a parpy trumpet note. 'Celebrities are parasites.'

'They're just people.'

'We're all *just people*, Elaine. But these people become hideous then work hard to be everywhere, at which point they work harder to become even more hideous and more . . . everywhere. *That's wrong.*'

'What about footballers?'

'What about them? They're paid salaries from heaven. They use whores.'

'It's true, Elaine,' Jess said. Her pump fell from her foot. She reclaimed it by briefly wearing it. A moment later, it was hanging from her toe and she was jiggling it again. 'I volunteer in a home for children with special needs. They're completely obsessed with famous people. It's all they talk about.'

'The point of knowledge is simple.' This was Mum. 'A choice isn't a choice unless you know what you're doing.'

'If that's true —' this was Elaine — 'then I've never made a choice, Mum.'

'Maybe you haven't, Elaine. There's a big skeleton on your back. It's wearing a top hat and smoking a cigarette.'

'Here's a choice for you.' Elizabeth Albright pushed her chair out from under the table. 'I choose to pee.'

'Celebrity is the West's only big idea.' Mum reached for the gravy boat as Elizabeth left the room. 'We will be judged by it. Just as communism is judged, or fascism, modernity . . . celebrity.' She used her fork to scrape slices of onion as well as thick gravy onto her plate. 'Celebrity is our system. It's our dream. We've had heaven, equality, peace, wealth. Now fame. *I* never *wanted* to be famous. Jess, you seem so much happier.'

Elizabeth Albright returned as Jess was describing her life in Bristol. 'We're so lucky,' Jess said, looking down at me briefly. 'We both run. There's a neighbourhood Italian we like. We've got our church, our charity work, Carter's board games. I *am* much happier. I don't want to be famous either.'

'Your life sounds dull, Jessica,' Elizabeth said, taking her seat. 'Why didn't we get crackers this year?' Her red high heels returned to their spot beneath the table. Jess's ballet pump continued to jiggle. 'Maybe I'm being harsh, but you don't know what being onstage is really like, Jess. Ladylike never played for an adoring public. You don't know either, Milly, because poetry's so unpopular. None of you, except Irene, truly know the bliss of hearing people cheering after you've entertained them. If any of you do, *he* does.' Elizabeth pointed to me and, as she did, she knocked over her wine glass. 'Oh, shit.' It didn't shatter, but red wine ran among the plates and bowls, soaking the cloth and causing Irene to stand to avoid it dripping into her lap. 'But, Lizzie —' Mum skipped across the room with a ream of kitchen roll – 'you don't know the bliss of being unknown.'

'Carter and I walk in Victoria Park every Saturday. It's heaven. Sometimes we play Scrabble or meet Mum and Dad in Pizza Express.'

'Meet Mum and Dad?' Mum said, standing up straight, holding a dripping wad of kitchen roll and looking at Irene. 'What's this?'

'Yes,' Irene said, squeezing past Mum and down into her seat. 'Edmund and I are back together.' The thick heels of Irene's boots slid through a small pool of red wine. 'He didn't dare come here because he knew you'd be horrible to him, Milly. He's having Christmas dinner with Carter's family in Chichester . . . It's the economy. They're coming for opera, too, you know – women with fake boobs, singing in quivery voices. I survive because there are so many parts for old hags. Otherwise, I'd be –'

'Fucked.' Elizabeth burped silently. 'Like I am,' she said. 'I'm sorry to swear, Elaine, but it's the truth.'

'Men,' Mum said, slowly. 'Irene, Edmund *cheated* on you.'

'It's a recession,' Irene said. 'We missed each other.'

Mum slowly spooned cranberry sauce onto her plate. 'I chose a cup size that matched the breasts I lost,' she said. 'For your information.' She licked the teaspoon clean. 'But do you know how I feel when men look at me? I feel like a diagram of a woman.'

The silence was the sound of our teeth and tongues, the clink of cutlery and breathing. On the adult table, they ate with bowed heads, only raising them occasionally to halfheartedly hum approval. Mum stood to carve more meat. Thomas's dinosaur lay on its side near to Jess's jiggling pump.

'I'm happy for you, Irene,' Elaine said. 'Edmund's a laugh.'

'I'm sorry, Milly, but just so we're clear –' This was Elizabeth – 'unless you know what it's like to be onstage, you can't talk about fame the way you do. I mean just so we're clear, people *should* love stars. But talented ones. I can do everything. Sing, dance, comedy, tragedy –'

'Oh, shut up, Elizabeth.' This was Elaine. She'd denied the

death of Kurt Cobain sitting at that table. She'd told Mum to fuck off once, too, on the morning after her house party in 1995, when young people had danced on that dining table and the air smelt of weed not turkey. Her tone was similar. 'Listen to yourself, Lizzie.'

'Edmund says we should manufacture huge oars and row England as far from Europe as we can.' This was Irene's attempt at changing the subject. 'We could row it to the West Coast of America, Jayne.'

'Edmund's a fool.'

'And so where would you row England to, Milly?' Elizabeth said. 'Come on. Where would you row England? You've got somewhere in mind, Milly, I can see it in your eyes. You're imagining somewhere. Somalia? Iran?' Elizabeth turned to my sister. 'I'm still your auntie, Elaine,' she said. 'Whether you're a mother or not, I'm *older* than you. Your art came to nothing because you −'

'You're drunk, Lizzie. Please don't talk about art.' Elaine stamped the floor softly with her black Doc Marten. 'You don't understand what art is.'

'Let's ask Daddy, shall we?' Elizabeth Albright leant forwards and raised her eyebrows expectantly towards the empty place at the head of the table. 'Well, Daddy? Entertainment. It's healed us, hasn't it?'

'We should all go for a walk.' This was Jess. 'Carter and I find walking makes us −'

'You and Daddy were disgusting.' Mum glared at Elizabeth. 'I've written poems about you and him.'

'Are they published? Let me read them.'

'Elizabeth, be quiet,' Jayne said.

'Why should I? And anyway, me and Daddy? What about you and him, Milly?' Elizabeth pointed at me with her empty fork. 'That's your son down there, sitting on your bread bin. He's nearly thirty. *Look at him.*' Elizabeth's nose, owing to its length, shook from side to side when she raised her voice. It came to a stop half a second later than her actual face.

'Why are we called the Albrights?' I said.

Snow began to fall in the Italian Courtyard. In the pocket of my jeans, my phone beeped to acknowledge receipt of a text. Thomas put his Legoman into his mouth and I did the same with mine.

'Because we're all stars,' Elizabeth said. 'There's no need to be ashamed. It's because we're *all* stars.'

'No phones at the dinner table, James.'

Walter died. Funeral tomorrow. I kept our baby.

Jess and Elaine were the first to kneel beside me and attempt to uncoil my body. I lay on the floor beside the bread bin and when I tried to breathe, I found I couldn't, and when I tried to be sick, the same. Wine glasses on the table were falling and shattering as the Albright sisters climbed to their feet and tried to help. 'He's choking,' Jess said, as she and Elaine lifted me. Mum wrapped her arms round my abdomen and began to squeeze me.

Eventually, Robbie Williams rejoins Take That. He and Gary Barlow release a single together, as a duo. It publicly marks the end of their long feud. The song is called 'Shame'.

The horrible thing about it, the thing that really made me sad, was the sound of Thomas Thorne crying. It must have looked pretty awful to a child, seeing a grown man squeezed like that. I expect we resembled wild animals making love on television. It was awful. It was awful because I wanted Mum to fail. Not because I wanted to die, but because I have always wanted her to fail. 'Breathe, James!' Her voice was distant. '*Breathe!*'

I pictured Harry, as he had been in 1992, pea-headed, before music, before fashion, even before table-tennis. At last, I remembered what it was that he contributed to the time capsule. It was a little stone.

Six times Mum squeezed me. On the sixth, the Legoman burst

out of my mouth and flew across the kitchen. The last thing I remember is Elizabeth Albright shrieking.

'Come and see where it landed! It's over here in the plughole!'

The song 'Praise You' is a number-one single in the UK for Fat Boy Slim in January 1999. Spike Jonze's video for the song is a stunt. A fictional dance troupe dance to the song in an American shopping centre without permission. It's filmed in an amateur way using one low-quality camera. At some stage, a security guard enters in a tuxedo to reprimand the group and confiscate their stereo.

The video anticipates an aesthetic that becomes common in the early twenty-first century. Footage of real life, funny stunts, even sex and petty crime is captured on camera phones and shared. This process accelerates in 2005 with the advent of YouTube.com. In 1999, the video for 'Praise You' is greeted with surprise. It shows you don't need lots of money to make a film. ('Anybody could have done it. Couldn't they though?') When cameras become so light that they can be held by an outstretched arm, individuals can film themselves. At the Adult Video Awards in 2005, Paris Hilton's sex tape, which is largely shot in night-vision, wins Best Overall Marketing Campaign – Individual Project, Best Renting Title of the Year and Best Selling Title of the Year. The official video for 'Praise You' currently has 74,223 views on YouTube. The most recent comment about the video was written one week ago by a person called hugeunit187. It reads: 'takes huge amount of balls to be yourself these days.' This comment has been given a 'liked' by forty-five people so far.

Walter's funeral was at Lancaster Crematorium. Jill still plays keyboards there, the woman who accompanied me at Dad's service, but she didn't recognise me and that was OK. Walter had planned his funeral service in advance. He stipulated that one of his old shopping lists be 'read aloud by my best friend, my wonderful girl, my Kate'. She read it well and got everyone laughing. Kate has a bump, not a massive one, but you can tell our child is growing inside her. She's given me permission to attend the birth and I look forward to that.

I dreamt last night that Kate gave birth to a girl and that she and I travelled to Florida to bathe in Disney's aquatic theme park, Typhoon Lagoon, where the theme is natural disaster and where the main pool boasts one of the largest man-made waves on earth. Each night there are firework displays at Disney parks all around the world, in Los Angeles, Tokyo, Paris, Hong Kong, Shanghai. Viewed from space these displays look like flares fired by old captains from the prows of lost ships, or else they look like splendour, like momentary explosions of happiness. It depends on what it actually means to hope.

In the main pool at Typhoon Lagoon, the ten-foot wave rises every ninety seconds, heralded by a wonderful bassy whoomph; it draws screams from the children and their parents. But it's harmless. It has none of the saltiness or undertow of a real wave. One day I'll describe the dream to my child. I'll describe how, as the wave lifted us, we clung to each other.

Walter requested that a live football game be played as his coffin disappeared from view. It was Manchester United versus Manchester City. As the curtains closed and his coffin rolled on castors into darkness, the commentator raised his voice to describe a shot at goal.

On New Year's Eve morning, Thomas Thorne and I stood at the kitchen window, looking out into the Italian Courtyard. Everything was coated in snow, except for Elaine, who stood in the middle of the yard wearing Mum's long coat, a red bobble-hat, scarf and gloves. She found her art in the cellar, behind a stack of bikes. She used a hacksaw to cut the large piece of chipboard into smaller pieces. She used pliers to remove the long nails and she put all of the used condoms into a bin liner. When she saw we were watching, she waved and smiled.

That night, around 11 p.m., she and I took Thomas for his

night-time pee. She held him under his arms and he dangled like a drunk cowboy in the bright bathroom light. His willy was the colour of eggshell. It was rock hard. I pushed its tip down using my index finger, and, though he was still sleeping, Thomas peed. Afterwards, I dabbed the tip with a piece of toilet paper and pulled his pyjama bottoms up. Elaine steered him away on his half-alive legs and I flushed.

Elaine has finally located Benny Giles. A friend bumped into him and texted. He was working in a bar in Brixton, wandering round selling sour shooters from a special rucksack with a little hose. He wouldn't admit to being him at first. In fact, for ages. He and Thomas are planning a trip to see the reptiles at London Zoo.

I intend to return to Manchester on 5 January. I quite enjoy life there. I will watch football in Walkabout on Sundays, when the air's still thick from Saturday night, and I'll drink soda water, perched on a high stool below the big screen. I spoke to Peta today and she says 'Top of the Morning!' remains our best-selling smoothie. Although she's invented a new one, she says. Banana, orange, coconut and lime is called 'Come Home Jim!'.

It's time for forgetting, the sister of remembering. I've heard she's more at ease with the world and that's encouraging. My youth was like that funfair Michael Jackson built for himself at Neverland. It was fun, I guess, for Michael and his friends, people like Elvis's daughter and child star Macaulay Culkin. I imagine there were some good rides and everything was free and there were no queues or rules. I quite liked Michael Jackson. It was reassuring, growing up knowing that the most famous man on earth was best friends with a chimp. It put things into perspective. The secret to Macaulay Culkin's career is that, as a child, he had the wit and the confidence to excel in the world of adults. That's something to aspire to.

Early this morning, Thomas spread out all his toys on the floor in the spare room. Jess joined us and we played Rock Band 2. Jess played the small plastic bass guitar with the coloured buttons instead of strings. Elaine crouched awkwardly behind the pretend drum kit, still in her beige silk pyjamas. I tried to teach Thomas how to hold the guitar. 'You sing, Jim,' Jess said, indicating the little plastic microphone.

'Hey, Jim,' Elaine said, as she struggled to get comfortable behind the little drum kit. 'Do you know Mum owns a horse? She wants to take Thomas to see it. It's got a name. Something really funny . . .'

'Santa Carlo Mist.'

'*Yes.* She says she can gallop!'

'She can.'

When people used to talk about the next generation of Albrights, they meant us. Me, my cousin Jess and my sister Elaine. We scored well on Rock Band 2 because we could all stay in time and in tune. Afterwards, I stood at the spare-room window, looking out into the square, which was quarter-lit by a feeble dawn and by the old lamp post, which stood, as it always has, in a pool of its own weak light. Across the road, Mum sat alone on the middle-step of the War Memorial, surrounded by snow. It hadn't settled on the road yet, but the War Memorial, the rooftops and the fields beyond were covered. I took one of Dad's winter coats from a hook by the cellar steps and walked out into the square. Chimney pots were silhouetted against the purple sky. The snow squeaked beneath my feet and I could see my breath. It was going to be one of those crisp winter days.

Mum patted the step of the Memorial. 'How's my son?' I wrapped the coat around myself and looked down the snowless road, where mist hung in the air, not moving at all. I sat beside her and she put her arm round me. 'I'm not bad,' I said. And I wanted to tell her I had very few plans except to keep living. To tell her that there's always next year and, as such, there's the seasons and the promises they keep, in spite of everything; in spite of my poor dress sense and my depleted hobbies, my lost table-tennis. There's the prospect of watching a baby emerge from Kate's beautiful beaver, me in a disposable, mint green tunic, cheering her on and reminding her to breathe as a small circle of lust completes. Your first home's your skull, that's what Walter used to say. I wanted to unleash love but I haven't.

It's over twenty years since the removal van collided with the wall around our doorstep. The replacement bricks still look quite new, relative to the old. They're like our birthmark. Mum and I sat in silence for a moment and then she clapped her hands once to warm them. The sound didn't reverberate because of the snow. Without ceremony, the light in the lamp post went out.

Thank you:

Marion Plowright, Beth Coates, Cathryn Summerhayes, Walter Donohue, Nicholas Royle, Chloe Johnson-Hill, Geraldine Osowska, Rob Dinsdale, James Sheard, Kristian Scott, Laura Marsden, Joe Cross, Hilary Marsden, Edward Evans, John Darby, Juliet Jacques, Adam Anderson, Socrates Adams, Chris Killen, Tom Darling, John Stretch, Laura Amiss, Paul Toogood, Malcolm Litson, Nicholas Reyland, Richard Milward, Cliff Jones, Jo Tatchell, Chris Carey, Tim Parry, Jazz Summers, Kat Kennedy, Becky Thomas, Callum Plowright, Richard Ridout, Steve Messer, Scott McCracken, Tim Lustig, Keele University and Tony Weymouth.